BLACK DAHLIA & WHITE ROSE

Haunted: Tales of the Grotesque
   (1994)

Will You Always Love Me? (1996)

The Collector of Hearts:
   New Tales of the Grotesque
   (1998)

Faithless: Tales of Transgression
   (2001)

High Lonesome:
   New and Selected Stories 1966–2006
   (2006)

Wild Nights! (2008)

Dear Husband, (2009)

Sourland (2010)

The Corn Maiden (2011)

BLACK DAHLIA & WHITE ROSE

JOYCE CAROL OATES

AN IMPRINT OF HARPERCOLLINSPUBLISHERS

BLACK DAHLIA & WHITE ROSE. Copyright © 2012 by The Ontario Review. All rights reserved. Printed in the United States of America. No part of this book may be used or reproduced in any manner whatsoever without written permission except in the case of brief quotations embodied in critical articles and reviews. For information address HarperCollins Publishers, 10 East 53rd Street, New York, NY 10022.

HarperCollins books may be purchased for educational, business, or sales promo-tional use. For information please write: Special Markets Department, HarperCollins Publishers, 10 East 53rd Street, New York, NY 10022.

FIRST EDITION

Designed by Suet Yee Chong

Library of Congress Cataloging-in-Publication Data has been applied for.

ISBN 978-0-06-219569-2

12 13 14 15 16   OV/RRD   10 9 8 7 6 5 4 3 2 1

TO BRAD MORROW

ACKNOWLEDGMENTS

Many thanks are due to the editors of the magazines and anthologies in which, often in slightly different versions, these stories were originally published.

"Black Dahlia & White Rose" in the anthology *L.A. Noire*.

"I.D." in *The New Yorker*; anthologized in *The Best American Short Stories 2011*.

"Deceit" in *Conjunctions*.

"Run Kiss Daddy" in the anthology *New Jersey Noir*.

"Hey Dad" in *Ellery Queen*.

"The Good Samaritan" in *Harper's*.

"A Brutal Murder in a Public Place" in *McSweeney's*.

"Roma!" in *Conjunctions*.

"Spotted Hyenas: A Romance" on The Atlantic online.

"San Quentin" in *Playboy*.

"Anniversary" in *Boulevard*.

CONTENTS

I

BLACK DAHLIA & WHITE ROSE

BLACK DAHLIA & WHITE ROSE: *Unofficial Investigation into the (Unsolved) Kidnapping-Torture-Rape-Murder-Dissection of Elizabeth Short, 22, Caucasian Female, Los Angeles, CA, January 1947 Material assembled by Joyce Carol Oates*

K. KEINHARDT—PHOTOGRAPHER:
They were lost girls looking for their fathers.
So I knew they'd come crawling back to *me*.

NORMA JEANE BAKER:
It is true that I was *lost*—but I knew that no one would find me except myself—if I became a Star in the sky of Hollywood where I could not be hurt.

He was the one—"K.K." we called him—who took pictures for the girlie mags & calendars—the one I begged *Please don't make me into a joke. Oh please that is all I ask of you.*

ELIZABETH—"BETTY"—SHORT:

Nasty lies told about me *post mortem* but none nastier than that I did not have an actual *father*—only just a pretend-father like Norma Jeane whose crazy mother would show her studio publicity photos of Clark Gable—whispering in the child's ear *Here is your father, Norma Jeane! But no one must know—yet.*

Poor Norma Jeane! Some part of her believed this craziness, why she was always looking for *Daddy.* Why Norma Jeane made bad mistakes seeking men like she did but that was not why I made my bad mistake winding up *post mortem* in a weedy vacant lot in a dingy neighborhood of Los Angeles so mutilated the hardened LAPD detectives shrank from seeing me & quickly covered my "remains" with a coat for I had an actual father named Cleo Marcus Short who favored me above my four sisters Kathryn & Lucinda & Agnes & Harriet & wrote to me solely, in 1940, when I was sixteen, to invite me to live with him in California—which Daddy would not have done if he had not truly loved me.

Post mortem—is the Latin term. *Post mortem* is this state I am in, now. That you do not know exists when you are "alive" & you cannot guess how vast & infinite *post mortem* is for it is all of the time—forever & ever—after you have *died.*

Later, Daddy would deny me. Daddy would be so shocked & disgusted by the newspaper headlines & photos—(which were not the coroner's photos or the LAPD crime scene photos which could not be published of course—too ugly & "obscene")—but photos of Elizabeth Short a.k.a. *THE BLACK DAHLIA*—(for since the age of eighteen when I came to L.A., I wore tight-fitting black dresses with dipping necklines & often black silk trimmed in lace & undergarments as well in black & my hair glossy-black & my skin pearly-white & my mouth flame-red with lipstick)—which were glamour photos striking as any stills from the studios—Daddy refused to identify me still less "claim" me—the (mutilated, dissected) remains of me in the L.A. coroner's morgue.

Or maybe Daddy thought he would have to pay some fee. He would have to pay for a burial, Daddy would fear.

Oh, that was mean of Daddy! To tell the L.A. authorities he would not drive to the morgue to make the "I.D." (For there is no law to compel a citizen in such circumstances, it seems.) If Daddy had not already broke my heart this sad news *post mortem* would do it.

But that was later. That was January 1947. When you were all reading of *THE BLACK DAHLIA* shaking your hypocrite heads in revulsion & chastisement *A girl like that. Dressing in all-black and promiscuous, it is what she deserves.*

When Daddy wrote to me, to summon me to him, it was three years before. I had dropt out of South Medford High School to work (waitress, movie house cashier) to help Momma with the household for we were five daughters & just Momma and no father to provide an income for we had thought that Daddy was dead & what a shock— Daddy was not dead but *alive.*

Cleo Short had been a quite-successful businessman selling miniature golf courses! All of us brought up swinging miniature golf clubs & hitting teeny golf balls & our photos taken—FIVE SHORT DAUGHTERS OF MEDFORD BUSINESSMAN CLEO SHORT TAKE TO THE "MINIATURE LINKS"—& published widely in Medford & vicinity for we were all pretty girls especially (this is a fact everyone acknowledged, this is not my opinion) "Betty" who was the middle sister of the five and the most beautiful by far.

& then the Depression which hit poor Daddy hard & soon collapsed into bankruptcy & utterly shamed so Daddy drove to the Mystic River Bridge & what happened next was never made clear but Daddy's 1932 Nash sedan was discovered on the riverbank & not Daddy, anywhere—so it was believed that Cleo Marcus Short was a tragic suicide of the Depression as others had been, & declared dead two years later, & Momma collected $3,000 insurance & was now officially a widow & we were bereaved for our beloved daddy, for years.

Oh but then one day a letter came postmarked Vallejo, Cal! & the shocking news like in a fairy tale that Cleo Short was not dead in the Mystic River as we had believed but "alive and well" in Vallejo, California!

Momma would not reply to this letter, Momma had too much pride. Momma's heart had turned to stone in the aftermath of such deception, as she called it.

& bitterness, for Momma had to pay back the $3,000 insurance which had been spent years before. In doing so Momma had to borrow from relatives & wherever else she could & out of our salaries we helped Momma pay & everyone in Momma's family was hateful toward Daddy for this trick as they called it of a callow heart.

Of the five daughters of Cleo Short only one would forgive him. Only one would write back to him & soon travel to live with him in faraway California in a new life that beckoned.

For the old life was used up & of no promise, in Medford, Mass. And the golden California life beckoned—Los Angeles & Hollywood.

Betty you're a terrific gal & sure the beauty of the Short females. Look at you!

It did not seem a far-fetched idea to Betty Short as to Cleo Short or anyone who knew them, that daughter Betty was pretty enough & "sexy" enough to be a movie star one day.

That was a happy time, those months then.

They did not last long but Norma Jeane said to me when we were new & shy to each other sharing a room in Mr. Hansen's "mansion" on Buena Vista Avenue *Oh Betty you are so lucky!* for Norma Jeane said she had not ever glimpsed her father even from a distance but now that she'd been on the covers of *Swank* & *Stars* & *Stripes* maybe he would see her & recognize her as *his*. & if ever she was an actress on-screen he would see & recognize her—she was sure of this.

(Poor Norma Jeane had faith, if she worked hard & made the right connections among the Hollywood men, like all of us, she would become a star like Betty Grable, Lana Turner, & earlier Jean Harlow, who was Norma Jeane's model & idol. It was so: Norma Jeane was very beautiful in a simpering-baby way with a white-rose-petal skin that was softer than my skin even & did not show fatigue in her face as I did, sometimes. We were not jealous of Norma Jeane for she was so young-seeming though at this time nineteen years old which is not so young in Hollywood. We laughed at Norma Jeane, she was so *trusting & innocent* & you had to think, hearing her weak whispery voice, Norma Jeane Baker was just not smart & mature enough to make her way in the shark-waters where her white limbs would be torn off in the predators' teeth.)

It was the New Year of 1947 when this terrible act was perpetrated upon me. That was a later time.

We did not *crawl back* to that bastard K.K.! Except he owed us money, he'd kept promising to pay. & he knew "gentlemen"—he said—of a "dependable quality" & not the kind waiting like sharks in the surf for some trusting person to wade out.

Anyway—I didn't crawl to K.K. like he boasted. *Betty Short did not crawl for any man not ever.*

So it was the Bone Doctor inflicted such hurt upon me: that I would not *submit* to him in the disgusting way he wished. For not even $$$ can be enough, in such a case.

Of course—I did not know what would befall me. I did not know what my little cries *No! No-no-NO!* would unleash in the man, who had seemed till then a sane & reasonable man, a man who might *be handled* by any shrewd girl like Betty Short!

Post mortem you would not guess that I had had dignity and poise in life as well as milky-skinned brunette beauty though it is true that I had not (yet) a film career—even a "starlet" contract like many girls of our acquaintance at the Hollywood Canteen. (Norma Jeane Baker had not a real contract yet, either—though she led people to think she did.) *Post mortem* seeing me naked & white-skinned (for my body had totally *bled out*) & covered in stab wounds & lacerations—my legs spread open in the most ugly & cruel way in mockery—& my torso separated from my lower body & twisted slightly from it as if in revulsion for the horror perpetrated upon me—*post mortem* you would not guess that I had been a vivacious young woman whom many men admired in Hollywood & L.A. & a favorite at parties & very popular with well-to-do older men & Hollywood producers & Mr. Mark Hansen who owned the Top Hat Club & Mesa Grande movie house & invited me to live in his "mansion" on Buena Vista with other girls—(some were "starlets" & others aspiring to that status)—to "entertain" guests.

Dr. M. was not one of these. Dr. M. was known by no one except K.K.—& Betty Short.

It was such cruelty—to ask if he might *kiss me* & when I shut my eyes, to press the chloroform cloth against my nose & mouth!

For in the romance movies always the kiss is with *shut eyes*—the camera is close up to the woman's beautiful smooth face & long-lashed shut eyes.

And the romance music.

Except in actual life—there is no music. Only the sound of the man's grunting & the girl trying to draw breath to scream, to scream, to scream—in silence.

& such cruelty, to slash the corners of my mouth smiling in terror & hope to "charm"—slashing my mouth to my ears so that my face that had been a beautiful face would become a hideous clown-face that can never cease grinning.

& my breasts that were milky-pale & beautiful—so stabbed & mutilated, the hardened coroner could barely examine.

& the autopsy revealed contents of my stomach too filthy & shameful to be stated—the man would subordinate the girl utterly in all ways, & *why* could not be imagined . . .

What I am hoping you will comprehend—if you would listen to my words & not stare in horror & disgust at the "remains" of me—(the morgue photos have been published & posted everywhere in the years following—there is no escape from shame & ignominy, in death—the two halves of me "separated" with a butcher knife the Bone Doctor wielded laying my lifeless body on two planks across a bathtub—in the house on Norfolk, that I had never seen before in all of my life—with this knife the cruel maniac tore & sawed at my midriff—my pearly-pale skin that was so beautiful & desirable—that my blood would fall & drain into the tub—& these halves of my body he would wrap in dirty plastic curtains to carry away to dispose of like trash in a public place to create a spectacle for all to stare at in revulsion & titillation enduring for years)—if you would listen to my words *post mortem*, I am trying to explain that though Norma Jeane has become famous throughout the world, as *MARILYN MONROE*, it was a chance thing at the time in January 1947, it was a wisp of a chance, fragile as those feathery spiraling seeds of trees in the spring blown in the wind & catching in your hair & eyelashes—it was not a decreed thing but mere chance that Norma Jeane would become *MARILYN MONROE* & Elizabeth Short would become *THE BLACK DAHLIA* pitied & scorned in death & not ever understood, & the cruelest lies spread about me. What I am saying is that if you'd known us, Betty Short & Norma Jeane Baker, in those days, when we were roommates & close as sisters you would not have guessed which one of us would ascend to stellar heights & which would be flung into the pits of Hell, *I swear you would not.*

K.K. had photographed Norma Jeane when she was working in a factory in Burbank—but she'd never do a nude for him, she said.

A "nude" is all the calendar men want—if you don't strip, forget it. No matter how gorgeous your face is—nobody gives a damn.

When K.K. saw us in the Canteen, & invited us to his studio to be photographed, it was Betty Short he stared at most, & not Norma Jeane he'd already photographed and had hit a dead-end—he thought. 'Cause she would not pose nude.

It was Betty Short who engaged K.K. in sparky repartee like Carole Lombard on the screen not Norma Jeanne who bit her thumbnail smiling & blushing like a dimwit.

It was Betty Short who said yes maybe. Can't promise but maybe, yes.

It was Norma Jeane who just giggled, and murmured something nobody could hear.

I was twenty then. I was so gorgeous, walking into the Top Hat—or the Canteen—or some drugstore—every eye turned on me in the wild thought—*Ohh Is that Hedy Lamarr?*

Norma Jeane said if she walked into some place eyes would flash on her and people would think—*Ohh is that Jean Harlow?*

Bullshit! Norma Jeane never was mistook for Jean Harlow, I can swear to it.

I was not jealous of Norma. In fact, Norma was like a sister to me. A true sister—she'd lend me clothes, money. Not like my bitch-sisters back in Medford, cut me out of their lives like I was dirt.

'Cause I left home, & went to live in California. 'Cause it was obvious to me, my destiny was in Hollywood not boring Medford.

'Cause I wore black. Know why? Black is *style*.

When I was just seventeen, in Vallejo, before I'd even caught on about *style*—something wonderful happened to me.

You would be led to believe it was the first of many such honors culminating in an Academy Award Oscar for Best Actress . . .

It was the nicest surprise of my life. It was a surprise to change my life.

I had not even entered my own self in the competition but some guys I knew, at Camp Cooke, entered pictures they'd taken of me, when I was cashier at the PX there—all of the soldiers & their officers voted & when the ballots were counted of twelve girls entered it was *ELIZABETH SHORT* who had won the title *CAMP CUTIE OF CAMP COOKE.*

This was June 1941. Six & a half years yet to live. On my grave marker it would've been such a kindness to carve ELIZABETH SHORT 1924–1947 CAMP CUTIE OF CAMP COOKE 1941 but not a one of you selfish bastards remembered.

K. KEINHARDT:

Looking through my camera lens sometimes I thought Betty Short was the one. Other times, I thought Norma Jeane Baker.

Betty was the dark-haired beauty—*THE BLACK DAHLIA.* Norma Jeane was *THE WHITE ROSE* to me—in secret—her skin like white-rose-petals & face like a china doll's.

Betty had the "vivacious" personality—Norma Jeane was shy and withdrawn almost—you'd have to coax her out, to meet the camera lens.

Betty was all over you—it felt like her hands were on you—like she was about to crawl onto your lap and twine her arms around your neck and suck at your mouth like one of Dracula's sisters.

Sometimes a man wants that. Sometimes not.

Norma Jeane was all quivery and whispery and holding-back even when she finally removed the smock I'd given her—to pose "nude" on the red velvet drapery. (You wouldn't say "naked"—"naked" is like a corpse. "Nude" is art.) Like if you reached out to position Norma Jeane, just to touch her—she'd be shocked and recoil. *Ohhh!* Norma Jeane's eyes widened, if I made a move toward her.

I'd just laugh—*For Christ's sake, Norma! Nobody's going to rape you OK?*

Fact is, I was afraid to touch *THE WHITE ROSE*—you could see the raw pleading in her blue eyes—the orphan-child pleading—no love any man could give Norma would be enough.

& I did not want to *love* any of them—there is a terrible weakness in *love* like a sickness that could kill you—but not "K. Keinhardt"!

THE BLACK DAHLIA was a different matter. I would not ever have loved Betty Short—but feared being involved with her, so anxious too for a *career*—& if you were close to Betty you would smell just faintly the odor of her badly rotted teeth—her breath was "stale"—so she chewed spearmint gum & smoked & learned to smile with her lips pursed & closed—a hard knowing look in her eyes.

Fact is, I discovered Norma Jeane Baker—*me*.

Lots of guys would claim her—seeing she'd one day be "Marilyn Monroe"—but in 1945 at the Radio Plane factory in Burbank, Norma Jeane was just a girl-worker in denim coveralls—eighteen—not even the prettiest girl at the factory but Norma had something—"photogenic"—nobody else had. I took her picture for *Stars & Stripes*—in those factory-girl coveralls seen from the front, the rear, the side—"to boost the morale of G.I.s overseas." And the phone rang off the hook—*Who's the girl? She's a humdinger.*

See, I made her take off her wedding band for the shoot.

All the girlie mags—*Swank, Peek, Yank, Sir!*—wanted Norma Jeane for their covers. But she'd never do a nude—*Ohhhh! Gosh I just c-can't . . .*

I knew she would, though. Just a matter of time—and needing money.

Young girls needing money to live and older guys with money—in L.A.—pretty good setup, eh? Always has been & always will be—that's human nature & the foundation of Civilization.

Norma Jeane was younger than Betty Short and a lot less experienced—so you'd think. (Actually she'd been married to some jerk at age sixteen—then divorced when he left her to join the Merchant

Marines.) Smaller than Betty and dreamy-eyed where Betty was sort of hard-staring and taking everything in with those dark-glassy eyes of hers all smudged in mascara—Norma Jeane was no more than a size two and her body perfectly proportioned—exquisite like something breakable. Betty Short's pinups were sexy in a crude eye-catching way, kind of sly, dirty-minded—like she's winking at you. *C'mon I know what you want big boy: do it!* Norma Jeane's pinups were sexy but angelic—her first nude photo "Miss Golden Dreams" I managed to coax out of her is *the* pinup photo of all recorded history.

See, the trick was getting Norma to lie on the crinkly-crimson-velvet like she was a piece of candy—to be sucked.

Getting Norma to *relax* & to *smile*—like she had not a care in the world & wasn't desperate for money & broken-hearted, her jerk of a husband had "left her."

& wasn't desperate, her movie career was stalled at *zero.*

Guess what I paid Norma Jeane? Fifty bucks.

I made nine hundred!—a record for me, at the time.

Later Norma would come back to me begging—she had not known what she was signing, the waiver I'd pushed at her that day—& I said it was out of my hands by then, the rights to "Miss Golden Dreams" had been bought by the calendar company & beyond that sold & sold & sold—millions of dollars for strangers to this very day.

Don't argue with me, I told Norma—this is the foundation of Civilization.

What I never told the L.A. detectives—or anyone who came around to ask about Betty Short—was that—(yes I am regretful of this, & wouldn't want it to get out publicly)—there was this guy, this "gentleman"-like character, called himself "Dr. Mortenson"—an "orthopedic surgeon"—I think that's what he called himself.

The Bone Doctor he came to be, to me.

Not my fault—all I did was bring them together.

In fact it was Norma Jeane Dr. M. wanted to meet—not the other girls who came through my studio at that time & definitely not Betty Short he thought was *somewhat common—vulgar.*

That's how the Bone Doctor would talk: this prissy way like there's a bad smell in the room.

Not the black-haired one—her chin is too wide for feminine beauty & she's got a cross-eye.

The little blond girl. That one. SHE is the feminine beauty like an angel in heaven.

(Did poor Betty Short have a "cross-eye"? Some photos you can see it, kind of—her left eye isn't looking at you exactly the way the right eye is. So you'd think—something isn't right about this girl, she's witchy.)

One day in September 1946 the phone rang—*Hello? Is this K. Keinhardt the pinup photographer I am speaking to?*—this prissy voice & I say *Who the fuck is this?* & he says *Excuse me I am hoping to speak with Mr. Keinhardt on a proposition* & I say *What kind of a proposition?* & he says *I have been led to believe that you take "pinup" photos for the calendars* & I say *I am a studio photographer in the tradition of Alfred Stieglitz and Paul Strand—"nudes" are a small part of my repertoire* & he says *My proposition is: in my profession I see almost exclusively injured, disfigured, or malformed human bodies—particularly the female body is a sorry sight when it is far from "perfect"—and so—I am wondering if I might make a proposition to you, Mr. Keinhardt, who photographs only "perfect" female bodies . . .*

The deal was, Dr. M. would pay me twenty-five bucks—(which I later upped to thirty-five)—just to be a secret "observer": looking through a peephole in the screen behind the camera tripod.

Sure, I said. *As long as you don't take pictures of your own.*

How many times did Dr. M. come to the studio on Vicente Blvd., that fall and into the winter of 1947?—maybe a dozen times—& he never caused any trouble, just paid me in cash.

Parked his shiny black 1946 Packard sedan across the street.

Sat in the back behind the screen. "Observed."

Dr. M. had a face like a smudged charcoal drawing of Harry Truman, say. Same kind of glasses as Truman. You could not imagine this man young but only middle-aged with a prim little mouth & sagging jowls.

Starched white shirt, no necktie but a good-quality coat and pressed trousers. Graying-brown hair trimmed and with a part on the left. Kind of stubby fingers for a surgeon but Dr. M. had that quiet air of "authority"—you could imagine this character giving orders to nurses and younger doctors in that voice.

You could imagine the man giving orders to women—in that voice.

Yes he was what you'd call a "gentleman"—"good breeding"—good taste too, he preferred the White Rose to the Black Dahlia—at least, that had been his wish.

Of Betty Short whom he saw photographed on three separate occasions Dr. M. said frowning afterward:

That black-haired vixen. She's got a dirty mind—you can see it in her eyes—that cross-eye. And always licking her lips like there's something on her lips she can't get enough of tasting.

Of Norma Jeane whom he saw photographed just once—(historic "Miss Golden Dreams" which was a session of just forty minutes, surprisingly)—Dr. M. did not speak at all as if tongue-tied.

Dr. M. did request the girls' names, telephone numbers & addresses & I told him NO.

NO I cannot violate the girls' privacy—that would be a considerable extra fee, Doctor!

Something in my manner discouraged him. The Bone Doctor mumbled sorry & did not pursue the issue, did not even ask how much the "extra fee" might be—which was unexpected.

After *THE BLACK DAHLIA* in all the papers the Bone Doctor

vanished. He did not ever call me again & no one would ever know of his visits to my studio except me—and Betty Short.

And how much Betty Short knew, I don't know.

Afterward I tried to find out who Dr. M. was—thinking maybe the Bone Doctor might find it worthwhile to pay me not to give the L.A. homicide detectives his name—but I couldn't track him.

So I thought *Could be just a coincidence.*

A year or so before in L.A. there'd been another girl murdered in what was called a "sex frenzy"—in fact a girl Betty Short had known from the Top Hat—ankles and wrists tied with rope in the same way as *The Black Dahlia*—some of the same kind of torture-stab-wounds—and left in a bathtub naked—(but not dissected at the waist like Betty)—so you might think the same guy did both murders—but the detectives couldn't come up with any actual "suspects"—there just wasn't evidence & in the meantime there's kooks confessing to the murder—not just men but some women too!

Could be just a coincidence, I thought then, & I think now. *Anyway— K.K. is not going to get involved.*

NORMA JEANE BAKER:

It was just a n-nightmare.

It was the awfulest—most horrible—thing . . .

You could not ever imagine such a—an awful thing . . .

When I came back to the room that night I was kind of m-mad at Betty 'cause she'd stood me up at the Top Hat—also Betty had not paid me back the thirty dollars she owed me—thirty dollars was a *lot*—also Betty was always in my things—she would "borrow" & never return what she took—like my lipsticks—*that* made me mad!

At 20th Century-Fox I went to auditions all the time. Betty was not on contract but got on a list to audition, too—it costs money for makeup & clothes—& hair—Betty dyed her hair that inky-black color—my hair, that was brown, about the color of Betty's natural hair, they made me bleach at the Blue Book Agency saying they could get twice as many shoots for me as with my brown hair & this turned out to be correct though an understatement—more like three times as many shoots. Like Anita Loos says—*Gentlemen Prefer Blondes*—this is a fact.

But Betty Short had the wrong complexion for blond—so dyed-black hair was perfect for her. & with white makeup & powder & dark lipstick she made herself look really glamorous—"sexy."

Always wearing black clothes—that wasn't Betty's idea but some agent. Trying to get Betty Short work in the studios. *Not who you are but who you know*—they'd tell us. To get a contract you'd have to "entertain" the producers & their friends & then to keep the contract renewed you'd be expected to live in one of their residences like Mr. Hansen's—he liked us to lie around the pool in the sun in teeny bathing suits & sunglasses—it was just party, party, party night after night & Betty Short thrived on it—& sleeping through the day—but I needed to get to my acting class & my dance class & that was no joke—you can't audition either, if you are hungover & have shadows under your eyes. So—Betty Short & me—we did not always get along 100 percent—being from different backgrounds too for Betty did actually have a "father"—she'd lived with him before coming to L.A.—she showed me pictures of him—& she said *Oh my father was pretty well-to-do in Medford, Mass. when I was a little girl—see, this is my sisters & me on Daddy's miniature golf course—then Daddy lost the business—people stopped buying miniature golf courses I guess—in the damn old Depression.*

And I was so jealous!—I said *Oh Betty at least you have a f-father—you could go to him in Vallejo even now* & Betty said with this hurt angry look *Like hell I would never crawl back to him or to any God-damn man, my drunk father kicked me out saying I was no good, I was not even a good*

housekeeper like my mother, & Daddy accused me of being a strumpet & a
whore—just on the evidence that I dated some boys.

    & I said *But maybe your father feels differently now, you are older now*
& maybe he needs you & Betty looks as me like I am an idiot saying
Maybe he needs me but I don't need him, & I don't need any man to boss
me around, I will marry a rich man who adores me & wants to please ME
not the other God-damn way around, see?

    So I backed off. I did not say that Betty had no idea how sad it is not
to have a father—even a drunk father—& not to have a mother—even
a sick mother like my mother who "could not keep me" because she had
"mental problems"—but still, I would live with her, if she was discharged
from the hospital . . . I did not say any of this because I did not want
Betty mad at me & screaming & swearing like she did. It was known
that Betty Short had a "short" temper! We were sharing a room at the
Buena Vista & already it was up to me to make her bed not just my own
& hang things up she'd throw down & take away laundry & wash it if I
did not want a demoralizing sight to greet me every time I opened the
door. & Betty owed me money, I was anxious she would not repay.

    Betty said *You can get money from men—if they're the right men not*
these God-damn bloodsuckers.

    Betty seemed angry at most men. She'd been engaged to a major
in the U.S. Army Air Corps she had met at Camp Cooke—this was
said of her by girls who'd known her longer than me—& her fiancé
had died in a plane crash—& she had been pregnant at the time—
(maybe)—& had lost the baby or—(maybe)—had had an abortion.
& there was something more—Betty had tried to sue her fiancé's
family—for what, it wasn't known.

    & I thought—we have that in common. As my husband Jim
Dougherty had left me to join the Merchant Marines because he could
not love me as I needed to be loved so Betty's fiancé had left her in a
terrible accident—in death.

Later I found out Betty's other roommates had evicted her! Coming home in the early morning & waking them & not giving a damn & worst of all stealing from them—they said.

You can't trust Betty Short. This "Black Dahlia" bullshit—what a laugh.

Betty was nice to me, though—she laughed at me & called me *Baby-face.* She laughed at me not wanting to pose for nude pictures—I told her if you do nude pictures it's like taking money from men for sex—it's a crossing-over & you can't go back. & she just laughed—*Of course Baby-face you can "go back"—who's to know?* & I said if you have a nude photo in your past, the studios will not touch you—(for this was true & well known)—& she said *Of course they will—if you are meant to be a star.*

Betty had great faith in this, more than any of us—if you could be a *star,* all would be changed for you.

Between Betty Short & Norma Jeane Baker, it could not have been predicted who would be a "star." Just looking at the two of us—you could not ever have guessed for sure.

Soon, the name "Marilyn Monroe" would be given me. For the studio did not like "Norma Jeane"—this was an Okie name, they said. (It was not an Okie name! No one in my family was Okie or anything near.) & the studio did not like "Baker"—this was a dull name. But even the new name—"Marilyn Monroe"—did not seem real but a concoction like meringue, that would melt in the slightest rain.

Betty was always looking at herself in a mirror. Betty would look right past your head & if you turned, you would see it was her reflection she was looking at like in a windowpane! Betty believed she was beautiful as Hedy Lamarr & that she would be a star soon—all she needed was the right break, the right audition.

Well—this is true! So many of us yearning for this "break"—which will make the sadness of our lives fade, we think—like shadows on a wall when the sun comes out.

& we will think then *Now the sadness of my life is forgotten. Now—there will be a new life.*

When Betty was in a bitter mood she said you have only a few years if you're a *female*. By twenty-five if you don't have a man to adore you & take care of you or a studio contract—you are through.

But Betty made a joke of it saying *You are kaput! Finito! Dead meat!*

When she died in that terrible way, Betty was twenty-two.

The saddest thing was—oh not the *saddest* maybe—but it was awful!—after Betty was found dead in a vacant lot in that terrible way a reporter for the *Enterprise* called her mother in Medford, Mass. & told Mrs. Short that her daughter "Elizabeth Short" had won a major beauty contest in California & please could Mrs. Short tell her anything she could of her daughter's background—& poor Mrs. Short talked & talked all excitedly for an hour—(Betty would have thought it ironic, her mother seemed to have "forgiven" her having heard she'd won a big beauty contest!)—& at the end, the reporter cruelly told her that the actual news was, her daughter Elizabeth Short had been *murdered* . . .

Reporters & photographers like K.K.—some cruelty enters their veins, like a parasite—they are not "human" any longer in their pursuit of prey.

What do you know of your roommate Elizabeth Short's life? "Secret" life?

But I could tell the detectives nothing that others had not told them. & I did not know nearly so much as others did—this was a surprise!

Who it could have been who'd taken Betty into captivity—if it was someone who knew Betty & had lain in wait for her—or someone who had never seen her before that night—was not revealed.

Three days before the morning she was found in the vacant lot dumped like trash, the kidnap must have happened. Betty had been last seen at the Biltmore Hotel at about 9 P.M. where she had gone to meet someone—maybe?

He must have h-hated her. This one. To hurt her so.

For days he had her tied up in secret, it was revealed in the newspapers. Tied by her wrists & her ankles & (it was speculated) hung "upside down"—"spread-eagled"—& tortured before he k-killed her . . .

He slashed her face—that was such a pretty face—& just a girl's face without the makeup—He cut the corners of Betty's mouth so it looked like she was crazy-smiling—like a mask . . .

& then he—did something else . . .

With sharp knives & it was speculated "surgical tools" . . .

It is too terrible for me to say. It is too terrible to think of Betty Short in this way, who was my friend & my s-sister . . .

Oh Betty what has happened to you! Who would do such a thing & why—why to you?

Oh Betty I am sorry—every unkind thought I had of you, & that last night when you "stood me up"—again . . .

Oh Betty forgive me—maybe I could have helped you s-somehow.

I was twenty then. I was a model & had a "starlet" contract at 20th Century-Fox—which the studio would let lapse at the end of the year.

Like Betty Short I was desperate for money & sometimes it did cross my mind—I would "do anything" for money . . .

Except of course—I *would not.*

BETTY SHORT:

Why he was so—*angry!*

This was such a shock to me I did not ever—comprehend—& then it was too late.

You would say *She asked for it. The Black Dahlia—a slut . . .*

She took $$$ from men, that makes her a *slut*—

Well I say a married woman is a slut too then—taking $$$ from a man except it is "blessed" by the church—hypocrites I hate you & wish that I could be revenged upon you from the grave especially those of you who have PROFITED FROM THE DAHLIA'S TERRIBLE FATE.

The Bone Doctor did appear to be a "gentleman" & not like most others. He did appear to be well groomed & thoughtful. Waiting for me in his shiny black Packard sedan outside K.K.'s studio on Vicente Blvd. & when I crossed the street in my black patent-leather high heels worn without stockings having some difficulty with the damn paving stones he called to me *Excuse me miss would you like a ride?*—& I knew who he was (for K.K. had mentioned to me, this "Bone Doctor" who paid to see girls photographed nude & who had a particular interest in Norma Jeane) though not his name of course—& when I saw him, the glittery glasses like some politician or public man, the smile that was strained but polite, the thought came to me *This one is well-to-do & can be trusted*—& maybe the thought came to me *This one is well-to-do & can be handled, by Betty Short.*

For always in that first instant if you are female an instinct comes to you: *can this one be handled, or no.* & if *no* you must flee.

But if *yes* it will be worth your while to advance to him, if he beckons.

& what happened was: Dr. M. drove me back to the Buena Vista in the beautiful black Packard car & said very few words to me—asked where I lived & was I a "starlet"—& stared straight ahead through the windshield of the car—(which I took note was sparkling clean & clear & the white sunshine of Los Angeles in January made my eyes water it was so bright)—& he said only that he was a resident of Orange County & had inherited a—(I am not certain of these fancy words, which I might mis-remember)—an "orthopedic surgical practice" from his father; but was an *artiste* in his heart & hoped to retire early & pursue his desires in that direction.

The starched white shirt-collar & cuffs—the stubby hands but nails manicured & very clean—the pressed trousers & shiny shoes not scuffed or battered in the slightest—the third finger of the left hand with a just-perceptible paleness & impress where—(Betty Short had a sharp eye for such clues!)—a wedding band had been removed—all this I absorbed without seeming to be staring. My hands were clasped on my knees & my nails were dark-maroon polish—to match my dark-maroon lipstick—& my face powdered very white like (as K.K. would say part-sneering & part-admiring) a geisha. & I am wearing black of course—a black satin flared skirt & a lacy black blouse & black "pearls" at my throat—each of these borrowed from friends at Buena Vista except the "pearls" a gift from Mr. Hansen—& I am smiling & mentioned to Dr. M. that the concrete in the sun glittered in my eyes reminding me of the snow of Medford Mass. of my childhood & Dr. M. said *You are from New England, Betty?*—(for I had told him my name Betty Short by this time)—*you do not seem like you are from New England.*

Where does it seem that I am from, then?—I asked him with a side-long smile.

He continued to drive the Packard slow along the street as other vehicles passed us & his forehead furrowed & he said finally—*I could not guess. I would think that you are born of Hollywood—you have stepped out of a movie—or of the night.*

Out of the night—this struck me, it was a strange thing to say & flattering to me & so I thought *He is attracted to me. He will fall in love with me—he will be in my power.*

& I smiled to think how K.K. would be surprised! That bastard treating us like shit on his shoes & taking such advantage of us.

Dr. M. let me out at Mr. Hansen's stucco "mansion" (as it would be called in the newspapers) asking did I have a roommate & I said yes & Dr. M. said with a catch in his throat *Is your roommate that little blond girl*—*"Norma Jeane"*—& I had to say yes.

What is her last name? he asked & I said stiffly *I am not comfortable talking about Norma Jeane, she is so dear to me. I'm sorry.*

Dr. M. asked me for my phone number—he did not ask for Norma Jeane's phone number—(which was identical to my own in fact—the phone did not belong to either of us but was shared by girls on the second floor of the house)—& so I thought maybe he would call me; & hoped that he would, for he did seem like a "gentleman" though old & starched-stuffy as hell but clearly he had $$$ & seemed kindly disposed & not a tightwad. & the next day a call did come for "Elizabeth Short"; & he was shy at first clearing his throat & saying did I remember him?—& I said yes of course—& he said he would like to see me again & also—if it was possible—my friend Norma Jeane; he would like to take us to dinner that night to a nice restaurant he knew of, on Sunset Boulevard, if we were free—& I said *Yes I believe we are both free, Norma Jeane & me—yes.* & a date was made, he would come to pick us up at the Buena Vista at 7 P.M.

& at 7 P.M. I was dressed & waiting—from our friend Phoebe who was away I borrowed a beautiful black satin dress with a "plunging" neckline—around my neck the black "pearls" Mr. Hansen gave me—& my black patent-leather shoes & silk stockings—(also borrowed from Phoebe, who had more than one pair)—& there came Dr. M. exactly on time—no one saw me depart, I think—I hurried to the curb & slipped into the front passenger seat of the shiny black Packard came & hoped not to see in the man's face a look of disappointment that Norma Jeane was not with me—(for I did not ask Norma Jeane to join us of course—& I would not have told Dr. M. that Norma Jeane was not coming for Dr. M. might have said he would not wish to see me alone)—& quickly said *Norma Jeane is not free after all*—& he said *Oh—but where is she?—she is not coming with us?*—like he was hard of hearing & I said in a louder voice smiling at him to put him at ease for he seemed stiff & unyielding—*Oh Norma Jeane leads a crazy life, you see—she has a former husband* very jealous of her—he is her "ex" but he is always spying on her & threatening to "beat to a pulp" her man-friends & after this, Dr. M. said nothing more of that simpering baby-face Norma; but paid attention to *me*.

Before the dinner we would stop by a place he knew, Dr. M. said. For he had forgot something essential—his wallet. (He said with an awkward wink.) & asked would I come inside & I said *Oh—I don't know . . .* for I did not want the "gentleman" to think that I was not shy & fearful of being alone with a strange man; & he said he was an *artiste* in his heart & was learning photography too—he would like to take photographs of me he said—for I was so beautiful—*But only with your consent, Betty.* & we entered into this house on Norfolk St.—which did not seem like a nice enough house for Dr. M. to be staying in & also did not seem to be furnished—& a strange smell came to my nostrils, a chemical-smell like some kind of strong disinfectant—but I was thinking how Dr. M.'s hair was the color of a sparrow's feathers & Dr. M. was not very tall so that in my high heels I was almost his height—& he was not a muscled man but lean & stringy—I was smiling thinking I could *handle him* if necessary; & he said, taking my elbow to help me up a step, in the most gentlemanly way as we further entered the house he said *Betty, may I kiss you? Just once please may I kiss you, you are so beautiful Betty Short* & his breath was quickened & his eyes moist & intense behind the glittery glasses & I leaned to him & held my breath against the starchy-stuffy smell & shut my eyes knowing how gorgeous the Black Dahlia was at this time of dusk, & in the wan light of a single lamp inside, & lifted my lips to be kissed that were dark-plum in hue & "kissable" as Hedy Lamarr's. & I thought—*Maybe he is the one. Maybe—this will be the one.*

NORMA JEANE BAKER:
In the Top Hat I waited for Betty & she did not come.
Oh gosh I was getting mad at Betty!

Ohhh damn you Betty I was thinking!

& my heart hardened against her for Betty had promised she would join me—there were two guys wanting to buy me drinks—& I needed to get home because I wanted to wash out some things & dry them on the radiator & in the morning iron—my flannel skirt & my white cotton eyelet blouse—I would wear these to acting class, the others wore slacks & cheap sweaters—I had the philosophy *It is always an audition, you don't know who is observing you* & so I needed to be in bed by midnight & needed at least seven hours sleep or there would be blue shadows beneath my eyes but damn Betty would come into the room later, I knew—for Betty was always coming home late & stumbling-drunk—& if you scolded her she would cry *Go to hell! Screw you!* like she did not even know me & did not care for me any more than she did for the other girls in the Buena Vista.

For her heart was broken Betty had said, she'd been engaged to a wonderful man she had loved so much, Major Matt Gordon of the U.S. Army Air Corps & they were to be married several years before but Major Gordon died in a plane crash far away in India & his body never recovered & Betty confessed she'd been so broken-hearted & a little crazed she had told her fiancé's family that they had actually been married—in secret—& had had a little baby that had died at birth; & the family refused to believe this & scorned her & kept her from them & finally pretended that "Elizabeth Short" did not exist—so she had ruined her chances with the Gordon family, & was sick to think of it— *So much that I have lost, I hate God sometimes He has cursed me.* & I said to Betty *Don't ever say that! Don't give God any reason to hurt you more.*

& Betty cried in my arms like a little girl as no one had ever seen her except me—for Betty did not wish anyone to know her weakness, she said—& swore me to secrecy, I would never tell; & I held her & said *We can help each other, Betty. We will!*

But then, you could not trust her. My new lipstick missing, & one of my good blouses—& I knew it was Betty doing what Betty did which was take advantage of a friend. & I knew a time was coming when we would split up—& Betty would have no place to stay for the girls of Buena Vista were getting sick of her & then what? Where would she go?

That January night it was cold & rainy & I came back to the Buena Vista finally in a taxi by 1 A.M. & climbed the stairs to the second floor & there was the door to our room shut & I thought *Maybe Betty is here: maybe Betty did not feel well & did not go out at all tonight*—& when I came inside I stumbled in the darkness & groped for the light switch & I could see someone in Betty's bed sprawled & helpless-seeming— limp & not-breathing—I was so scared!—then managed to switch on the light & saw that it was just bedclothes twisted in Betty's messy bed, coiled together like a human body.

"Oh Betty! Gosh I thought it was *you*."

II

I.D.

For *eiii-dee* they were saying.
       If your name is *Lisette.*
This was weird! This was unexpected.

In second-period class, 9:40 A.M., some damn Monday in some damn winter month she'd lost track of and even the year—a "new" year—was weird to her, like a movie set in a faraway galaxy.

It was one of those school mornings—some older guys had got her high on beer, for a joke. Well, it was funny—not just the guys laughing at her but Lisette laughing at herself—not mean-laughing—she didn't think so—but, like, they *liked her.* "Liz-zette"—"Lizzzz-ette"—was their name for her, high-pitched piping like bats, and they'd touch her—run their fingers, fast, along her arms, her back—like she was scalding-hot to the touch.

Picked her up on the way to school. The middle school was on the way to the high school. This wasn't the first time. Most times, she was with a girlfriend—Keisha, or Tanya. They were mature girls for their age—Keisha especially—and not shy like other middle-school girls—they knew how to talk to guys, and guys knew how to talk to them, but it was just talk mostly, the girls were so young, just eighth graders.

Funny to see the young girls swilling beer out of cans, taking a drag from a cigarette, or a joint trying not to cough till they were red-faced. *Funny!*

Now this was—math?—damn math class Lisette hated—made her feel so stupid—not that she was *stupid*—only just, sometimes, her thoughts were snarled bad as her hair—eyes leaking tears behind her dark-purple-tinted glasses—*pres-ciption lenses*—so she couldn't see what the hell the teacher was scribbling on the board, even the shape of it—"triangle"—"rectangle"—was fuzzy to her. And Mz. Nowicki would say in her bright hopeful voice *Who can help me here? Who can tell us what the next step is here?*

Most of the class just sat on their asses, staring. Smirking. Not wanting to be called on—but then, Lisette was rarely called on in math class—Lisette might shut her eyes pretending she was thinking really hard—frowning and thinking really really hard—and when she opened her eyes there was one of the three or four smart kids in the class at the board taking the chalk from Nowicki.

She tried to watch, and she tried to comprehend. Something about the chalk clicking on the board—not a *blackboard*, for it was *green*—and the numerals she was expected to make sense of—she'd begin to feel dizzy, sickish.

Math, mathematics. Just the sound made her feel funny. Like when you know you're going to fuck up, and you're going to feel bad, and there is nothing you can do about it.

Her mother, Yvette Mueller, was a blackjack dealer at the Tropicana.

You had to be smart, and you had to think fast—you had to know what the hell you were doing—to be a blackjack dealer.

Counting cards. This was forbidden. If you caught somebody *counting cards* you signaled for help. Yvette liked to say how one day soon she would change her name, her hair color, all that she could about herself, drive out to Vegas, or some lesser place, like Reno, and play blackjack in such a way they'd never catch on—*counting cards like no amateur could do.*

But if Lisette said *Any time you're going take me with you Momma, OK?* her mother would frown as if Lisette had said something really stupid, and laugh—*Sweetie I am joking. Obviously—you don't fuck with these casino guys—I am* JOKING.

Vegas or Reno wasn't where she'd gone. Lisette was certain. She'd gone so far away, where it wasn't winter the way it was in New Jersey, she'd have taken lots more clothes, and a different kind of clothes.

In seventh grade the previous year Lisette hadn't had trouble with *arithmetic.* She hadn't had trouble with any of her school subjects, she'd gotten mostly B's and her mother had placed her report card, opened like a greeting card, on top of the refrigerator. All that seemed long ago like in another galaxy.

She was having a hard time sitting still. Like red ants were crawling inside her clothes, in her armpits, groin, and between her legs. Stinging, and tickling. Making her itch. Except she couldn't scratch as she wanted, with her fingernails really hard, to draw blood, so there was no point in just touching where her skin itched. That would only make it worse.

And her eye—her left eye. And the ridge of her nose where the cartilage/bone had been "rebuilt." A numb sensation there, except the eye leaked tears continuously. *Liz-zette's cry-ing! Hey—Liz-zette's cry-ing! Why're you cry-ing Liz-zz-zette—hey?*

They liked her, the older guys. That was why they teased her. Like she was some kind of cute little animal, like—*mascot?*

First time she'd seen J-C—(he'd transferred into their class in sixth grade)—she'd nudged Keisha saying *Ohhhh*—like in some MTV video, a moan to signal *sex-pain.*

She didn't know what it was, exactly. She had an idea.

Her mother's favorite music videos were *soft rock, retro rock, country and western, disco.* You'd hear her in the shower singing-moaning in a way you couldn't decipher was it angry, or happy—outside the bathroom Lisette listened transfixed. Momma never revealed such a raw yearning secret-self to *her.*

Oh she hated math class! Hated this place! Her school desk in the outside row by the windows, at the front of the classroom, made Lisette feel like she was at the edge of the glarey-bright-lit room looking *in*—like she wasn't a part of the class—Nowicki said it's to keep you involved, up close like this, so Lisette wouldn't daydream or lose her way but just the opposite was true, most days Lisette felt like she wasn't there at all.

Swiped at her eyes. Shifted her buttocks hoping to alleviate the red-stinging-ants. Nearly fifteen damn minutes she'd been waiting for their teacher to turn her fat back so Lisette could flip the folded-over note across the aisle to her friend Keisha—for Keisha to flip over to J-C—(Jimmy Chang)—who sat across the aisle from Keisha—this note that wasn't paper but a Kleenex—and on the Kleenex a lipstick-kiss—luscious grape-colored lipstick-kiss for J-C from Lisette.

She'd felt so dreamy blotting her lips on the Kleenex. A brand-new lipstick *Deep Purple* which her mother knew nothing about for like her girlfriends Lisette wore lipstick only away from home, giggling together they smeared lipstick on their lips and it was startling how different they looked within seconds, how mature and how *sexy.*

Out of the corner of her eye she was watching Keisha in the desk beside her and past Keisha's head there was J-C in the next row—J-C seemingly oblivious of either girl, or indifferent—stretching his long legs in the aisle, silky black hair falling across his forehead and when J-C's eyes moved onto Lisette—which happened sometimes, like by accident—(but it couldn't always be just accident)—she felt a sensation in her lower belly like you feel when there's a lightning flash and deafening thunder a second later—you're OK, you didn't get killed, but almost not.

J-C wasn't a guy you trifled with. That was a fact. Not J-C or his friends—his "posse." She'd been told. She'd been warned. These were older guys by a year or maybe two—they'd been kept back in school, or had started school later than their classmates. Except the beer-buzz at the back of Lisette's head—that made her careless, reckless. Or could be, a few drags from some guy's joint, or a diet pill, or two—or glue sniffing—(which was what little kids did, younger than eighth grade)—Lisette would blurt out some word she shouldn't know—or she'd do some weird impulsive thing to make her girlfriends scream with laughter, like waving to get the attention of a stranger driving a car, or actually running out into the street, narrowly missing being hit; lately, it seemed to be happening more frequently—making people laugh, and making them stare.

From older girls at the high school she'd picked up the trick of pursing her lips tight like for kissing—*Kiss-kiss!*—poking her pink tongue out—just a peep of her tongue—*Look look look at me damn you.* But J-C wouldn't glance at her—no matter how hard she tried.

I can make you look at me. I can make you love me. Look!

J-C's father worked at the Trump Taj Mahal. Where he'd come from, somewhere called *Bay-jing*, in China, he'd driven a car for some high government official. Or, he'd been a bodyguard. J-C boasted that his father carried a gun, J-C had held in his hand. Man, he'd fired it!

A girl asked J-C if he'd ever shot anybody and J-C shrugged and laughed.

Lisette's mother had moved Lisette and herself from Edison, New Jersey, to Atlantic City when Lisette was nine years old. She'd been separated from Lisette's father but later, Daddy came to stay with them in Atlantic City when he was on leave from the army.

Later, they were separated again. Now, they were *divorced*.

Lisette liked to name the places her mother had worked, that had such special names: Trump Taj Mahal—Bally's Atlantic City—Harrah's—the Tropicana.

Except it wasn't certain if Yvette worked at the Tropicana any longer—if she was a blackjack dealer any longer. Could be, Yvette was back to being a cocktail waitress.

It made Lisette so damn—fucking—*angry!*—you could ask her mother the most direct question like *Exactly where the hell are you working now Momma* and her mother would find a way to give an answer that made some kind of sense at the time but afterward you would discover it had melted away like a tissue dipped in water.

But J-C's father was a security guard at the Taj. That was a fact. J-C and his friends never approached the Taj or any of the new glittery hotel-casinos where security was tight and there were cameras on you every step of the way but hung out instead at the south end of the Strip where there were cheap motels, fast-food restaurants, pawnshops and bail-bond shops and storefront churches, sprawling parking lots and not parking garages so they could cruise the lots and side streets after dark and break into parked vehicles if no one was watching. The guys laughed how easy it was to force open a locked door or a trunk where people left things like for instance a woman's heavy handbag she didn't want to carry walking on the boardwalk. Assholes! Some of them were so dumb you almost felt sorry for them.

All this while Lisette had been waiting, for Nowicki to be distracted. The beer-buzz was fading, she was beginning to lose her nerve. Passing a lipstick-kiss to J-C. like saying *All right if you screw me, fuck me—whatever. Hey here I am.*

Except maybe it was just a joke—so many things were jokes—you'd have to negotiate the more precise meaning, later.

If there was a *later*. Lisette wasn't into thinking too seriously about *later*.

Wiped her eyes with her fingertips like she wasn't supposed to do since the surgery—*Your fingers are dirty Lisette you must not touch your eyes with your dirty fingers there is the risk of infection*—oh God she hated how both her eyes filled with tears in cold months and in bright light like this damn fluorescent light in all the school rooms and corridors so her mother had got permission for Lisette to wear dark-purple-tinted sunglasses to school, that made her look—like, *cool*—like she's in high school not middle school, sixteen or seventeen not thirteen.

Hell you're not thirteen—are you? You?

One of her mother's man friends eyeing her suspiciously. Like, why'd she want to play some trick about her *age*?

He'd been mostly an asshole, this friend of her mother's. Chester— "Chet." But kind of nice, he'd lent Momma some part of the money she'd needed for Lisette's eye doctor.

Now Lisette was as tall as her mother. It was hard to get used to seeing Momma just her height—a look of, like, fright in Momma's face, that her daughter was catching up with her, fast.

They'd said she was *slow. Slow learner*. They'd said *mild dyslexia*. But with glasses, she could read better up close. Except if her eyes watered and she had to keep blinking and blinking and sometimes that didn't even help.

That morning she'd had to get up by herself. Get her own breakfast—sugar-glaze Wheaties—eating in front of the TV—and she hated morning-TV, cartoons and crap or worse yet "news"—she'd slept in her clothes for the third night—black T-shirt, underwear, wool socks—dragged on her jeans, a scuzzy black-wool sweater of her mother's with *TAJ* embossed on the back in turquoise satin. And her boots.

Checked the phone messages but there were none new.

Friday night 9 P.M. her mother had called, Lisette had seen the caller ID and hadn't picked up. *Fuck you going away, why the fuck should I talk to you.*

Later, feeling kind of scared hearing loud voices out in the street she'd tried to call her mother's cell phone number. But the call didn't go through.

Fuck you I hate you anyway. Hate hate hate you!

Unless Momma brought her back something nice—like when she and Lisette's father went to Fort Lauderdale for their *second honeymoon* and Momma brought Lisette back a pink-coral-colored outfit—tunic top, pants.

Even with all that went wrong in Fort Lauderdale, Momma remembered to bring Lisette a gift.

Now it happened—and it happened fast.

Nowicki went to the door—classroom door—where someone was knocking and quick!—with a pounding heart Lisette leaned over to hand the wadded Kleenex-note to Keisha who tossed it onto J-C's desk like it was a hot coal—and J-C blinked at the note like it was some weird beetle that had fallen from the ceiling—and without glancing over at Keisha, or at Lisette peering at him through the dark-purple-tinted glasses, with a gesture like shrugging his shoulders—J-C was *so cool*—all he did was shut the wadded Kleenex in his fist and shove it into a pocket of his jeans.

Any other guy, he'd open the note to see what it was. But not Jimmy Chang. Like J-C was so accustomed to girls tossing him notes in class, he hadn't much curiosity what it was the snarl-haired girl in the dark glasses had sent him, or maybe he had a good idea what it was. *Kiss-kiss. Kiss-kiss-kiss.* The main thing was, J-C hadn't just laughed and crumpled it up like trash.

By now Lisette's mouth was dry like cotton. This was the first time she'd passed such a note to J-C—or to any boy. And the beer-buzz that had made her feel so happy and hopeful was rapidly fading.

Like frothy surf withdrawing with the tide, the beach is left littered with pathetic putrid crap like desiccated jellyfish, fish heads and bones, hypodermic needles from what the newspapers called *medical waste* dumped in the ocean off New York City, borne to the New Jersey coast.

Voices scolded but were mostly admiring, envious—*Y'know Lisette Mueller—she's hot.*

She'd had a half-beer, maybe. Swilling it down outside in the parking lot behind where the buses parked and fouled the air with exhaust stinging the eyes but the guys didn't seem to notice loud-talking and loud-laughing and she could see, the way they looked at her sometimes, Lisette Mueller was *hot.*

Except: she'd spilled beer on her jacket. Beer stains on the dark-green corduroy her mother would detect, if she sniffed at it. When Momma returned home probably that night.

This Monday, in January—it was January—she'd lost track of the actual date like what the fuck'd she do with the little piece of paper her mother'd given her, from the eye doctor, *pres-ciption* it's called, for the drugstore, for the eyedrops. This her mother'd given her last week last time she'd seen Momma, maybe Thursday morning. Or Wednesday. And this was some kind of *steroid-solution* she needed for her eye after the surgery but the damn *pres-ciption* she couldn't find now not in any pocket in her jacket or backpack or in the kitchen at home, or in her bedroom, or—like on the floor by the boots—in the hall where they hung their coats—not anywhere.

Nowicki was at the door now turned looking at—who?—Lisette?—like a bad dream where you're singled out—some stranger, and this looked like a cop, coming to your classroom to ask for *you.*

"Lisette? Can you step out into the hall with us, please."

Next to Nowicki was a woman, in a uniform—had to be Atlantic City PD—Hispanic features and skin-color and dark hair drawn back tight and sleek in a knot; and everybody in the classroom riveted now, awake and staring and poor Lisette in her seat like she's paralyzed, stunned—"Lis-sette Muel-ler? Will you step out in the hall with us, please"—like waking from a dream Lisette tried to stand, biting at her lip trying to stand, fuck her feet were tangled in her backpack straps, a roaring in her ears through which the female cop's voice penetrated—repeating what she'd said in a sharper voice and adding *personal possessions, please*—meaning that Lisette should take her things with her—she was going to be taken out of school—wouldn't be returning to the classroom.

So scared, she belched beer. Sour-vomity-beer taste in her mouth and—oh Christ!—what if the female cop smelled her breath.

And in the corridor a worse roaring in her ears as in a tunnel in which sounds are amplified so loud you can't distinguish anything clearly—out of the Hispanic woman's lips came bizarre sounds *eiii-dee*—*if you are Lisette Mueller—come with me.*

EIII-DEE—EIII-DEE—like a gull's cry borne on the wind rising and snatched-away even as you strained desperately to hear.

*

Turned out, there were two cops who'd come for her.

If you are Lis-ette Mueller. Come with us!

Now her head was clearing a little, she began to hear *I.D.*

The Hispanic policewoman introduced herself—Officer Molina. Like, Lisette was going to remember this name, let alone use it—*Officer Molina!* That had to be a joke.

The other cop was a man—a little younger than the Hispanic

woman—his skin so acne-scarred and smudged-looking you'd be hard put to say he was *white*.

Both of them looking at Lisette like—what? Like they felt sorry for her, or were disgusted with her, or—what? She saw the male cop's eyes drop to her tight-fitting jeans with a red-rag-patch at the knee, then up again to her blank scared face.

It wouldn't be note-passing in math class, they'd come to arrest her for. Maybe at the Rite Aid—the other day—plastic lipstick tubes marked down to sixty-nine cents in a bin—almost, Lisette's fingers had snatched three of them up, and into her pocket, without her knowing what she did . . .

"You are—'Lisette Mueller'—daughter of 'Yvette Mueller'—yes?"

Numbly Lisette nodded—yes.

"Resident of—'2991 North Seventh Street, Atlantic City'—yes?"

Numbly Lisette nodded—yes.

Officer Molina did the talking. Lisette's heart was beating hard and quick. She was too frightened to react when Molina took hold of her arm at the elbow—not forcibly but firmly—as a female relation might; walking Lisette to the stairs, and down the stairs, talking to her in a calm kindly matter-of-fact voice signaling *You will be all right. This will be all right. Just come with us, you will be all right.*

"How recently did you see your mother, Lisette? Or speak with your mother? Was it—today?"

Today? What was today? Lisette couldn't remember.

"Has your mother been away, Lisette? And did she call you?"

Numbly Lisette shook her head—no.

"Your mother isn't away? But she isn't at home—is she?"

Lisette tried to think. What was the right answer. A weird scared smile made her mouth twist in the way that pissed her mother who mistook the smile for something else.

They'd been to the house, maybe. They'd been to the house looking for Yvette Mueller and knew she wasn't there. Molina said:

"When did you speak with your mother last, Lisette?"

This was hard to determine. It wouldn't be the right answer, Lisette reasoned, to say that her mother had called and left a phone message—would it?

Shyly Lisette mumbled she didn't know.

"But not this morning? Before you went to school?"

"No. Not—this morning." Lisette shook her head grateful for something to say that was definite.

They were outside, at the rear of the school. A police cruiser was parked in the fire lane. Lisette felt a taste of panic—were they taking her to the cruiser? She was being arrested, taken to *juvie court*. The boys in J-C's posse joked about *juvie court, fam'ly court*.

In the cold wet air smelling of the ocean Lisette felt the last of the beer-buzz evaporate. She hated it how the cops—both cops—were staring at her like they'd never seen anything so sad, so pathetic, maybe disgusting before—like some sniveling little mangy dog. They could see her pimply skin at her hairline and every snarl in her dirt-colored frizz-hair she hadn't taken the time to comb, or run a brush through, let alone shampoo for four, five days. And she hadn't had a shower, either.

That long, her mother had been *away*.

Away for the weekend with—who?—that was one of Momma's secrets. Could be a new friend—"Exciting new friend" Yvette always described them on the phone—some man she'd met at the casino probably—there were lots of roving unattached men in Atlantic City—if they won in the casino they needed to celebrate with someone, and if they lost in the casino they needed to be cheered up by someone—Yvette Mueller was the one!—honey-colored hair not dirt-colored (which was her natural hair color) in waves to her shoulder, sparkly eyes, a quick nice soothing laugh that was what a man wanted to hear, not something sharp and ice-picky driving him up the wall.

Lisette had asked her mother who this was she was *going away for the weekend* with and Momma'd said nobody you know; but some way she'd smiled, not at Lisette but to herself, some unfathomable look like the expression of the face of one about to step into mid-air—step off the diving board, or into the (empty) elevator shaft—made Lisette think suddenly—*Daddy?*

She knew that her mother was still in contact with her father. Some way she knew this, though Momma would not have told her. Even after the divorce which had been a nasty divorce, they'd been in contact.

That was because—(as Daddy had explained to her)—she would always be his daughter.

All else might be changed, like where Daddy lived, and if Daddy and Mommy were married—but not that. Not ever.

So Lisette persisted asking her mother was it Daddy she was going away with, was it Daddy, *was it?*—nagging at Momma until Momma laughed saying *Hell no! No way I'm seeing that asshole again.*

But something in the way her mother laughed, some slide of her eyes like she was excited, and feeling good about it, and reckless-seeming, like she'd been drinking though Lisette didn't think she had been, just then—something made Lisette think *Daddy!*

Lisette mumbled she wasn't sure—when she'd seen her mother last. "I guess—maybe—Saturday . . ."

It hadn't been Saturday. More like Thursday. But she was thinking—with a part of her mind almost calmly thinking—that there might be some New Jersey state law, an adult parent could not leave an underage child alone and unsupervised for more than a day or two—maybe even a single day—and she did not want her mother to get into trouble.

Sure she hated Momma sometimes, she was pissed at Momma lots of times but she did not want Momma to get into trouble with the cops.

They were staring at her now guiltily faltering, fumbling, "—could've been, like, just yesterday—or—day before—"

Her heart thumped in her chest like a crazed sparrow throwing itself against a window like she'd seen in a garage once, the little brown bird trapped inside the garage up by the ceiling beating its wings and exhausting itself.

Yvette Mueller was in trouble with the law—was that it?

In trouble with the law—*again?*

Christmas before last Lisette's mother had been ticketed for DWI—*driving while intoxicated*—and for failing to have her auto registration and insurance in the car.

Earlier, when Lisette was a little girl, there'd been some other charges, too. Whatever came of these, Lisette never knew.

The only court Lisette had been in, with her mother, was Ocean County Family Court. Here, the judge had awarded *custody* to Yvette Mueller and *visitation privileges* to Duane Mueller. If something happened to Yvette Mueller now, Lisette would be removed from their rented house and placed in a foster home. It wasn't possible for Lisette to live with her father who was now a sergeant in the U.S. Army and last she'd heard was about to be deployed to Iraq for the third time.

Deployed was a strange word—a strange sound. *De-ployed.*

Daddy hadn't meant to hurt her, she knew. Even Momma believed this which was why she hadn't called 911. And when the doctor at the ER asked Lisette how her face had been so bruised, the *temporal bone* broken, her nose and eye socket broken, she'd said it was an accident on the stairs, she'd been running, and she fell.

Which was true. She'd been running, and she fell. And Daddy shouting behind her, swiping with his fists—not meaning to hit her, or to hurt her. But he'd been pissed.

And all the things Daddy said afterward were what you wanted to hear, what made you cry, you wanted so badly to hear. Though knowing even as you were hearing them that Daddy was going away soon again—*de-ployed*. And so it would not matter whether the things that Daddy promised were true or not-so-true.

"And your father? Have you seen your father, Lisette? How recently have you seen your father?"

So she could wear dark-purple-tinted glasses at school. And Momma had let her pick out the frames she'd wanted. And J-C had an older brother paralyzed from the waist down, victim of a drive-by shooting, so J-C was cool with people looking freaky, if anything this would call J-C's attention to the snarl-haired girl who gazed at him like a lovestruck puppy and who blushed red when he caught her.

Pain like gulls picking at something alive, in her *repaired* face. But it was worth it, if J-C took notice. If any of the guys took notice. *Liz-ette! Liz-zzzette!*

Her mother had gone away for the weekend—"I can trust you, Lisette—right?"—and Lisette said sure, sure you can.

Alone in the house meant that Lisette could stay up as late as she wanted watching TV. And she could watch as much TV as she wanted. And any channel she wanted. And lie sprawled on the sofa talking on her cell phone as much as she wanted.

It was a short walk to the minimall—Kentucky Fried Chicken, Vito's Pizzeria, Taco Bell. Though alone in the house it was easier just to defrost frozen suppers in the microwave and eat in the living room watching TV.

The first night, Friday, Yvette was gone just a few hours when Lisette's friend Keisha came over. The girls watched a DVD Keisha brought over and ate what they could find in the refrigerator.

"It's cool, your mother gone away. Where's she gone?"

Lisette shrugged. Philadelphia, New York—who gave a damn?

"Wow! New York?" Keisha was impressed. "Who'd she go with?"

Lisette thought. Possibly, her mother had gone to Vegas after all. With her man friend, or whoever. This time of year, depressing-cold and wet by the ocean, the smartest place you'd want to go would be Vegas.

"She's got lots of friends there, from the casino. She's welcome to go out there, anytime. She'd have taken me except for damn, dumb school."

In the cruiser, the male cop drove. Molina sat in the passenger's seat turned to look at Lisette. Her cherry-red lips were bright in her face like something on a billboard that was otherwise weatherworn and raddled. The sleek black hair shone like a seal's coat, the sharp dark eyes shone with a strange unknowable unspeakable knowledge. It was a look Lisette had seen often in the faces of women—usually, women older than her mother—when they looked at you not in disgust or disapproval but sudden sympathy seeing *you*.

Lisette was uneasy with that look. She'd seen it in Nowicki's face, too. Better was the look of quick disgust, dismay—the woman seeing the girl like somebody she'd never been, or could even remember.

Must've been two, three times Molina explained to Lisette where they were taking her—to the Ocean County Hospital—for the I.D. But the words hadn't come together in a way that was comprehensible.

Eiii-dee. Eiii-dee. Long she would hear these syllables like a gull's cry lifting into the asphalt-colored clouds above the ocean.

"We will just stay as long you wish. Or, not long at all—it's up to you. Maybe it will be over in a minute. Or maybe . . ."

Molina spoke to Lisette in this way, that was meant to soothe, but did not make sense. No matter the words, there was a meaning beneath that Lisette could not grasp. Often adults were uncomfortable with Lisette because she gave an impression of smirking but it was just the skin around her left eye, the eye socket that had been shattered and repaired, and a frozen look to that part of her face because the nerve-muscles were dead. *Such a freak accident* her mother said *told her and told her not to—not to run—on the stairs—you know how kids are.* And half-pleading with the surgeon though she knew the answer to her question *Will the life return to them, ever? The broken nerves?*

Not broken but *dead*. Momma knew!

At the hospital they parked again at the rear of the building. This was the hospital Yvette had brought Lisette to, last fall, to visit one of her casino friends dying of AIDS. But Lisette pretended not to know what the hospital was. Especially Lisette pretended not to know that the basement—you pressed *B* on the elevator—took you to MORGUE.

Some reason she was being taken here. The roaring in her head was like a wind blowing any clear thought away.

In a lowered voice Molina conferred with the male cop who was grimacing like her father sometimes did—mostly around the mouth. She could go into a dream recalling *Daddy*—but this wasn't the place.

Couldn't hear what the cops were saying. She had no wish to hear. But she wanted to believe that the Hispanic woman was her friend and could be trusted—it was like that with Hispanic women, the mothers of her classmates, mostly they were nice, they were *kind*. Molina was a kind woman, you could see how she'd be with children and possibly grandchildren. Weird that she was a cop, and carried a gun—*packed heat* it was said. Molina was not a beautiful woman with thick heavy brows like a man's but a smooth almost unlined face of some dark-taffy color beginning to thicken at the jawline. This kind of woman who'd be stern and frowning with you then wink, so you laughed, startled.

Molina didn't *wink*. Lisette had no reason to laugh.

They were standing just inside the hospital, on the first floor by the elevators. People moved around them, past them. Like blurs in the background of a photograph, or in a film. It seemed urgent now to listen to what Molina was telling her in a soothing/confiding voice as Molina gripped Lisette's arm again. Did Molina think that Lisette would try to shake her off, and escape? The male cop held himself a little apart, frowning. Lisette's mother knew some cops—she'd gone out with a cop—she'd said how the life of a cop is so fucking boring except once in a while something happens and happens fast and you could be shot down in that second or two but mostly it was very very boring like dealing blackjack cards to assholes thinking they could win against the house. *You never win against the house.*

What Molina was saying did not seem to Lisette relevant to the situation but later, Lisette would see that yes, all that the policewoman said was relevant—asking Lisette about Christmas, which was maybe two weeks ago, or three weeks ago, and New Year's—how much "business" the police had at this time of year; and what had Lisette and her mother done over the holidays, anything special?

Lisette tried to think. *Holidays* wasn't a word she or Momma would use.

"Just saw some people. Nothing special."

"You didn't see your father?"

No. Didn't.

"When was the last time you saw him?"

Last time! Lisette tried to think: it was back beyond the face surgery, and the eye surgery. But she'd been out of school.

Maybe in the summer. Like, around July Fourth.

"Not more recently than that?"

Lisette swiped at her eye. Wondering was this some kind of trick like you saw on TV cop shows?

"On New Year's Eve, did your mother go out?"

Yes. Sure. Momma always went out, New Year's Eve.

"Do you know who she went out with?"

No. Did not know.

"He didn't come to the house, to pick her up?"

Lisette tried to think. If whoever it was came to the house for sure Lisette wasn't going to see him like she hid from Momma's woman-friends and why—no reason, just wanted to.

Lisette how big you're getting!

Lisette taller than your mom, eh?

They took the elevator down. Down to MORGUE.

Here the hospital was a different place. Here the air was cooler and smelled—smelled of something like chemicals. There were no visitors here. There were very few hospital staff people here. A female attendant in white pants, white shirt and a cardigan sweater told them that the *assistant coroner* would be with them soon.

They were seated. Lisette was between the two cops. Feeling weak in the knees, sick—like she'd been arrested, she was *in custody* and this was a trick to expose her. As casually—for she'd been talking of something else—Molina began to ask Lisette about a motel on the south edge of the city—the Blue Moon Motel on South Atlantic—had Lisette heard of the Blue Moon Motel?—and Lisette said no—she had never heard of the Blue Moon Motel—there were motels all over Atlantic City and some of them sleazy places and she did not think—as Molina seemed to be saying—that her mother had worked at any one of these motels, ever—if it'd been the Blue Moon Motel, she'd have heard of it. Since when was Yvette Mueller working *there*? She was not. Her mother was not.

Lisette said her mother was not a motel maid or a cocktail waitress but a blackjack dealer and you had to be trained for that.

Lisette said maybe her mother had to fly out to Las Vegas—maybe there was a job for her there.

Lisette said, like one groping for a light switch: "Is Momma in—some kind of trouble?"

A twisty little knot of rage in her heart, against Mommy. Oh she *hated that woman!*—all this was Momma's fault.

Molina said they weren't sure. That was what the I.D. might clear up.

"We need your cooperation, Lisette. We are hoping that you could provide—*identification.*"

Weird how back at school she'd heard *eiii-dee* not I.D. Like static was interfering, to confuse her. Like after she'd fallen on the stairs and hit her face and hit her head and she hadn't been able to walk without leaning against a wall she'd been so dizzy, and she'd forgotten things. Some short-circuit in her brain.

"Can you identify—these? Do these look familiar, Lisette?"

A morgue attendant had brought Molina a box containing items of which two were a woman's handbag and a woman's wallet which Molina lifted carefully from the box, with gloved hands.

Lisette stared at the handbag and at the wallet. What were these? Were they supposed to belong to her mother? Lisette wasn't sure if she had ever seen them before and wondered was this some kind of cop-trick, to see if she was telling the truth.

Lisette shook her head no—but slowly. Staring at the brown-leather handbag with some ornamentation on it, like a brass buckle, and straps; and the black wallet shabby-looking, like something you'd see on a sidewalk or by a Dumpster and not even bother to pick up to see if there's money inside.

Molina was saying these "items" were "retrieved" from a drainage ditch behind the Blue Moon Motel.

Also behind the drainage ditch was a woman's body—a "badly damaged" woman's body for which they had no identification, yet.

Carefully Molina spoke. Her hand lay lightly on Lisette's arm, which had the effect of restraining Lisette from swiping and poking at her left eye as she'd been doing. It had the effect also of restraining Lisette from squirming in her seat like red ants were stinging inside her clothes.

"The purse has been emptied out and the lining is ripped. In the wallet was a New Jersey driver's license issued to 'Yvette Mueller' but no credit cards or money—no other I.D. There was a slip of paper with a name and a number to be called 'in case of emergency' but that number has been disconnected—it belonged to a relative of your mother's who lives, or lived, in Edison, New Jersey? 'Iris Pedersen'?"

Lisette shook her head as if all this was too much—just too much for her to absorb. She didn't recognize the handbag and she didn't recognize the wallet—she was sure. She resented being asked, for these items were so grungy-looking it was an insult to think that they might belong to her mother.

Close up she saw that Molina's eyes were beautiful and dark-thick-lashed the way Lisette's mother tried to make her eyes, with a mascara brush. The skin beneath Molina's eyes was soft and bruised-looking and on her throat were tiny dark moles. Molina's lips were the exposed red-fleshy part of her, swollen-looking, moist. It did not seem natural that a woman like Molina who you could see was a *mother*—her body was a mother's body for sure, spreading hips and heavy breasts straining at the front of her jacket—and in her earlobes, small gold studs—could be a *cop*; it did not seem natural that this person was carrying a gun, in a holster attached to a leather belt, and that she could use it, if she wanted to. Anytime she wanted to. Lisette went into a dream thinking, if she struck at Molina, if she kicked, spat, bit, Molina might shoot *her*.

The male cop, you'd expect to have a gun. You'd expect he would use it.

Daddy had showed them his guns, he'd brought back from Iraq. These were not *army-issue* but *personal guns,* a pistol with a carved-wood handle and a heavier handgun, a *revolver.* He'd won these in a card game, Daddy said.

Maybe it hadn't been from Iraq he'd brought them. Maybe this was Fort Bragg, where he'd been stationed.

Lisette was saying that, if her mother's driver's license had been in that wallet, maybe it was her mother's wallet—but definitely, she didn't recognize it.

As for "Iris Pedersen"—"Aunt Iris"—this was her mother's aunt not hers. Aunt Iris was old enough to be Lisette's grandmother and Lisette hadn't seen her in years and did not think that her mother had, either. For all they knew the old lady was dead.

"We tried to contact her and the Edison police tried to contact her. But . . ."

Molina went on to tell Lisette that they had tried to locate her father—"Duane David Mueller"—to make the I.D. for them but he was no longer a resident in Atlantic City or so far as they knew in the State of New Jersey.

An I.D. by someone who knew Yvette Mueller well was necessary to determine if, in fact, the dead woman was Yvette Mueller—or another woman of her approximate age. The condition of the body and the injuries to the face made it difficult to judge, from the driver's license photo. And from photos on file at the casinos in which Yvette Mueller had worked.

Condition of the body. This was the first Lisette had heard of a *body.*

Unless Molina had been telling her, this was some of what Molina had been telling her, Lisette hadn't heard.

Body! She didn't know anything about any *body.*

Lisette said, "My father's in the U.S. Army. My father is a sergeant in the U.S. Army, he used to be stationed at Fort Bragg but now he's in

Iraq," and Molina said, "No, Lisette. I'm afraid that that has changed. Your father is no longer a sergeant in the U.S. Army, and he is no longer in Iraq."

Lisette wanted to say *That's bullshit! That is not true.*

"The army has no record of 'Duane Mueller' at the present time—he's been AWOL since December twenty-sixth of last year."

Lisette was so surprised she couldn't speak. Except for Molina gripping her arm she'd have jumped up and run away.

Her stomach felt sick. Deep in her stomach. Like the bad kind of flu, with diarrhea.

Molina was speaking of other relatives of Yvette Mueller they'd tried to locate, in New Jersey and Maryland, to come to Atlantic City for the I.D.—for they'd hoped to spare Lisette—but these relatives seemed to have moved away, or vanished. None were listed in the phone directory.

Lisette wanted to say with a jeering laugh *Yeah. There's nobody left except Momma and me.*

She was shivering so hard, her teeth were chattering. The corduroy jacket wasn't really for winter—this nasty wet cold. There hadn't been Momma that morning scolding her *Dress warm! For Christ's sake it's January.*

Another morgue attendant, an Indian-looking man—some kind of doctor—*assistant coroner*—had come to speak in a lowered voice to the police officers. Quickly Lisette shut her eyes not listening. This was not meant for her to hear and she did not want to hear! Trying to remember where she was exactly, and why—why they'd been asking her . . . Trying to picture the classroom she'd had to leave—she had not wanted to leave—there was Nowicki at the board with her squeaky chalk, and there was J-C slouched in his desk, silk hair falling into his face—and Keisha, who breathed through her mouth when she was excited, or scared—and there was Lisette's own desk, empty—but now it was later, it was third period and J-C wasn't in English class with Lisette—but—there was the cafeteria—when the bell rang at 11:45 A.M., it was lunchtime and you lined up outside the doors—bright-lit fluorescent lights and a smell of greasy fried food—french fries . . . Macaroni and cheese, chili on buns . . . Lisette's mouth flooded with saliva.

Smiling seeing the purple-lipstick kiss on the Kleenex, as J-C would see if when he unfolded it—a surprise!

Actually the lipstick-kiss was kind of pretty, on the Kleenex. She'd blotted her lips with care.

Her mother didn't want her to wear lipstick but fuck Momma, all the girls her age did.

Last time she'd seen Momma with Daddy, Daddy had been in his soldier's dress uniform and had looked very handsome. His hair had been cut so *short*.

Not then but an earlier time when Daddy had returned from Iraq for the first time Lisette's mother had covered his face in purple-lipstick-kisses. Lisette had been so young she'd thought the lipstick-kisses were some kind of wounds, her daddy was hurt and bleeding and it was a bearded face she hadn't known too well, she had not recognized at first so it scared her.

The times were confused. There were many times. You could not "see" more than one time though there were many.

There were many Daddys—you could not "see" them all.

There was the time Daddy took Momma to Fort Lauderdale for what they called their *second honeymoon*. They'd wanted to take Lisette but—it hadn't worked out—Lisette had to be in school at that time of year, in February.

She'd gone to stay with her mother's friend Misty who'd worked at Bally's at that time. But when Momma called from Florida, Lisette refused to come to the phone. They'd planned on ten days in Florida but Lisette's mother surprised her by returning after just a week saying that was it, that was the end, she'd had to call the police when he'd gotten drunk and beat her, and in a restaurant he'd knocked over a chair he was so angry, that was it for her, no more.

At Thanksgiving, he'd returned. Not to live in Atlantic City but to visit before he was *deployed* again to Iraq.

Yvette had man friends she met in the casinos. Most of them, Lisette never met. Never wished to meet. One of them was a *real estate agent* in Monmouth County, Lisette could remember just the first name which was some unusual name like *Upton, Upwell . . .*

The Indian-looking man was speaking to Lisette but she could not comprehend a word he said. He was very young-looking to be a doctor. He wore a neat white jacket and white pants, crepe-soled shoes. Behind wire-rimmed glasses his eyes were soft-black, somber. His hair was black, but coarse and not silky-fine like J-C's hair.

He was leading the cops and Lisette into a fluorescent-lit refrigerated room. Firmly Molina had hold of Lisette's hand—the icy fingers.

"We will make it as easy for you as we can, Lisette. All you have to do is squeeze my hand—that will mean *yes*."

Yes? Yes what? Desperately Lisette was picturing the school cafeteria—the long table in the corner where the coolest guys sat— J-C and his friends—his "posse"—and sometimes certain girls were invited to sit with them—today maybe J-C would call over to Lisette to sit with them—*Lisette! Hey Liz-zette!*—because he'd liked the purple-lipstick kiss, and what it promised. *Lisette c'mere*—this would be *so cool . . .*

"Take your time, Lisette. I'll be right beside you."

*

Then—so quick it was over!

The female body she was meant to I.D. was not anyone she knew let alone not her mother.

This one was not Yvette's size, and not Yvette's shape. This one had hair that was darker than Yvette's hair, and the roots of the hair were brown, and it was all snarled like a cheap wig, and really ugly—and the forehead was so bruised and swollen, and the eyes—you could hardly see the eyes—and the mouth was, like, broken—and swollen, and purple—you could not make sense of the face, almost. It was a face that would need to be straightened out, like with a pliers.

A face like Hallowe'en. A face hardly female.

"No. Not Momma."

Lisette spoke sharply, decisively. Molina was holding her hand— she was tugging to get free.

This was the *morgue*: this was a *corpse*.

This was not a woman but a *thing*—you could not believe really that it had ever been a *woman*.

Only just the head and the face were exposed, the rest of the body was covered by a white sheet but you could see the shape of it, the size, and it was not Lisette's mother—obviously. Older than Momma and something had happened to the body to make it small—smaller. Some sad pathetic broken female-like debris washed up on the shore.

It was lucky, the sheet was drawn up over the chest. The breasts. And the belly, and pubic hair—fatty-raddled thighs of a woman of such an age, you would not want to look at.

The guys were quick to laugh, and to show their contempt. Any girl or woman not good-looking, and if her chest was flat, or she was a little heavy—you would walk fast to avoid their eyes—if you were fast enough, you could hide.

"This is not Momma. This is no one I know."

Molina was close beside Lisette instructing her to take her time, this was very important Molina was saying, to make an *eiii-dee* of the woman was very important, to help the police find who had done these terrible things to her.

Lisette pulled free of Molina. "I told you—this is not Momma! *It is not.*"

Something hot and acid came up into her mouth—she swallowed it down—she gagged again, and swallowed and she was shivering so hard her teeth chattered like ivory dice shaken. Badly she wanted to run from the damn nasty room which was cold like a refrigerator, and smelly—a faint chemical smell—a smell of something sweet, sickish—like talcum powder and sweat—but Molina detained her.

They were showing her clothes now, out of the box. Dirty blood-stained clothes like rags. And a coat—a coat that resembled her mother's red suede coat—but it was filthy, and torn—it was not Momma's stylish coat she'd bought a year ago, in the January sales at the mall.

Lisette said she'd never seen any of these things before. She had not. She was breathing funny like her friend Keisha who had asthma and Molina was holding her hand and saying things to comfort her, bullshit things to comfort her, telling her to be calm, it was all right . . . if she did not think that this woman was her mother, it was all right: there were other ways to identify the victim.

Victim. This was a new word. Like *body, drainage ditch.*

Molina led her to a restroom. Lisette had to use the toilet, fast. Like her insides had turned to liquid fire and had to come out. At the sink she was going to vomit but could not. Washed and washed her hands. In the mirror a face hovered—a girl's face—in dark-purple-tinted glasses and her lips a dark grape color—around the left eye the scarring wasn't so visible if she didn't look closely and she had no wish to look closely. There had been three surgeries and after each surgery Momma had promised *You'll be fine! You will look better than new.*

They wanted to take her somewhere—to Family Services. She said she wanted to go back to school. She said she had a right to go back to school. She began to cry, she was resentful and agitated and she wanted to go back to school and so they said all right, all right for now Lisette, and they drove her to the school, and it was just after the bell had rung for lunchtime at 11:45 A.M.—so she went directly to the cafeteria, not waiting in line but into the cafeteria without a tray and still in her jacket and in a roaring sort of blur she was aware of her girlfriends at a nearby table—there was Keisha looking concerned calling, "Lisette, hey—what was it? You OK?" and Lisette laughed into the bright buzzing blur, "Sure I'm OK. Hell why not?"

DECEIT

Not by e-mail but by phone which is so God-damned more intrusive the call comes from someone at Kimi's school—*Please call to make an appointment urgent need discuss your daughter.*

No explanation! Not even a hint.

Candace has come to hate phone calls! Rarely answers phone calls! If she happens to be near the phone—the kitchen phone—quaint old soiled-plastic that has come to be called, in recent years, as by fiat, a "land phone"—she might squint at the I.D. window to see who the hell is intruding in her life, for instance the ex-husband, but rarely these months, could be years, does Candace *pick up.*

Cell phones she keeps losing. Or breaking.

Cell phones are useful for keeping in (one-way) contact with Kimi—*crummy substitute for an umbilical cord*—and a pause, a beat, the signature wincing laugh that crinkles half her face like pleated paper, then—*ha ha: joke*—if the assholes don't get Candace's wit.

And more it seems to be happening, assholes don't *get it.*

Well, the cell phone. Unless she has lost it, she has it—somewhere.

Could be in a pocket of a coat or a jacket, could be on the floor of her car beneath the brake or gas pedal, or in the driveway; could be in a drawer, or atop a bureau; could be, as it was not long ago, fallen down inside one of Candace's chic leather boots; the cell phone is a great invention but just too damned small, slight, impractical. Could be sitting on the God-damned thing and not have a clue until the opening notes of Beethoven's Fifth Symphony come thundering out of your rear.

Not that Kimi answers Mom's calls all that readily—the docile-daughter reflex seems to have atrophied since Kimi's thirteenth birthday—but the principle is, getting voice mail on her cell through the day at school, text messages from MOM, Kimi at least has to acknowledge that MOM exists even if MOM is no longer one of those desirable individuals for whom Kimi will eagerly *pick up*.

"YOUR DAUGHTER."

"Y-yes? What about my daughter?"

Cool-calm! Though Candace's voice is hoarse like sandpaper and her heart gives a wicked lurch in her chest despite that morning's thirty-milligram lorazepam.

"Has Kimi spoken with you, Mrs. Waxman, about—yesterday?"

"Y-yesterday?"

"Kimi was to speak with you, Mrs. Waxman, about an issue—a sensitive issue—that has come up—she hadn't wanted us to contact you first."

Weedle, Lee W.—"Doctor" Weedle since there's a cheesy-looking psychology Ph.D. diploma from Rutgers University at Newark on the wall behind the woman's desk—speaks in a grave voice fixing her visitor with prim moist blinking lashless bug-eyes.

Why are freckled people so *earnest*, Candace wonders.

"Your daughter has been reported by her teachers as—increasingly this semester—'distracted.'"

"Well—she's fourteen."

"Yes. But even for fourteen, Kimi often seems distracted in class. You must know that there has been a dramatic decline in her academic performance this semester, especially in math . . ."

"I was not a good math student, Dr. Wheezle. It might be simply—genetics."

" 'Weedle.' "

"Excuse me?"

"My name is 'Weedle,' not 'Wheezle.' "

"Is it! I'm sorry."

Candace smiles to suggest that she isn't being sarcastic, sardonic—"witty." Though *Weedle* is a name for which one might be reasonably sorry.

" . . . have seen your daughter's most recent report card, haven't you, Mrs. Waxman?"

"Did I sign it?"

"Your signature is on the card, yes."

Weedle fixes Kimi's mother with suspicious eyes—as if Candace might have forged her own signature. The woman is toughly durable as polyester—like the "pantsuit" she's wearing—short-cropped graying hair and a pug face like an aggressive ex-nun.

"If my signature is on the card, it is my signature."

Candace speaks bravely, defiantly. But this isn't the issue—is it?

Hard to recall, in the lorazepam haze, what the issue *is*.

"You can't expect children to leap through flaming hoops each semester. Kimi has been an A student since day care—it's cruel to be so *judgmental*. I don't put pressure on my daughter to get straight A's any more than I'd put pressure on myself at her age."

Since the ex-husband is the one to praise their daughter for her good grades at school, as a sort of sidelong sneer at Kimi's mother whom he'd taken to be, even in the days when he'd adored her, as an essentially *frivolous person*, Candace takes care never to dwell upon Kimi's report cards.

Now the thought comes to Candace like a slow-passing dirigible high overhead in the lorazepam haze—she hadn't done more than glance at Kimi's most recent report card. She'd had other distractions at the time and so just scrawled her signature on the card having asked Kimi if her grades were OK and Kimi had shrugged with a wincing little smile.

Sure Mom that smile had signaled.

Or maybe *Oh Mom* . . .

For this visit to the Quagmire Academy—i.e., Craigmore Academy—which is Candace's first visit this term—Candace is wearing a purple suede designer jacket that fits her tight as a glove, a matching suede skirt over cream-colored spandex tights, and twelve-inch Italian leather boots; her streaked-blond hair has been teased, riffled, blow-dried into a look of chic abandon and her eyebrows—recklessly shaved off twenty years before when it had seemed that youth and beauty would endure forever—have been penciled and buffed in, more or less symmetrically. Her lipstick is Midnight Plum, her widened, slightly bloodshot eyes are outlined in black and each lash distinctly thickened with mascara to resemble the legs of daddy longlegs. It's a look to draw attention, a look that startles and cries *Whoa!*—as if Candace has just stumbled out of a Manhattan disco club into the chill dawn of decades ago.

Weedle is impressed, Candace sees. Having to revise her notion of what Kimi Waxman's mom must be like, based upon the daughter.

For Candace has style, personality, wit—Candace is, as the ex-husband has said, *one-off*. Poor Kimi—"Kimberly"—(a name Candace now regrets, as she regrets much about the marriage, the fling at motherhood and subsequent years of dull dutiful fidelity)—has a plain sweet just slightly fleshy and forgettable face.

Weedle is frowning at her notes. Which obviously the cunning psychologist has memorized that she might toss her dynamite material, like a grenade, at the stunned-smiling mother of Kimi Waxman facing her across the desk.

" . . . at first Kimi convinced us—her teachers, and me—that her injuries were accidental. She told us that she'd fallen on the stairs and bruised her wrist—she'd cut her head on the sharp edge of a locker door, in the girls' locker room, when she was reaching for something and lost her balance. The more recent bruises—"

Injuries? More recent? Candace listens in disbelief.

"—are on her upper arms and shoulders, as if someone had grabbed and shaken her. You could almost see the imprint of fingers in the poor child's flesh." Weedle speaks carefully. Weedle speaks like one exceedingly cautious of being misunderstood. Weedle pauses to raise her eyes to Candace's stricken face with practiced solemnity in which there is no hint—not even a glimmer of a hint—of a thrilled satisfaction. "I am obliged to ask you, Mrs. Waxman—do you know anything about these injuries?"

The words wash over Candace like icy water. Whatever Candace has expected, Candace has not expected *this*.

And there are the moist protuberant eyes which are far steelier than Candace had thought.

The lorazepam, like the previous night's sleep medication, provides you with a sensation like skiing—on a smooth slope—but does not prepare for sudden impediments on the slope like a tree rushing at you, for instance.

Warning signs are needed: SLOW. DANGER.

"Excuse me, w-what did you say, Dr. Wheezle?"

Weedle repeats her question but even as Candace listens closely,

Candace doesn't seem to hear. In her ears a roaring like a din of locusts.

"Then—you don't know anything about Kimi's injuries? Neither the older ones on her legs, nor the more recent?"

Candace is trying to catch her breath. The oxygen in Weedle's cramped little fluorescent-lit office is seriously depleted.

" 'Kimi's injuries'—I j-just don't . . . I don't know what you are talking about, Dr. Wheezle—*Weedle*."

"You haven't noticed your daughter's bruised legs? Her wrist? The cut in her scalp? The bruises beneath her arms?"

Candace tries to think. If she says *no*—she is a bad mother. But if she says *yes*—she is a worse mother.

"Mrs. Waxman, how are things in your home?"

"—home? Our *home*?"

"Do you know of anyone in your household—any adult, or older sibling—who might be abusing your daughter?"

Abusing. Adult. Candace is sitting very still now. Her eyes are filling with tears, her vision is splotched as it often is in the morning, and in cold weather. In order to see Weedle's scrubbed-nun face clearly Candace has to blink away tears but if Candace blinks her eyes tears run down her face in a way that is God-damned embarrassing; still worse, if Candace gives in, rummages in her purse for a wadded tissue. *She will not.*

"N-No. I do not—know . . . I don't k-know what you are talking about, I think I should see Kimi now . . ." Wildly the thought comes to Candace: her daughter has been taken from school. Her daughter has been taken into the custody of Child Welfare. Her daughter has falsely informed upon *her*.

"Mrs. Waxman—may I call you 'Candace'?—I'm sorry if this is a shock to you, as it was to us. That's why I asked you to come and speak with me. You see, Candace—we are obliged to report 'suspicious injuries' to the police. In an emergency situation, we are obliged to use the county family services hotline to report suspected child abuse in which the child's immediate well-being may be in danger."

Candace is gripping her hands in her lap. Why she'd chosen to wear the chic suede skirt, matching jacket with gleaming little brass buttons and the leather boots, to speak with the school psychologist/guidance counselor, she has no idea. Her heart feels triangular in her chest, sharp-edged. Despite the lorazepam and last night's medication she'd had a premonition of something really bad but no idea it could be—*this bad.*

Eleven minutes late for the appointment with Weedle. Taking a wrong turn into the school parking lot and so shunted by one-way signs onto a residential street—God damn!—returning at last to the entrance to the school lot which she'd originally missed impatient now and would've been seriously pissed except for the lorazepam— (which is a new prescription, still feels experimental, tenuous)—and a hurried cigarette simultaneously first/last cigarette of the day, Candace vows—and inside the school building which looks utterly unfamiliar to her—*Has she ever been here before? Is this the right school, or is her daughter enrolled at another school?*—bypassing the front office in a sudden need to use a girls' lavatory at the far end of the corridor— praying *Dear God dear Christ!* that Kimi will not discover her mother slamming into one of the stalls, needing to use the toilet and yet, on the toilet, cream-colored spandex tights huddled about her ankles like a peeled-off skin, there is just—*nothing.*

God-damned drugs cause constipation, urine retention. If excrement is not excreted, where does it *go?*

Once a week or so, Candace takes a laxative. But sometimes forgets if she has taken it. Or forgets to take it.

Candace recalls another lavatory she'd hurried into recently on a false alarm, at the mall. This too a place where girls—high-school, middle-school—hang out. She'd been shocked to see a poster depicting a wan adolescent girl with bruised eyes and mouth staring at the viewer above a caption inquiring ARE YOU A VICTIM OF VIOLENCE, ABUSE, THREAT OF BODILY HARM? ARE YOU FRIGHTENED? CALL THIS NUMBER. At the bottom of the poster were small strips of paper containing a telephone number and of a dozen or more of these, only two remained. Candace wanted to think that this was some kind of prank—tearing off the paper strips as if they'd be of use.

Weedle is inquiring about Kimi's father: does he lose his temper at times, lose control, does he ever *lay hands* on Kimi?

" 'Kimi's father'—?"

Candace has begun to sound like a deranged parrot echoing Weedle's questions.

"Yes—Kimi's father Philip Waxman? According to our records, he is your daughter's father?"

Some strange tortured syntax here. *Your daughter's father.*

"Well, yes—but this 'Philip Waxman' no longer lives with us, Dr. Weedle. My former husband has moved to Manhattan, to be nearer his place of employment in which he occupies a sort of low-middle-echelon position of shattering insignificance."

"I see. I'm sorry to hear that . . ."

"Sorry that he has moved to Manhattan, or that he occupies a low-middle-echelon position of shattering insignificance? He's in the insurance scam—I mean, 'game'—should you be curious."

Candace speaks so brightly and crisply, Candace might be reciting a script. For very likely, Candace has recited this script concerning the *former husband* upon other occasions.

Usually, listeners smile. Or laugh. Weedle just stares.

"The question is—does Kimi's father share custody with you? Does she spend time alone with him?"

"Well—yes. I suppose so. She is in the man's 'custody' on alternate weekends—if it's convenient for him. But Philip is not the type to 'abuse' anyone—at least not physically." Candace laughs in a high register, a sound like breaking glass. Seeing Weedle's disapproving expression Candace laughs harder.

Once it is *dialogue* Candace is doing, Candace can do it. *Earnest conversation* is something else.

Weedle asks Candace what she means by this remark and Candace says that her former husband has refined the art of *mental abuse*. "But indirectly—Philip is passive-aggressive. It's as if you are speaking to a person who does not know the English language—and he is deaf! He becomes stony-quiet, he will not *engage*. You can speak to him—scream at him—clap your hands in his face, or actually slap his face—only then will he acknowledge you, but you will be *at fault*. It is impossible for the man to lose at this game—it's his game. And if you stand too close to him you're in danger of being sucked into him—as into a black hole." Candace laughs, wiping at her eyes. *Black hole* is new, and inspired. Wait till Candace tells her women friends! " 'Abusive men' are 'provoked' into violent behavior but my former husband can't be provoked—*he* is the one who provokes violence."

But is this a felicitous thing to have said? With Weedle staring at Candace from just a few feet away, humorless, and slow-blinking?

"What do you mean, Candace—'provokes violence'?"

"Obviously not what I said! I am speaking figuratively."

"You are speaking—in 'figures'?"

"I am speaking—for Christ's sake—analytically—and in metaphor. I am just trying to communicate what would seem to be a simple fact but—I am having great difficulty, I see."

Breathing quickly. Trying not to become exasperated. Her hands have slipped loose of their protective grip and are fluttering about like panicked little birds.

"What I mean is that, through his extreme passive-aggressive nature, the man provokes others, his former wife for instance, to rage."

"*You* experience 'rage'? And how does this 'rage' manifest itself?"

This is coming out all wrong. It's like Weedle is turning a meat grinder and what emerges is *wrong*.

"It doesn't! Not me."

Candace's voice is trembling. Tiny scalding-hot bubbles in her blood, she'd like to claw at the imperturbable freckled-nun-face.

"It doesn't? Not *you*? Yet you seem very upset, Mrs. Waxman—Candace..."

"I think I want to see my daughter. Right now."

" 'See' her? Take her out of class, for what purpose? So that the three of us can talk?"

"No—take her home."

There is a pause. Candace is breathing quickly in the way that a balloon that has been pricked by numerous small puncture wounds might breathe, to keep from deflating.

"Take her home! I think that—yes. Take her home."

More weakly now. For, having taken Kimi *home*—assuming that Kimi would agree to come home in the middle of the school day—what would follow next?

Imperturbable Weedle does not advise such an act. Imperturbable Weedle is telling Candace that taking Kimi out of school—"interrupting her school-routine"—would be "counter-productive"—especially if Kimi's friends knew about it.

"Yesterday Kimi was quite defensive—she insists that the injuries are 'accidental.' It was the girls' gym instructor Myra Sinkler who noticed the leg bruises, initially—this was about ten days ago—then, just yesterday, the shoulder and upper-arm bruises. Then Myra discovered the head injury—a nasty-looking little wound in Kimi's scalp, which should have been reported at the time, if it took place, as Kimi claims, in school—in the girls' locker room, after gym class. But no one informed Myra Sinkler at that time and no one can verify the account that Kimi gives—so we are thinking, Myra and I, that the 'accident' didn't happen when Kimi says it did, but at another time. And somewhere else. When Kimi was questioned she became excited, as I've said 'defensive'—it's never good to upset a traumatized child further, if it can be avoided." Weedle paused. *Traumatized* hovered in the air like a faint deadly scent. "Kimi promised us that she would tell you about the situation, Candace, but evidently she didn't. That was about the time I'd called you and left a message. In the interim—you didn't ask Kimi anything?"

"Ask her—anything? No, I—I didn't know what to ask her . . ."

"You don't communicate easily with your daughter?"

"Well—would you, Dr. Weedle? If you had a fourteen-year-old daughter? Do you think that mothers of fourteen-year-old daughters and fourteen-year-old daughters commonly communicate *well*?"

Candace speaks with sudden vehemence. The moist protuberant nun-eyes blink several times but the freckled-nun-face remains unperturbed.

"Well—let me ask you this, Candace: what is Kimi's relationship with her father?"

"Dr. Weedle—is this a conversation, or an interrogation? These questions you are firing at me—I find very hard to answer . . ."

"I understand, Candace, that you're upset—but I am obliged to ask, to see what action should be taken, if any. So I need to know what Kimi's relationship has been with her father, so far as you know."

"Kimi's relationship with her father is—the man is her father. I was very young when we met and arguably even more naïve and 'optimistic' than I am now—obviously, I wasn't *thinking*. The two look nothing alike and have very little in common—Kimi is clearly my daughter—one glance, you can see the resemblance—though Kimi is just a few pounds overweight, and a much sweeter girl than I'd been at that age. Is she ever! Too sweet for instance to say she doesn't much want to spend time with her very dull father—but she isn't, I think, *frightened* of him."

Was this so? Candace never asks Kimi about her weekends with Philip out of a sense of—propriety, you could say.

Or dignity, indifference. Rage so incandescent, it might be mistaken for an ascetic purity.

But mostly boredom. Candace is *so bored* by all that—enormous chunk of her "life"—like a clumsily carved male-likeness on Mount Rushmore—the features crude, forgettable.

You can't just erase me from your life. How can you imagine you can do such a thing . . .

Easily. Once Candace makes up her mind, breaking off relations with certain people, it's like an iron grating being yanked down, over a storefront window. And the store darkened, shut up tight.

"She sees her father, you'd said, on alternate weekends? Does she seem happy with this arrangement?"

"'Happy'? For Christ's sake, no one I know is 'happy.' This is the U.S.A. Are you 'happy'?"

Candace is perspiring—something she never does! Not if she can help it.

Relenting then, before Weedle can respond, "Well—yes—frankly yes, I think Kimi *is*. Happy, I mean. She's happy with her classes, her teachers—her life . . . She's an only child—no 'sibling'"—(with a fastidious little wince to signal that, in normal circumstances, Candace would never utter so tritely clinical a term)—"therefore, no 'sibling rivalry.'"

Weedle allows Candace to speak—fervently, defiantly. Hard not to concede that what she is saying mimics the speech of the mother of an adolescent who doesn't know what the hell she is talking about— hasn't a clue. Can't even remember exactly what the subject is except she's the object of an essentially hostile interrogation and not doing so well—Lee W. Weedle, Ph.D., is one of those individuals, more frequently female than male, to whom Candace Waxman is *not so very impressive.*

When she escapes back home she will take another thirty-milligram lorazepam with a glass of tart red wine and maybe go to bed.

Except: what time is it? Not yet 11:30 A.M. Too early for serious sleep.

"And what about boys, Candace?"

"No—no boys. Kimi doesn't hang out with boys."

"She doesn't have a boyfriend? She says not."

"You've seen Kimi. What do you think?"

A sharp crease between Weedle's unplucked brows signals that this is not a very nice thing for Kimi's mother to say, however frank, candid and adult-to-adult Candace imagines she is being. Quickly Candace relents: "I'm sure that Kimi doesn't have a boyfriend—even a candidate for a boyfriend. She's—shy . . ."

"And what about other boys? In her class? Or older boys, from the high school, possibly?"

"Kimi never mentions boys. The subject hasn't come up."

"You are sure, Candace?"

"Yes, I am sure."

Poor Kimi! Candace is embarrassed for her.

Grimly Weedle says: "Of course, there are boys even at Craigmore who intimidate girls—harass them sexually, threaten them. There have been—among the older students—some unfortunate incidents. And there is this new phenomenon—'cyberbullying.' Has Kimi ever mentioned being upset by anything online?"

"No. She has not."

"It's a strange new world, this 'cyberspace' world—where children can 'friend' and 'unfriend' at will. We are committed to protecting our students here at Craigmore from any kind of bullying."

"Committed to stamping out bullies. I like that."

They will bond over this—will they? Candace feels an inappropriate little stab of hope.

"But Kimi hasn't mentioned being harassed? Bullied? 'Teased'?"

"I've said *no*."

But Candace is remembering—vaguely, like a photo image coming into just partial clarity—something Kimi mentioned not long ago about older boys saying *gross things* to the ninth grade girls, to embarrass them; pulling at their hair, their clothes; *bothering* them. On the school bus, this was. Candace thinks so.

Candace asked Kimi if any of these boys were bothering her and stiffly Kimi said, "No, Mom. I'm not *popular*."

Candace knows that terrible things are said about the behavior of some of the middle-school students—both girls and boys—at Craigmore. Oral sex in the halls and beneath the bleachers, girls younger than Kimi exploited by older boys with a hope of becoming "popular"; boys bragging online about girls' lipstick smeared on their penises. Not at this private suburban school perhaps but at nearby public schools— boys physically mistreating girls, sexually molesting them in public; grabbing and squeezing their breasts, even between their legs. Some of this behavior is captured on cell phones—and posted online. From the mothers of Kimi's classmates Candace has heard these things—she'd been so shocked and disgusted, not a single joke had occurred to her. Where Candace can't joke, Candace can't linger. It is very hard for Candace to do *earnest*.

She'd been upset at the time. Seeing poor sweet moon-faced Kimi, a shy girl, with not-pretty features, hair so fine it sticks up around her head like feathers—among such crude jackals.

"If Kimi says she hurt herself accidentally, then Kimi hurt herself accidentally. My daughter does not lie. She is not *deceitful*."

"I'm sure she is not, Candace. But if she has been coerced, or threatened—"

"Kimi has always been accident-prone! As a small child she had to be watched every minute, or . . ." Candace has a repertoire of funny-Kimi stories to testify to the child's clumsiness though the stories don't include actual injuries, of which there had been a few. Just, Candace wants this hateful suspicious "school psychologist" to know that her dear sweet daughter is *prone to self-hurt*.

"And Kimi's friends are all girls. They're all her ninth grade class-mates. She's known most of them since elementary school. Great kids, and I don't think they 'hang out' with boys."

As if unhearing, or unimpressed, Weedle says: "Adolescent boys can be terribly predatory. They can sense weakness, or fear. At almost any age, however young, if there's a ringleader—an 'alpha male'—with a tendency to bully, he can manipulate the behavior of other boys who wouldn't ordinarily behave in such a way. These boys can harass girls like a pack. And girls can turn against girls . . ."

Candace protests: "Kimi has never said anything to me about any of this! I really don't think what you are saying pertains to my daughter and I—I resent being . . ."

Candace feels a sensation of something like panic: really she doesn't know what Kimi is doing much of the time, after school for instance upstairs in her room, with the door shut; frequently Kimi is at her lap-top past bedtime, or texting on her cell phone, as if under a powerful enchantment; sometimes, one of Kimi's girlfriends is with her, suppos-edly working on homework together, but who knows what the girls are really doing on laptops or cell phones.

If Candace knocks at the door, at once the girls' voices and laughter subside—*Yes Mom? What is it?*

A careful neutrality in Kimi's voice. So Mom is made to know that this is not *little-girl-Kimi* at the moment but *teenager-Kimi*.

The interview—interrogation—is ending, at last. Weedle shuf-fles papers, slides documents into a manila file, glances at the cheap little plastic digital clock on her desk. Candace sees a pathetic little array of framed photos on the desk—homely freckled earnest faces, in miniature—Weedle's parents, siblings, little nieces and nephews. Not one of Weedle with a *man*.

"You will call me, Candace, please, after you've spoken with your daughter this evening? I hope she will allow you to examine her injuries. We didn't feel—Kimi's teachers and I—that the injuries were serious enough to warrant medical attention any longer. But you may feel differently."

Feel differently? Meaning—what? In a haze of eager affability Candace nods *yes*.

Yes she will call Weedle—of course.

Yes she is an attentive, vigilant, loving and devoted mother—who could doubt this?

(Wondering: is this interview being recorded? Videotaped? Will Weedle use it against Candace as evidence, in a nightmare court case?)

(Is the former husband Philip Waxman in some way involved? *Is Weedle on Waxman's side?*)

Faintly now Weedle manages a smile. As if to mitigate the harshness of her words:

"I will wait until I hear from you before making a decision about reporting your daughter's injuries, Candace. Kimi is certainly adamant that they were 'accidental' and we have no proof that they are not. But, you see, if I don't report 'suspicious injuries' to a child, and there are more injuries, that are reported, I will be held to account and I may be charged with dereliction of duty."

"Well, Dr. Weedle, we wouldn't want that—would we! 'Dereliction of duty.' Absolutely not."

Candace bares her beautiful teeth in a smile to suggest—to *insist*— that her words are lightly playful merely. But Weedle reacts as if stung:

"Mrs. Waxman, this is not a joke. This is a serious matter. Anything involving the well-being of a vulnerable child is serious. I would think you might be grateful that the staff at Craigmore is alert to a situation like this, rather than reacting defensively."

"I am grateful—very! The tuition I pay for Kimi's education here suggests how grateful! But I warn you—and Kimi's teachers—if you over-react about something harmless—if you call the 'hotline' and involve the police—I promise, I will sue you. I will sue you, and the others involved, and the school board. I will not allow my daughter to be humiliated and used as a pawn in some sort of 'politically correct' agenda."

Feeling triumphant at last, Candace is on her feet. Weedle struggles to her feet. With satisfaction Candace sees that Weedle is shorter than Candace, and at least a decade older; Weedle is a homely woman, exuding the sexual allure of one of those inedible root vegetables—turnip, rutabaga.

"Good-bye! Thank you! I know, Dr. Weedle—you mean well. In fact I am impressed, the school staff is so *vigilant*. I will talk with Kimi this afternoon—as soon as she returns from school—and clear all this up. Shall I make an appointment now to see you next week—Monday morning? At this time?"

So brightly and airily Candace speaks, it seems she must be making a gesture of reconciliation. Such abrupt turns of mood are not unusual in Candace but Weedle is slow to absorb the change. Warily she tells Candace that Monday is a school holiday—Martin Luther King, Jr.'s birthday. But Tuesday morning—

Candace laughs almost gaily. Something *so funny* about this.

" 'Martin Luther King, Jr.'s birthday'! Every month there's a 'great man's' birthday! Sometimes there's 'Presidents' Day'—three for one. And how many 'great women' birthdays do we have? Is Eleanor Roosevelt so honored? Emily Dickinson? Amelia Earhart? What about—Circe? Circe is a goddess—that's big-time. Or was there more than one of her? Is 'Circe' the singular—or the plural? Is there a 'Circ' and the plural is 'Cir-say'? Like goose and geese—ox and oxen?"

Weedle stares at Candace with an expression of absolute perplexity.

"All right! Tuesday, then. Same time, same place—I promise, I will be on time."

Candace thrusts out a glittery-ringed hand to shake Weedle's pallid hand—one of those warm-friendly-intimidating gestures Candace has perfected, like a sudden parting social kiss to the cheek of someone who has been entranced by her, yet guarded.

Strides out of Weedle's office. Already she is feeling much, much better.

At the front entrance of Craigmore Academy Middle School Candace has her cigarettes in hand and by the time Candace locates her car, on the far side of a lot she doesn't remember parking in, she has her cigarette lighted.

IT'S SO: Kimi's friends are all girls she has known since grade school. A small band of not-pretty/not-popular girls of whom at least two—Kimi and Scotia Perry—are invariably A students.

Friendships of girls unpopular together. Candace hopes that her daughter's friends will remain loyal to one another in high school which looms ahead for them next year like an ugly badlands terrain they will have to cross—together, or singly.

Scotia is not Candace's favorite among Kimi's friends—there is something subtly derisive about the girl, even as she politely asks Mrs. Waxman how she is, and engages her in actual conversations; Scotia is stocky and compact as a fire hydrant, with a ruddy face, deceptively innocent blue eyes and thick strong ankles and wrists—a girl-golfer!

(Candace has never seen Kimi's friend play golf but she has been

hearing about the golf "prodigy" for years.) Scotia is an all-round athlete who plays girls' basketball, field hockey and volleyball with equal
skill, while poor Kimi takes aerobics for her phys-ed requirement—
Kimi shrinks from sports and has difficulty catching balls tossed to
her so slowly they seem to float in mid-air. Though not a brilliant student, Scotia so thrives on competition that she maintains an A average
in school; she also takes Mandarin Chinese at the local language im-
mersion school and she has been a savior of sorts for Kimi, as for their
other friends, helping them with malfunctioning computers.

(Scotia has helped Candace, too!) From a young age Scotia exuded a
disconcerting air of mock-maturity: Candace recalls when, after Kimi's
father had moved out of the house in the initial stage of what was to be,
from Candace's perspective, an ordeal like a protracted tooth extrac-
tion, both painful and intensely boring, Scotia said with a bright little
smile,

"Hope you had the locks changed on the door, Mrs. Waxman!
That's what women do."

(In fact, Scotia's parents are not divorced. This droll bit of information must have come to Scotia from other sources.)

Last year, in eighth grade, Kimi's closest friend seemed to have
been a girl named Brook, displaced over the summer by Scotia Perry.
Now it's Scotia who spends time in Kimi's room as the girls prepare
class projects together, or work on homework; watch DVDs, do email,
text-messages, Myspace and Facebook; snack on cheese bits, trail mix,
Odwalla smoothies which Candace keeps stocked in the refrigerator—
*Strawberry Banana, Red Rhapsody, Super Protein, Mango Tango, Blue-
berry B Monster*. Often Candace is out—with friends—for the evening
and returns to discover that Scotia is still on the premises, though the
hour is getting late—past 9 P.M. She can hear, or half-hear, the mur-
mur of their girl-voices, and their peals of sudden girl-laughter; she's
grateful that Kimi has a friend though Scotia Perry seems too mature

for Kimi, and too strong-willed; and Scotia's mother hasn't made any effort to befriend Candace, which feels like a rebuke.

Once, Candace thought she'd overheard Scotia say to Kimi in a laughing drawling voice—a mock-male voice, was it?—what sounded like *fat cunt*—but Candace hadn't really heard clearly for Candace *was not eavesdropping* on her daughter and her daughter's friends. And afterward when Scotia had departed and Kimi came downstairs flush-faced and happy Candace had asked what Scotia had said and Kimi replied, with averted eyes, "Oh, Scotia's just kidding, teasing—'fat cow' she calls me, sometimes—but not, y'know, mean-like. Not mean."

"'Fat cow.' That girl who looks like a young female twin of Mike Tyson has the temerity to call my daughter *fat*. Well!"

Candace pretended to be incensed though really she was relieved. Very relieved. *Fat cunt* was so much worse than *fat cow*.

Conversely, *fat cow* was so much less disturbing than *fat cunt*.

Another time, just the previous week, after Scotia came over to do homework with Kimi, next morning Candace was shocked to discover that, in the refrigerator, not a single smoothie remained of six she'd bought just the day before.

"Kimi! Did you and Scotia drink *six smoothies between you?*"

Kimi's face tightened. The soft round boneless face in which large brown eyes shimmered with indignation.

"Oh *Mom*. I hate you counting *every little thing*."

"I'm not counting—I'm recoiling. I mean, it was a visceral reaction—pure shock. I just went shopping yesterday and this morning all the smoothies are gone. No wonder you're overweight, Kimi. You really don't need to put on more pounds."

This was cruel. Unforgiveable.

Kimi made a sound like a small animal being kicked and ran upstairs.

———

"KIMI? MAY I COME IN, please?"

This is a tip-off: something is seriously wrong. For Mom is behaving politely—almost hesitantly. Instead of rapping briskly on the door and opening it before Kimi can reply.

Kimi's voice lifts faintly—whether inviting Mom in, or asking Mom not to interrupt her right now, she's working; but the door isn't locked, and Mom comes in.

"Hiya!"

"Hi."

Candace's eyes clutch at the girl—sprawled on her bed with her laptop opened before her, a shimmering screen that, as Candace slowly approaches, vanishes and is replaced with drifting clouds, exquisitely beautiful violet sky. Candace wonders what was just on Kimi's screen but has decided she will not ask, even playfully. Kimi bristles when Candace is too inquisitive.

Kimi is lying on top of her bed surrounded by the stuffed animals of her childhood: Otto the one-eyed panda, Carrie the fuzzy camel, Molly the big-eyed fawn. Since returning home from school Kimi has changed into looser-fitting clothes—sweatpants, sweatshirt. Her feet are bare and her toes twitching.

Last summer Kimi painted her toenails iridescent green, and still flecks of shiny green remain on her toenails, like signs of leprosy.

On the pink walls of Kimi's room are silly, lewd rock posters: Lady GaGa, Plastic Kiss, Raven Lunatic.

There is music in Kimi's room—some sort of chanting, issued out of her laptop. Kimi brings a forefinger to her lips to silence her mom who nonetheless speaks: "Sweetie . . ."

When Kimi, frowning at her music, doesn't glance up, Candace says she'd been summoned to Kimi's school that morning—"D'you know Dr. Weedle?—she has some sort of psychological counseling degree."

Kimi's surprise seems genuine. Her eyes widen in alarm.

"Dr. *Weedle?* What's she want with *you?*"

"She said that you were going to speak to me about an issue that came up at your school yesterday. But you didn't."

"Mom, I *did*. I mean, I certainly tried."

"You did? When?"

In a flurried breathless voice that is an echo of Candace's girl-voice Kimi tries to explain. She'd started to say something to Candace but Candace had been in a hurry and on her way out of the house and now belatedly Candace recalls this exchange but details are lost—crucial words are lost—Kimi had drifted away, and later that evening Candace heard Kimi in her room laughing, on her cell phone with a friend.

Candace has changed from her designer clothes into pencil-leg jeans, a magenta silk blouse, flannel slippers. She sits on the edge of Kimi's bed with less abandon than usual. Bites her lip ruefully saying, to enlist her daughter's sympathy, "I'm not good at whatever this is—a TV scene. If I can't be original, I hate to even try."

Kimi smiles to signal *yes*, she knows that her mother is a funny woman, and clever, and original; but Kimi is tense, too. For Mom has let herself into Kimi's room for a purpose.

"Kimi, I have to ask you—is someone hurting you?"

Candace is hoping that this will not turn out to be the horror film in which the perpetrator of evil turns out to be the protagonist—or maybe, on a somewhat loftier plane, this is Sophocles' *Oedipus Rex*.

Though knowing—*She has never touched her child in anger still less has she abused her child. Or any other child.*

Kimi sits up, indignant. Kimi tugs her sweatshirt down over her fleshy midriff. "'Hurting me'? You mean—making me cry? Making me *feel bad?*"

"Yes. Well—no. I don't mean 'hurting' your feelings—exactly— but 'hurting' *you*. Physically."

Kimi squirms and kicks, this is so—ridiculous! Candace sees a paperback book on the bed—Kimi's English class is reading *To Kill a Mockingbird* and this is consoling, to Candace.

"Mom, for God's sake! That is so *not cool.*"

"Sweetie, this is serious. You are saying that no one has hurt you? No one at your school? Or—anywhere?"

"No one, Mom. Jeez!"

Yet Kimi's voice is faltering, just perceptibly. You would have to be Kimi's mom to hear.

"Will you—let me examine you?"

"Examine me!" Kimi laughs hoarsely, an uncanny imitation of her mother's braying laugh. "What are you—a doctor? Psychiatrist? Examining me?"

Nonetheless, Candace is resolved. The roaring in her ears is a din of deranged sparrows.

"Will you let me look, Kimi? I promise that—I—I won't be—won't over-react. Dr. Weedle said something about a head injury—"

Kimi is scuttling away, crab-fashion, on the bed. Stuffed animals topple onto the floor with looks of mute astonishment.

"You hit your head on a—locker at school, and cut it? Did you go to the school nurse? Did you tell anyone? Did you tell *me?*"

Kimi would swing her hips around to kick at her mother but Mom has captured her, kneeling on the bed. The mattress creaks. Another stuffed animal falls to the floor, and the paperback *To Kill a Mockingbird*. Candace is panting gripping Kimi's head between her spread fingers—not hard, but hard enough to keep the girl from wresting free—as Kimi hisses, "Mom, you *smell*! Disgusting cigarettes, wine— you *smell*!"—as Candace peers at the girl's scalp through a scrim of fine feathery pale-brown hair at first seeing nothing, then—"Oh! My God"—Candace sees the dark zipperlike wound, something more than a simple scratch, about four inches long, at the crown of Kimi's head.

Candace is stunned, staring.

Feebly Kimi protests, like a guilty child.

"I didn't mention it to you because it's *just nothing*, Mom! I was stooping to get one of my shoes, in the locker room, after gym, and banged my head on the edge of a locker door—it didn't even hurt, Mom. It's *just nothing*."

"But it must have bled, Kimi—head wounds bleed . . ."

"Well, sure—but I didn't just let it *bleed*. I had tissues in my backpack and some girls brought me toilet paper, I just pressed it against the cut. After a while it stopped bleeding. Scotti had some kind of disinfectant, we went to her house after school, and she put it on the cut with an eyedropper." Kimi smiled, recalling. A guarded look came into her face. "Scotti's going to be a doctor, she thinks. Neurosurgeon."

"Is she! I wouldn't doubt, that girl could do it . . ."

But Candace doesn't want to get sidetracked into talking about Scotia Perry, whom Kimi hero-worships. Not right now.

Staring at the dark wound in her daughter's scalp, that had existed for how many days, without Candace knowing, or in any way suspecting, beneath the feathery child's-hair, Candace feels a sensation of utter chill futility—emptiness: the way she'd felt, just for a moment, in the women's restroom where she'd seen the poster with the photo of the bruised and battered girl—ARE YOU A VICTIM OF VIOLENCE, ABUSE, THREAT OF BODILY HARM? ARE YOU FRIGHTENED?

How awful the world is. No joke can neutralize it.

She has failed as a mother. She has not even begun to *qualify as a mother*.

Maybe just, oh Christ—cash in your chips. Tune out.

Suicide: *off-self*. Candace has always wondered why more people don't do it.

Candace is stammering—not sure what Candace is stammering—

drawing a forefinger gingerly along the scabby cut in her daughter's scalp—"Not to have a doctor look at it, Kimi—it should have had stitches—I should have known . . ."

Not even begun to *qualify as a mother.*

Kimi pushes Candace's hands away. Kimi is flush-faced as if her soft smooth cheeks have been slapped.

"Mom, I told you—it's *just nothing.* If there'd been stitches—they'd have shaved my head, think how ugly that would be." Kimi makes a fastidious little face, in unconscious mimicry of her mother.

"But, Kimi—not to tell me about it, even . . ."

Kimi scuttles away drawing her knees to her chest. Candace is surprised as always by the fleshiness of her daughter's thighs, hips—the swell of her breasts. And now the hostility in Kimi's eyes, that are red-rimmed, thin-lashed as if she has been rubbing at them irritably with a fist.

You don't know this child. This is not your child.

See the hate in her eyes! For you.

"That really bothers you, Mom—doesn't it? That you were not *told.*"

"Yes of course. Of course—it bothers me. I was summoned to this terrible woman's office—in your school—'Lee W. Weedle, Ph.D.' It was an occasion for your school psychologist to terrify and humiliate me—and to threaten me."

"Threaten you? How?"

"She might report your 'injuries' to—some authority. 'Abuse hotline'—something like that."

"But—I told them—my 'injuries' are *accidental.* They can't make me testify to anyone hurting me because *no one did.*"

"This cut in your scalp—does it hurt now? Does it throb?"

"No, Mom. It does not *throb.*"

"It could become infected . . ."

"It *could not* become infected. I told you—Scotti swabbed disinfectant on it. And anyway it doesn't hurt. I've forgotten about it, actually."

Candace lunges—clumsily—*this is what a mom would do, impulsively*—to hug Kimi and to kiss the top of Kimi's head, the ugly zipper-scab hidden beneath the feathery hair as Kimi stiffens in alarm, then giggles, embarrassed—"Jeez, Mom! I'm OK."

Candace shuts her eyes, presses her warm face against Kimi's warm scalp, disheveled hair. She is fearful of what comes next and would like to clutch at Kimi for a little longer but the girl is restless, perspiring—resisting.

"Mom, hey? OK please? I need to work now, Mom—I have homework."

"Yes, but—it can wait for a minute more. Please show me your shoulders now, and your upper arms. Dr. Weedle said—you're bruised there . . ."

"What? Show you—*what*? No!"

Now Kimi shrinks away, furious. Now Kimi raises her knees to her chest, prepares to use her elbows against Mom.

Candace is trembling. Is this abuse?—*this*? Asking her fourteen-year-old daughter to partly disrobe for her, to submit to an examination?

Candace is in terror, for maybe she is to blame. In her sleep, in an alcoholic-drug blackout, abusing her own daughter and forgetting it?

Kimi is more fiercely protective of her body beneath her clothes than she was of the wound in her scalp. Panting, crying—"Leave me alone! Don't touch me! You're crazy! I hate you!"

Candace kneels on the bed, in the twisted comforter, straddling the resisting daughter. Kimi is shrieking, furious—Candace is trying to pull Kimi's sweatshirt up—has to pull it partly over her head so that she can see the girl's shoulders and upper arms—oh this is shocking! frightening!—the bruises Weedle described, on Kimi's pale soft shoulders—ugly rotted-purple, yellow. In order to see Kimi's upper arms, Candace has to tug the sweatshirt off Kimi's head as the girl kicks, curses—"I hate you! I hate *you!*" Kimi's fine soft hair crackles with static electricity—Kimi's eyes are widened, dilated—like a furious snorting animal Kimi brings a knee against Candace's chest, knocking the breath out of her. Candace is disbelieving—how can this be happening? She, who loves her daughter so much, and Kimi who has always been so sweet, docile . . . "You fat cunt! I hate you."

Candace stares at the bruises on her daughter's shoulders and upper arms—beneath her arms, reddened welts—and on the tops of her breasts which are smallish hard girl-breasts, waxy-pale, with pinprick nipples just visible through the cotton fabric of her bra— (Junior Miss 34B: Candace knows because Candace purchased the bra for Kimi). For several seconds Candace is unable to speak—her heart is pounding so violently. It does look as if someone with strong hands—strong fingers—had grabbed hold of Kimi and shook, shook, shook her.

"Your f-father? Did he—is this—? And you're protecting him?"

"Don't be ridiculous, Mom! You know Dad would never touch me," Kimi says scornfully. "I mean, Dad never even *kisses* me! How'd he get close enough to 'abuse' me?" Kimi's laughter is awful, like something being strangled.

"Then—who? Who did this?"

"Nobody *did anything*, Mom. Whatever it was, I *did to myself.* I'm a klutz—you always said so. Always falling down and hurting myself, breaking things—my own damn fault."

Kimi's eyes shine with tears. *Damn* is out of character, jarring.

Klutz. Such words as *klutz, wimp, dork, nerd* are just slightly more palatable than the cruder more primitive and unambiguous *asshole, fuckup, fuckhead, cunt.* Or maybe the equivalent would be *stupid cunt.*

So to call your daughter a *klutz*, or to conspire with others, including the daughter herself, in calling her *klutz*, however tenderly, fondly, is to participate in a kind of child molestation.

This seems clear to Candace, like a struck match shoved into her face.

"Kimi, you are not a 'klutz.' Don't say that about yourself."

"Mom, I am! You know I am! Falling, tripping, spilling things, ripping my clothes—banging my damn head, my legs"—with furious jocosity Kimi speaks, striking her ample thighs with her fists. "And a *fat cow-klutz* on top of it."

Family joke was that Kimi was a little butterball, chubby legs and arms, fatty-creased face like a moon-pie, and so *eager*—spilling her milk glass, toppling out of a high chair, spraining wrist, ankle in falls off tricycle, bicycle, down a flight of stairs.

Philip! Our baby daughter is a piglet. Cutest little piglet. With red eyes, red snub nose like a miniature snout, funny little pig-ears but—too bad!—no sweet little tail.

Young mother high on Demerol, entranced with her baby. *Oh Jesus it is a—baby! But—mine? Not mine!*

The horror washing over her, even as she felt love for the little piglet so powerful, could scarcely breathe and even now—fourteen years later—a muscle constricts in her chest, in the region of her heart—*Can't breathe can't breathe love comes too strong.*

And it was so—nursing started off so wonderfully—*Peak experience of my life*—then something went wrong. Little Kimberly ceased nursing as a baby is supposed to nurse, spat out precious milk, tugged at Candace's sensitive nipples and the nipples became chafed and cracked and bled and now, not so much fun. More, like—ordeal, obligation. More, like—who needs this. Milk turned rancid, baby puked a lot, cried and kicked at the wrong times. Young mother *freaking God-damned depressed.*

Fourteen years later not that much has changed. Except the baby's father is out of the picture even more than he was then.

That day returning home from Weedle and yes, Candace took another thirty-milligram lorazepam reasoning that she will not be engaged in *operating heavy machinery* for the remainder of the day and yes, Candace washed down the capsule with a (only two-thirds full) glass of tart red wine but no, Candace did not sleep but spent headachy hours at her computer clicking onto *abuse, girls* drawn to read of *abuse, rape, female cutting, slaughter* in Africa until she became faint thinking, where were the girls' mothers? how do they bear living? Thinking, jokes cease when little girls are raped, strangled, left to die in the bush.

Exactly as Weedle said: you can see the imprints of fingers in Kimi's skin.

"I'm asking you again, Kimi—who did this to you?"

Kimi grabs her sweatshirt back from Candace and pulls it furiously over her head.

"Please tell me, was it a boy? I hope not a—teacher?"

Candace hears herself beg. Candace wants to gather Kimi in her arms for another hug but knows that the girl will elbow her impatiently away.

"Mom, for God's sake cool it."

"But honey—I want to protect you. I want to be a good mother. It isn't too late—is it? Don't push me away."

Kimi yanks the sweatshirt down over her breasts, as far as it will go. Kimi is exasperated and embarrassed but seeing the expression in Candace's face, Kimi says: "Well, see—what happened wasn't primary. It was, like, a secondary factor."

"What do you mean—'secondary'?"

"The cut in my head wasn't on purpose. Nobody actually hit me. I was slow doing something and she pushed me from behind and I stumbled and hit my own damn head myself on something sharp—not a locker door but a chrome table edge. And she stopped the bleeding, and put disinfectant on it, and kissed it, and was sorry. So—it's OK. It's, like, nothing."

"Who did this? She?"

"Scotti. Who've we been talking about?"

"Scotia? Scotia did this to you? What do you mean?"

"Oh, Mom. Jeez! Just forget it."

"But—what did Scotia do to you? Pushed you? So you fell, and hit your head? Why?"

Kimi shrugs. Kimi's eyes shine with a sort of defiant merriment but her skin is flushed-red, smarting.

"Why would Scotia do such a thing? What were the circumstances?"

"Probably some stupid thing I said. Or didn't answer fast enough. Scotti has a problem with *slow*. Half the kids in our class, Scotti says, are *retards*."

"That terrible cut in your scalp—Scotia caused? But why are you protecting her?"

"Yes, my scalp. Mom. And my damn arms—you're so excited about—Scotti was helping me on the bars. Gymnastics."

"Scotia did that, too? 'Gymnastics'?"

"We were fooling around at her house. She's got all this Nautilus equipment her dad bought for her. You're always telling me to lose weight so I'm doing exercises at Scotti's. There're these, like, bars you hang on—Scotti was showing me how. No big deal, Mom—will you stop staring at me? I hate it."

"I'll call Scotia's mother. This has got to stop."

"It's *stopped*, Mom. I told you—it wasn't anyone's fault."

"It was Scotia's fault. And it isn't going to happen again."

"No! Don't you dare call Mrs. Perry! Scotti is the only thing in my life that means anything—the only person who gives a damn about me. If you take Scotti from me, I will kill myself."

Kimi begins crying, sobbing. Her swollen face seems to be melting. When Candace moves to embrace her, Kimi shoves her away as Candace expected—which doesn't make the hurt less painful.

Candace stumbles downstairs. Rapidly her mind is working— thoughts fly at her, through her, like neutrinos—can't quite comprehend the significance of these thoughts or what they are urging her to do—for a mom must *do*, a mom must more than simply *be*—until she's in the kitchen peering into the refrigerator: no Odwalla smoothies? *None?*

But there are ingredients for smoothies, Candace can make her own for Kimi, and for herself; strawberries and raspberries, banana, a dollop of orange juice, the remains of a container of yogurt blended together in Candace's shiny, rarely used twelve-speed blender. She is thrilled to be preparing something *homemade* for Kimi which she knows Kimi will love, and she knows that Kimi is hungry for Kimi is always hungry at this time of day, after school and before dinner which isn't always on the table until—well, after 8 P.M. Or then. The blender yields two tall glasses of strawberry-tinged smoothies, rich with nutrients, and delicious. Candace thinks *But more*. She goes to a kitchen drawer where there's an old stash of pills, pre-lorazepam, a handful of anti-anxiety meds, with tremulous fingers she empties one of the tall brimming glasses into the blender, tosses in a pill or two—or three— and whips the liquid again, grinds the pills to a froth, repours into the glass; then, who knows why, a neutrino-thought has pierced her brain with the cunning of desperation, she empties the other glass into the blender, tosses in a pill or two—or three—and whips the liquid again into a strawberry-hued froth.

Upstairs there is Kimi sprawled on her bed still wet-faced, panting and indignant—under the pretext of squinting into *To Kill a Mocking-*

bird she's been texting on her cell phone, which with clumsy childish deceit she tries to hide beneath the book so that Mom can't see. Of course Mom can see but Mom smiles radiant and forgiving as if not-seeing, carrying the glasses of strawberry-raspberry-banana smoothies—"For you, sweetie. And for me." Kimi is sullen but surprised and pleased—Kimi can't resist of course. Mumbling *Thanks Mom* for truly Kimi is a very well behaved and polite girl and always hungry.

Without waiting to be invited Candace sits cautiously on the edge of the badly rumpled bed and both Kimi and Candace drink their smoothies which are in fact delicious—"Better than what you get in the store, isn't it?"—and Kimi has to concede, yes.

"Just so you know I love you, honey. You do, don't you?—know this?"

Kimi shrugs, maybe. Yes.

Soon Kimi is yawning and blinking in a futile effort to keep her eyes open and Candace says yes, why don't you have a nap before dinner sweetie, a nap is a very good idea as Kimi whimpers faint as a kitten sighing and curling up to sleep unprotesting amid the stuffed animals which Candace has retrieved, to arrange on the bed around her daughter; as Candace, grunting with effort, beginning to be light-headed, straightens the comforter, fluffs up the flattened tear- and mucus-dampened pillow. Kimi's face is still puffy, flushed—her lips are swollen like labia—there's a babyish glisten at her nostrils Candace wipes tenderly with a tissue. With her new caution Candace takes away the smoothie glasses, makes her way swaying into the hall into the bathroom to wash each glass thoroughly in hot water, rub her fingers around inside the glasses and again hold them beneath the hot-gushing water and then returning to Kimi's room making her way carefully now knowing it is crucial not to slip, not to fall heavily onto the floor Candace returns to the white-wicker girl's bed where Kimi is now snoring faintly, lying on her side with her head flung back and her fine pale-brown hair in a halo on the pillow, beads of sweat at her fore-head; the sweatshirt has been pulled down as if to flatten her breasts, showing a soiled neckline. Carefully Candace climbs onto the bed and gathers Kimi in her arms, her heart is suffused with love for her limp unresisting daughter, sweet little piglet, Mommy's own piglet, she has forgotten to switch off the light, the God-damned light is in her eyes. But what the hell.

RUN KISS DADDY

"Tell Daddy hello! Run kiss Daddy."

He'd been gone from the lake less than an hour but in this new family each parting and each return signaled a sort of antic improvised celebration—he didn't want to think it was the obverse of what must have happened before he'd arrived in their lives—the daddy departing, and the daddy not returning.

"Sweetie, h'lo! C'mere."

He dropped to one knee as the boy ran at him to be hugged. A rough wet kiss on Kevin's forehead.

The little girl hesitated. Only when the mother pushed more firmly at her small shoulders did she spring forward and run—wild-blue-eyed suddenly, with a high-pitched squeal like a mouse being squeezed—into his arms. He laughed—he was startled by the heat of the little body—flattered and deeply moved kissing the excited child on the delicate soft skin at her temple where—he'd only just noticed recently—a pale blue vein pulsed.

"What do you say to Daddy when Daddy comes back?"

The mother clapped her hands to make a game of it. This new

family was so new to her too, weekends at Paraquarry Lake were best borne as a game, as play.

"Say 'Hi Daddy!'—'Kiss-kiss Daddy!'"

Obediently the children cried what sounded like *Hi Daddy! Kiss-kiss Daddy!*

Little fish-mouths pursed for kisses against Daddy's cheek.

Reno had only driven into the village of Paraquarry Falls bringing back semi-emergency supplies: toilet paper, flashlight batteries, mosquito repellent, mousetraps, a gallon container of milk, a shiny new garden shovel to replace the badly rusted shovel that had come with the camp. Also small sweet-fruit yogurts for the children though both he and the mother weren't happy about the children developing a taste for sugary foods—but there wasn't much of a selection at the convenience store.

In this new-Daddy phase in which unexpected treats are the very coinage of love.

"Who wants to help Daddy dig?"

Both children cried *Me!*—thrilled at the very prospect of working with Daddy on the exciting new terrace overlooking the lake.

And so they helped Daddy excavate the old, crumbled-brick terrace a previous owner had left amid a tangle of weeds, pebbles and broken glass, or tried to help Daddy—for a while. Clearly such work was too arduous for a seven-year-old, still more for a four-year-old, with play-shovels and rakes; and the mild June air too humid for much exertion. And there were mosquitoes, and gnats. Despite the repellent. For these were the Kittatinny Mountains east of the Delaware Water Gap in early June—that season of teeming buzzing fecundity—just to inhale the air is to inhale the smells of burgeoning life.

"Oh!—Dad-dy!"—Devra recoiled from something she'd unearthed in the soil, lost her balance and fell back onto her bottom with a little cry. Reno saw it was just a beetle—iridescent, wriggling—and told her not to be afraid: "They just live in the ground, sweetie. They have special beetle-work to do in the ground."

Kevin said, "Like worms! They have 'work' in the ground."

This simple science—earth science—the little boy had gotten from Reno. Very gratifying to hear your words repeated with child-pride.

From the mother Reno knew that their now-departed father had often behaved "unpredictably" with the children and so Reno made it a point to be soft-spoken in their presence, good-natured and unexcitable, predictable.

What pleasure in being *predictable*!

Still, Devra was frightened. She'd dropped her play shovel in the dirt. Reno saw that the little girl had enough of helping Daddy with the terrace for the time being. "Sweetie, go see what Mommy's doing. You don't need to dig any more right now."

Kevin remained with Daddy. Kevin snorted in derision, his baby sister was so *scaredy*.

Reno was a father, again. Fatherhood, returned to him. A gift he hadn't quite deserved the first time—maybe—but this time, he would strive to deserve it.

This time, he was forty-seven years old. He—who'd had a very hard time perceiving himself other than *young, a kid*.

And this new marriage!—this beautiful new family small and vulnerable as a mouse cupped trembling in the hand—he was determined to protect with his life. Not ever *not ever* let this family slip from his grasp as he'd let slip from his grasp his previous family—two young children rapidly retreating now in Reno's very memory like a scene glimpsed in the rearview mirror of a speeding vehicle.

"Come to Paraquarry Lake! You will love Paraquarry Lake."

The name itself seemed to him beautiful, seductive—like the Delaware River at the Water Gap where the river was wide, glittering and winking like shaken foil. As a boy he'd hiked the Appalachian Trail in this area of northeastern Pennsylvania and northwestern New Jersey—across the river on the high pedestrian walkway, north to Dunfield Creek and Sunfish Pond and so to Paraquarry Lake which was the most singular of the Kittatinny Ridge lakes, edged with rocks like a crude lacework and densely wooded with ash, elm, birch and maples that flamed red in autumn.

So he courted them with tales of his boyhood hikes, canoeing on the river and on Paraquarry Lake, camping along the Kittatinny Ridge where once, thousands of years ago, a glacier lay like a massive claw over the land.

He told them of the Lenni Lenape Indians who'd inhabited this part of the country for thousands of years!—far longer than their own kind.

Though as a boy he'd never found arrowheads at Paraquarry Lake or elsewhere, yet he recalled that others had, and so spoke excitedly to the boy Kevin as if to enlist him in a search; he did not quite suggest that they might discover Indian bones, that sometimes came to the surface at Paraquarry Lake, amid shattered red shale and ordinary rock and dirt.

In this way and in others he courted the new wife Marlena, who was a decade younger than he; and the new son, Kevin; and the new daughter who'd won his heart the first glimpse he'd had of her—tiny Devra with white-blond hair fine as the silk of milkweed.

Another man's lost family. Or maybe *cast off*—as Marlena said in her bright brave voice determined not to appear hurt, humiliated.

His own family—Reno had hardly cast off. Whatever his ex-wife would claim. If anything, Reno had been the one to be *cast off* by her.

Yet careful to tell Marlena, early in their relationship: "It was my fault, I think. I was too young. When we'd gotten married—just out of college—we were both too young. It's said that if you 'cohabit' before getting married it doesn't actually make any difference in the long run—whether you stay married, or get divorced—but our problem was that we hadn't a clue what 'cohabitation' meant—means. We were always two separate people and then my career took off . . ."

Took off wasn't Reno's usual habit of speech. Nor was it Reno's habit to talk so much, and so eagerly. But when he'd met a woman he believed he might come to seriously care for—at last—he'd felt obliged to explain himself to her: there had to be some failure in his personality, some flaw, otherwise why was he alone, unmarried; why had he become a father whose children had grown up largely without him, and without seeming to need him?

At the time of the divorce, Reno had granted his wife too many concessions. In his guilty wish to be generous to her though the breakup had been as much his wife's decision as his own. He'd signed away much of their jointly owned property, and agreed to severely curtail visitation rights with the children. He hadn't yet grasped this simple fact of human relations—the more readily you give, the more readily it will be taken from you as what you owe.

His wife had appealed to him to be allowed to move to Oregon where she had relatives, with the children; Reno hadn't wanted to contest her.

Within a few years, she'd relocated again—with a new husband, to Sacramento.

In these circuitous moves, somehow Reno was cast off. One too many corners had been turned, the father had been left behind except for child-support payments which did not diminish.

Trying not to feel like a fool. Trying to remain a gentleman long after he'd come to wonder why.

"Paraquarry Lake! You will all love Paraquarry Lake."

The new wife was sure, yes she would love Paraquarry Lake. Laughing at Reno's boyish enthusiasm, squeezing his arm.

Kevin and Devra were thrilled of course. Their new father—new

Daddy—so much nicer than the old, other *Daddy*—eagerly spreading out photographs on a tabletop like playing cards.

"Of course," the new Daddy said, a sudden crease between his eyes, "this cabin in the photos isn't the one we'll be staying in. This is the one—" Reno paused, stricken. It felt as if a thorn had lodged in his throat.

This is the one I have lost was not an appropriate statement to make to the new children and to the new wife listening so raptly to him, the new wife's fingers lightly resting on his arm.

These photographs had been selected of course. Reno's former wife and former children—of course, "former" wasn't the appropriate word!—were not shown to the new family.

Sixteen years invested in the former marriage! It made Reno sick—just faintly, mildly sick—to think of so much energy and emotion, lost.

Though there'd been strain between Reno and his ex-wife—exacerbated when they were in close quarters together—yet he'd insisted upon bringing his family to Paraquarry Lake on weekends through much of the year and staying there—of course—for at least six weeks each summer. When Reno couldn't get off from work he drove up weekends. For the "camp" at Paraquarry Lake—as he called it—was essential to his happiness.

Not that it was a particularly fancy place: it wasn't. Several acres of deciduous and pine woods, and hundred-foot frontage on the lake—*that* was what made the place special.

Eventually, in the breakup, the Paraquarry Lake camp had been sold. Reno's wife had come to hate the place and had no wish to buy him out—nor would she sell her half to him. In the woman's bitterness, the camp had been lost to strangers.

Now, it was nine years later. Reno hadn't seen the place in years. He'd driven along the Delaware River and inland to the lake and past the camp several times but became too emotional staring at it from the road, such bitter nostalgia wasn't good for him, and wasn't, he wanted to think, typical of him. So much better to think—to tell people in his new life *It was an amicable split-up and an amicable divorce over all. We're civilized people—the kids come first!*

Was this what people said, in such circumstances? You did expect to hear *The kids come first!*

Now, there was a new camp. A new "cabin"—an A-frame, in fact—the sort of thing for which Reno had always felt contempt; but the dwelling was attractive, "modern" and in reasonably good condition with a redwood deck and sliding glass doors overlooking both the lake and a ravine of tangled wild roses to the rear. The nearest neighbor was uncomfortably close—only a few yards away—but screened by evergreens and a makeshift redwood fence a previous owner had erected.

Makeshift too was the way in which the A-frame had been cantilevered over a drop in the rocky earth, with wooden posts supporting it; if you entered at the rear you stepped directly into the house but if you entered from the front, that is, facing the lake, you had to climb a steep flight of not-very-sturdy wood steps, gripping a not-very-sturdy railing. The property had been owned by a half-dozen parties since its original owner in the 1950s. Reno wondered at the frequent turnover of owners—this wasn't typical of the Water Gap area where people returned summer after summer for a lifetime.

The children loved the "Paraquarry camp"—they hugged their new Daddy happily, to thank him—and the new wife who'd murmured that she wasn't an "outdoor type" conceded that it was really very nice—"And what a beautiful view."

Reno wasn't about to tell Marlena that the view from his previous place had been more expansive, and more beautiful.

Marlena kissed him, so very happy. For he had saved her, as she had saved him. From what—neither could have said.

Paraquarry Lake was not a large lake: seven miles in circumference.

The shoreline was so distinctly uneven and most of it thickly wooded and inaccessible except by boat. On maps the lake was L-shaped but you couldn't guess this from shore—nor even from a boat—you would have to fly in a small plane overhead, as Reno had done many years ago.

"Let's take the kids up sometime, and fly over. Just to see what the lake looks like from the air."

Reno spoke with such enthusiasm, the new wife did not want to disappoint him. Smiling and nodding yes! What a good idea—"Sometime."

The subtle ambiguity of *sometime*. Reno guessed he knew what this meant.

In this new marriage Reno had to remind himself—continually—that though the new wife was young, in her mid-thirties, he himself was no longer that young. In his first marriage he'd been just a year older than his wife. Physically they'd been about equally fit. Reno had been stronger than his wife of course, he could hike longer and in more difficult terrain, but essentially they'd been a match and in some respects—caring for the children, for instance—his wife had had more energy than Reno. Now, the new wife was clearly more fit than Reno who became winded—even exhausted—on the nearby Shawangunk Trail that, twenty years before, he'd found hardly taxing.

Reno's happiness was working on the camp: the A-frame that needed repainting, a new roof, new windows; the deck was partly rotted, the front steps needed to be replaced. Unlike Reno's previous camp of several acres the new camp was hardly more than an acre and much of the property was rocky and inaccessible—fallen trees, rotted lumber, the detritus of years.

Reno set for himself the long-term goal of clearing the property of such litter and a short-term goal of building a flagstone terrace beside the front steps, where the earth was rocky and overgrown with weeds; there had once been a makeshift brick terrace or walkway here, now broken. Evidence of previous tenants—rather, the negligence of previous tenants—was a cause of annoyance to Reno as if this property dear to him had been purposefully desecrated by others.

During the winter in their house in East Orange Reno had studied photos he'd taken of the new camp. Tirelessly he'd made sketches of the redwood deck he meant to extend and rebuild, and of the "sleeping porch" he meant to add. Marlena suggested a second bathroom, with both a shower and a tub. And a screened porch that could be transformed into a glassed-in porch in cold weather. Reno would build—or cause to be built—a carport, a new fieldstone fireplace, a barbecue on the deck. And there was the ground-level terrace he would construct himself with flagstones from a local garden supply store, once he'd dug up and removed the old, broken bricks half-buried in the earth.

Reno understood that his new wife's enthusiasm for Paraquarry Lake and the Delaware Water Gap was limited. Marlena would comply with his wishes—anyway, most of them—so long as he didn't press her too far. The high-wattage smile might quickly fade, the eyes brimming with love turn tearful. For divorce is a devastation, Reno knew. The children were more readily excited by the prospect of spending time at the lake—but they were children, impressionable. And bad weather in what was essentially an outdoor setting—its entire raison d'être was *outdoors*—would be new to them. Reno understood that he must not make with this new family the mistake he'd made the first time—insisting that his wife and children not only accompany him to Paraquarry Lake but that they enjoy it—visibly.

Maybe he'd been mistaken, trying so hard to make his wife and young children *happy*. Maybe it's always a mistake, trying to assure the happiness of others.

His daughter was attending a state college in Sacramento—her major was something called communication arts. His son had flunked out from Cal Tech and was enrolled at a "computer arts" school in San

Francisco. The wife had long ago removed herself from Reno's life and truly Reno rarely thought of any of them, who seemed so rarely to think of him.

But the daughter. Reno's daughter. *Oh hi Dad. Hi. Damn I'm sorry— I'm just on my way out.*

Reno had ceased calling her. Both the kids. For they never called him. Even to thank him for birthday gifts. Their e-mails were rudely short, perfunctory.

The years of child support had ended. Both were beyond eighteen.

And the years of alimony, now that the ex-wife had remarried.

How many hundreds of thousands of dollars . . . But of course, Reno understood.

But the new children! In this new family!

Like wind rippling over the surface of Paraquarry Lake emotion flooded into Reno at the thought of his new family. He would adopt the children—soon. For Kevin and Devra adored their new daddy who was so kind, funny, patient and—yes—"predictable"—with them; who had not yet raised his voice to them a single time.

Especially little Devra captivated him—he stared at her in amazement, the child was so *small*—tiny rib cage, collarbone, wrists—after her bath, the white-blond hair thin as feathers against her delicate skull.

"Love you—I love you—all—so much."

It was a declaration made to the new wife only in the dark of their bed. In her embrace, her strong warm fingers gripping his back, and his hot face that felt to him like a ferret's face, hungry, ravenous with hunger, pressed into her neck.

At Paraquarry Lake, in the new camp, there was a new Reno emerging.

It was hard work but thrilling, satisfying—to chop his own firewood and stack it beside the fireplace. The old muscles were reassert-

ing themselves in his shoulders, upper arms, thighs. He was developing
a considerable ax-swing, and was learning to anticipate the jar of the ax
head against wood which he supposed was equivalent to the kick of a
shotgun against a man's shoulder—if you weren't prepared, the shock
ran down your spine like an electric charge.

Working outdoors he wore gloves which Marlena gave him—"Your
hands are getting too calloused—scratchy." When he caressed her, she
meant. Marlena was a shy woman and did not speak of their lovemak-
ing but Reno wanted to think that it meant a good deal to her as it
meant to him, after years of pointless celibacy.

He was thrilled too when they went shopping together—at the
mall, at secondhand furniture stores—choosing Adirondack chairs,
a black leather sofa, rattan settee, handwoven rugs, andirons for the
fireplace. It was deeply moving to Reno to be in the presence of this attractive woman who took such care and turned to him continually for
his opinion as if she'd never furnished a household before.

Reno even visited marinas in the area, compared prices: sailboats,
Chris-Craft power boats. In truth he was just a little afraid of the
lake—of how he might perform as a sailor on the lake. A rowboat was
one thing, even a canoe—he felt shaky in a canoe, with another passenger. With this new family vulnerable as a small creature cupped in
the palm of a hand—he didn't want to take any risks.

The first warm days in June, a wading pool for the children. For
there was no beach, only just a pebbly shore of sand hard-packed as
cement. And sharp-edged rocks in the shallows at shore. But a plastic
wading pool, hardly more than a foot of water—that was fine. Little Kevin splashed happily. And Devra in a puckered yellow spandex
swimsuit that fitted her little body like a second skin. Reno tried not to
stare at the little girl—the astonishing white-blond hair, the widened
pale-blue eyes—thinking how strange it was, how strange Marlena
would think it was, that the child of a father not known to him should

have so totally supplanted Reno's memory of his own daughter at that age; for Reno's daughter, too, must have been beautiful, adorable—but Reno couldn't recall. Terrifying how parts of his life were being shut to him like rooms in a house shut and their doors sealed and once you've crossed the threshold, you can't return. Terrifying to think except waking in the night with a pounding heart Reno would catch his breath thinking *But I have my new family now. My new life now.*

Sometimes in the woods above the lake there was a powerful smell—a stink—of skunk, or something dead and rotted; not the decaying compost Marlena had begun which exuded a pleasurable odor for the most part, but something ranker, darker. Reno's sinuses ached, his eyes watered and he began sneezing—in a sudden panic that he'd acquired an allergy for something at Paraquarry Lake.

That weekend, Kevin injured himself running along the rocky shore—as his mother had warned him not to—falling, twisting his ankle. And little Devra, stung by yellow jackets that erupted out of nowhere—in fact, out of a hive in the earth, that Reno had disturbed with his shovel.

Screaming! High-pitched screams that tore at Reno's heart.

If only the yellow jackets had stung *him*—Reno might have used the occasion to give the children some instruction.

Having soothed two weeping children in a single afternoon Marlena said ruefully, " 'Camp' can be treacherous!" The remark was meant to be amusing but there was seriousness beneath, even a subtle warning, Reno knew.

Reno swallowed hard and promised it wouldn't happen again.

This warm-humid June afternoon shading now into early evening and Reno was still digging—"excavating"—the old ruin of a terrace. The project was turning out to be harder and more protracted than Reno had anticipated. For the earth below the part-elevated house was a rocky sort of subsoil, of a texture like fertilizer; moldering bricks were everywhere, part-buried; also jagged pieces of concrete and rusted spikes, broken glass amid shattered bits of red shale. The previous owners had simply dumped things here. Going back for decades, probably. Generations. Reno hoped these slovenly people hadn't dumped anything toxic.

The A-frame had been built in 1957—that long ago. Some time later there were renovations, additions—sliding glass doors, skylights. A sturdier roof. Another room or two. By local standards the property hadn't been very expensive—of course, the market for lakeside properties in this part of New Jersey had been depressed for several years.

The new wife and the children were down at the shore—at a neighbor's dock. Reno heard voices, radio music—Marlena was talking with another young mother—several children were playing together. Reno liked hearing their happy uplifted voices though he couldn't make out any words. From where he stood, he couldn't have said with certainty which small figure was Kevin, which was Devra.

How normal all this was! Soon, Daddy would quit work for the evening, grab a beer from the refrigerator and join his little family at their neighbor's dock. How normal Reno was—a husband again, a father and a homeowner here at Paraquarry Lake.

Of all miracles, none is more daunting than *normal*. To be—to become—*normal*. This gift seemingly so ordinary is not a gift given to all who seek it.

And the children's laughter, too. This was yet more exquisite.

With a grunt Reno unearthed a large rock, he'd been digging and scraping at with mounting frustration. And beneath it, or beside it, what appeared to be a barrel, with broken and rotted staves; inside the barrel, what appeared to be shards of a broken urn.

There was something special about this urn, Reno seemed to know. The material was some sort of dark red earthenware—thick, glazed—inscribed with figures like hieroglyphics. Even broken and coated with grime, the pieces exuded an opaque sort of beauty. Unbroken, the urn would have stood about three feet in height.

Was this an Indian artifact? Reno was excited to think so—remains of the Lenni Lenape culture were usually shattered into very small pieces, almost impossible for a non-specialist to recognize.

With the shiny new shovel Reno dug into and around the broken urn, curious. He'd been tossing debris into several cardboard boxes, to be hauled to the local landfill. He was tired—his muscles ached, and there was a new, sharp pain between his shoulder blades—but he was feeling good, essentially. At the neighbor's dock when they asked him how he was he'd say *Damn good! But thirsty.*

His next-door neighbor looked to be a taciturn man of about Reno's age. And the wife one of those plus-size personalities with a big smile and a greeting. To them, Marlena and Reno would be a *couple.* No sign that they were near-strangers desperate to make the new marriage work.

Already in early June Reno was beginning to tan—he looked like a native of the region more than he looked like a summer visitor from the city, he believed. In his T-shirt, khaki shorts, waterstained running shoes. He wasn't yet fifty—he had three years before fifty. His father had died at fifty-three of a heart attack but Reno took care of his health, he had nothing to worry about. Reno had annual checkups, he had nothing to worry about. He would adopt the woman's children—that was settled. He would make them his own children: Kevin, Devra. He could not have named the children more fitting names. Beautiful names for beautiful children.

The Paraquarry property was an excellent investment. His work was going well. His work was not going badly. His job wasn't in peril—yet. He hadn't lost nearly so much money as he might have lost in the recent economic crisis—he was far from desperate, like a number of his friends. Beyond that—he didn't want to think.

A scuttling snake amid the debris. Reno was taken by surprise, startled. Tossed a piece of concrete at it. Thinking then in rebuke *Don't be ridiculous. A garter snake is harmless.*

Something was stuck to some of the urn shards—clothing? Torn, badly rotted fabric?

Reno leaned his weight onto the shovel, digging more urgently. A flash of something wriggling in the earth—worms—cut by the slice of the shovel. Reno was sweating now. He stooped to peer more closely even as the cautionary words came *Maybe no. Maybe not a good idea.*

"Oh. God."

Was it a bone? Or maybe plastic?—no, a bone. An animal bone?

Covered in dirt, yet a very pale bone.

A human bone?

But so small—had to be a child's bone.

A child's forearm perhaps.

Reno picked the bone up, in his gloved hands. It weighed nothing—it might have been made of Styrofoam.

"It is. It really . . . is."

Numbly Reno groped amid the broken pottery, tossing handfuls of clumped dirt aside. More bones, small broken rib-bones, a skull . . . A skull!

It was a small skull of course. Small enough to cup in the hand.

Not an animal-skull but a child's skull. Reno seemed to know—*a little girl's skull.*

This was not believable! Reno's brain was struck blank, for a long moment he could not think . . . The hairs stirred at the nape of his neck and he wondered if he was being watched.

A makeshift grave about fifteen feet from the base of his house.

And when had this little body been buried? Twenty years ago, ten years ago? By the look of the bones, the rotted clothing and the broken urn, the burial hadn't been recent.

But these were not Indian bones of course. Those bones would be much older—badly broken, dim and scarified with time.

Reno's hand shook. The small teeth were bared in a smile of sheer terror. The small jaws had fallen open, the eye sockets were disproportionately large. Of course, the skull was broken—it was not a perfect skull. Possibly fractured in the burial—struck by the murderer's shovel. The skeleton lay in pieces—had the body been dismembered? Reno was whispering to himself words meant to console—*Oh God. Help me God. God!* As his surprise ebbed Reno began to be badly frightened. He was thinking that these might be the bones of his daughter—his first daughter; the little girl had died, her death had been accidental, but he and her mother had hurriedly buried her . . .

But no: ridiculous. This was another time, not that time.

This was another camp-site. This was another part of Paraquarry Lake. This was another time in a father's life.

His daughter was alive. Somewhere in California, a living girl. He was not to blame. He had never hurt her. She would outlive him.

Laughter and raised voices from the lakeshore. Reno shaded his eyes to see—what were they doing? Were they expecting Daddy to join them?

Kneeling in the dirt. Groping and rummaging in the coarse earth. Among the broken pottery, bones and rotted fabric faded to the no-color of dirty water, something glittered—a little necklace of glass beads.

Reno untangled it from a tangle of small bones—vertebrae? The remains of the child's neck? Hideous to think that the child-skeleton might have been broken into pieces with a shovel, or an ax. An ax! To fit more readily into the urn. To hasten decomposition.

"Little girl! Poor little girl."

Reno was weak with shock, sickened. His heart pounded terribly—he didn't want to die as his father had died! He would breathe deeply, calmly. He held the glass beads to the light. Amazingly, the chain was intact. A thin metallic chain, tarnished. Reno put the little glass-bead necklace into the pocket of his khaki shorts. Hurriedly he covered the bones with dirt, debris. Pieces of the shattered urn he picked up and tossed into the cardboard box. And the barrel staves . . . Then he thought he should remove the bones also—he should place the bones in the box, beneath the debris, and take the box out to the landfill this evening. Before he did anything else. Before he washed hurriedly, grabbed a beer and joined Marlena and the children at the lakefront. He would dispose of the child's bones at the landfill.

No. They will be traced here. Not a good idea.

Frantically he covered the bones. Then more calmly, smoothing the coarse dirt over the debris. Fortunately there was a sizable hole—a gouged-out, ugly hole—that looked like a rupture in the earth. Reno would lay flagstones over the grave—he'd purchased two dozen flagstones from a garden supply store on the highway. The children could help him—it would not be difficult work once the earth was prepared. As bricks had been laid over the child's grave years ago, Reno would lay flagstones over it now. For Reno could not report this terrible discovery—could he? If he called the Paraquarry police, if he reported the child-skeleton to county authorities, what would be the consequences?

His mind went blank—he could not think.

Could not bear the consequences. Not now, in his life.

Numbly he was setting his work-tools aside, beneath the overhang of the redwood deck. The new shovel was not so shiny now. Quickly then—shakily—climbing the steps, to wash his hands in the kitchen. A relief—he saw his family down at the shore, with the neighbors— the new wife, the children. No one would interrupt Reno washing the little glass-bead necklace in the kitchen sink, in awkward big-Daddy hands.

Gently washing the glass beads, that were blue—beneath the grime a startling pellucid blue like slivers of sky. It was amazing, you might interpret it as a sign—the thin little chain hadn't broken, in the earth.

Not a particle of dirt remained on the glass beads when Reno was finished washing them, drying them on a paper towel on the kitchen counter.

"Hey—look here! What's this? Who's this for?"

Reno dangled the glass-bead necklace in front of Devra. The little girl stared, blinking. It was suppertime—Daddy had grilled hamburgers on the outdoor grill, on the deck—and now Daddy pulled a little blue-glass-bead necklace out of his pocket as if he'd only just discovered it.

Marlena laughed—Marlena was delighted—for this was the sort of small surprise Marlena appreciated.

Not for herself but for the children. In this case, for Devra. It was a good moment, a warm moment—Kevin didn't react with jealousy but seemed only curious, as Daddy said he'd found the necklace in a "secret place" and knew just who it was meant for.

Shyly Devra took the little glass-bead necklace from Daddy's fingers.

"What do you say, Devra?"

"Oh Dad-dy—thank you."

Devra spoke so softly, Reno cupped his hand to his ear.

"Speak up, Devra. Daddy can't hear"—Marlena helped the little girl slip the necklace over her head.

"Daddy *thank you!*"

The little fish-mouth pursed for a quick kiss of Daddy's cheek.

Around the child's slender neck the blue-glass beads glittered, gleamed. All that summer at Paraquarry Lake Reno would marvel he'd never seen anything more beautiful.

HEY DAD

Almost wouldn't recognize you. And you wouldn't recognize *me*.

Your face is gaunter than your photo-face. Your eyes are hidden by dark-tinted glasses. The goatee looks like Brillo-wires pasted on your jaws.

Hey Dad: congratulations!

Hey Dad: me.

I'm in the third row. I'm the face with the smile.

Hey Dad this is *coincidence*.

You are one of five Honorary Doctorate awardees.

I am one of 233 Bachelor of Arts awardees.

You are sixty-two years old. I am twenty-one years old.

We both look ridiculous don't we Dad? You in the black academic gown on this sweltering-hot day in May, in New England. Me in the black academic gown on this sweltering-hot day in May, in New England.

You in shiny black leather shoes, proper black silk socks.

Me in black leather sandals, sockless.

You in a folding chair on the commencement platform. First row of the select—president's party.

Me in the third row of 223 graduating seniors. Seated on the hard hard stone of the quasi-Greek amphitheater.

One of a small sea of black-robed kids. Some of us in T-shirts and swim trunks beneath the black robes 'cause it's God-damn hot in mid-May on our little Colonial-college campus in New England.

Some of us hungover from last night's partying. Some of us high.

Some of us God-damn sober.

Confronting the rest-of-our-lives, God-damn sober.

But hey Dad: it's cool.

Don't worry that I will make a scene. That I will confront you.

Though crossing the platform to have my hand shaken by the president. Though crossing the platform in my black academic robe and mortar-board cap passing within eighteen inches of your knees.

Though I seem to be, if your biographies are accurate, your *only son*.

That is, biographies indicate that you are the father of two daughters, from your first, long-ago marriage.

Biographies of M——— V——— are respectful. Mostly noting your *controversial work in ethics, political commentary*. Briefly noting your several marriages. And no record of your numerous *liaisons*.

Hey Dad relax: I'm not the type to confront, or to confound. I have never been the type, I think.

You have not shied away from public pronouncements that have caused dissension, controversy. Your books on the "ethics of killing"—(war, abortion, euthanasia)—that made your early reputation. Your books on "American imperialism" in the Third World, your scathing attacks on "colonization in new forms."

You are the egalitarian, the friend of the oppressed. *You* speak for those in the Third World who can't speak for themselves.

You would not "colonize" anyone—of course.

Your (thinning, graying-coppery) hair is still long, in the style of the 1960s. Signaling to youth in the audience that, for all his academic distinction, and the Brillo-goatee threaded with gray, M——— V——— is one *cool dude*.

Already when my mom knew M——— V——— in the long-ago, you were a person of distinction. And, for sure, one *cool dude*.

Not that Mom talked about you. Never.

Not that Mom thought about you. In recent years.

Not that my stepfather knew (much) about you.

Hey Dad this isn't about them. This is about *me*.

And this is about you.

This is about *coincidence*.

What a brainteaser to calculate the odds: not just M——— V——— receiving an honorary doctorate at his (unacknowledged, unknown?) son's commencement but the son *existing*.

For that hadn't been your intention, hey Dad?

It isn't an operation, it isn't surgery. It's a medical procedure. It's common like going to the dentist.

And, later. More sternly, losing patience: *Don't be ridiculous. There is nothing to be frightened of.*

Mom did not tell me. Mom did not ever tell me. If Mom talked about her life of long-ago when she'd been a graduate student at the distinguished Ivy League university in which you've been on the faculty for thirty years it was not to me.

The quasi-Greek amphitheater looks like it has been hacked out of stone in some primitive time of public ritual, sacrifice.

In a lurid TV melodrama I would have brought a weapon with me to commencement. A weapon hidden beneath the ridiculous black robe.

But this is not TV, and it is not melodrama. The mood is too measured, stately, and *slow* for melodrama.

"Pomp and Circumstance" played by the college orchestra. Very brassy, militant. Ridiculous old music but hey Dad, your mean old heart quickens, I bet!

Your picture in the papers, your squinting-smiling photo-face.

Maybe the face is wearing out, a little. Corroding from within.

Decades now you've been winning awards. Decades you've been a *known figure*.

Graduate students and post-docs and interns and assistants. And young untenured professors. You are their General. They do your bidding.

Hey Dad it's a strain, isn't it: listening to other people speaking.

But hey no one is going to confront you here.

No one is going to accuse you.

She hadn't accused you. Maybe by the standards of that long-ago era you hadn't violated university policy. Maybe there were no rules governing the (sexual, moral) behavior of faculty members and their students in those days.

It just isn't going to happen—that we can be together. Not just now.

I will pay for the procedure. I can't accompany you for obvious reasons but I will pay and I suggest that you make arrangements to have it done out of town and not here; and I will pay for your accommodations there of course.

Which you did not, Dad. Because Mom refused.

Which pissed you considerably, Dad. Because Mom refused.

Because Mom wanted *me*. If it meant pissing you considerably, and losing you—still, Mom wanted *me*.

Hey Dad guess how I know this? Reading Mom's journal.

Mom's journal—journals—she's been keeping since 1986 when she was a freshman at the university and first enrolled in your famous lecture course.

More than three hundred students in that legendary course.

The Ethics of Politics. From Plato to Mao.

But it was later, Mom met you. When Mom was a graduate student in your seminar. And Mom became your dissertation advisee—a *coup* for the twenty-three-year-old since it's known that M——— V——— chooses few students to work closely with him.

Hey Dad we know: you've forgotten Mom's name.

Or if you haven't forgotten the name exactly, you've forgotten Mom.

For there were so many of them, in your life.

Though Mom went on to teach in universities herself. Mom has a career not so distinguished as yours but Mom too has published articles, reviews, and books.

Has, or had. Mom isn't working now, Mom is pretty sick.

Mom has been pretty sick for a while. *Struggling* as they say.

Determined to beat it as they say.

And maybe she will. Odds are a little better than fifty-fifty she can make it.

Which is why Mom isn't here this morning. Mom and my step-dad. Why I am alone here this morning.

With my friends, I'm a popular guy. Girls like me pretty much, too.

But mostly I'm alone. My truest self is alone.

Mom doesn't know that I've been reading her journals. They are handwritten notebooks kept on a high shelf in her study. They are not for anyone's eyes except Mom's.

And if Mom dies—it isn't clear what will become of the journals.

Mom isn't famous or distinguished enough for the journals to be published, I think.

So you don't have to worry, Dad. Not that you're worried.

And not much chance is there, Dad?—you're going to peruse the columns of names of the class of 2011 in the commencement program you've been given. For no name listed there could interest M——— V——— in the slightest.

Even my name with its little red asterisk to indicate *summa cum laude.*

Hey Dad here's a question: if you had known *me,* if you'd foreseen *me,* including the *summa cum laude* and the Rhodes scholarship for next year at Oxford, would you have insisted upon the procedure, just the same?

No? Yes?

"The ethics of killing." Did you ever wonder what it feels like to be *the killed*—hey Dad?

I'm curious, I think. Passing within eighteen inches of M——— V——— on the platform maybe I will pause, for just a moment—a "dramatic" moment.

In the phosphorescent-heat of the sun. Nearing noon, the sun will be overhead. Even the shade beneath the stage canopy will be hot, humid. Perspiration will run in little trickles down your face, Dad. Inside your clothes, Dad.

You aren't a young man any longer. You may notice a shortness of breath, climbing stairs. A shimmering wave of vertigo at the top of the stairs. A dark place in your heart opening—*I have been a shit. My life is shit. Whatever terrible death awaits me, I deserve.*

I'm thinking now, yes I will. After the President shakes my hand and the dean hands me my diploma and I am crossing the platform in a slow steady stream of Bachelor of Arts awardees all in ridiculous black robes flapping about our ankles and I pass no more than eighteen inches from M——— V——— in dark-tinted glasses and goatee. I will stop, I will turn to you, only a moment, a fleeting moment, and among the buzz and hum of this part of commencement not many will notice. And if they notice, they will have no idea what I've said to you to so shock and disconcert you—*Hey Dad it's me.*

THE GOOD SAMARITAN

On the train from Utica in the late fall of 1981 I found the wallet.

Wedged between the soiled cushion-seat and the metallic strip beneath the window, so that it wasn't visible to the casual eye, but I felt it nudging against my hip, a hard object, as I'd sat down heavily, books spilling out of my bookbag onto my lap and onto the floor.

Just by accident! For I'd intended to sit in another car but seeing in the corner of my eye someone I knew from school—not well, but she knew me, she'd have wanted me to sit with her so that she could tell me about her boyfriend(s), her sorority sisters, how "terrific" our college was—the prospect filled me with dismay and quickly before she could see me I'd headed in the opposite direction.

The object jutting against my hip was a woman's wallet, a too-bright green, meant to resemble crocodile skin. Surreptitiously I examined it, hoping that no one was watching.

Clearly this was a "lost" object—it was not mine.

I was twenty years old—still young enough and needy enough to

feel a little stab of elation that someone had left her wallet behind—
for me.

There is a romance of lost objects, I think. Like abandoned houses,
junked cars. Objects once valuable and cherished and now ownerless.
Lost-and-found in our high school was a closet with shelves adjacent
to the front office, for which a secretary had the key. Searching for a
lost mitten you were surprised to see so many single, lost mittens and
gloves, glasses with cracked lenses, soiled change purses, notebooks,
sweaters, socks, a single sneaker. How could such sizable objects be
lost? I'd gone with a friend who was looking for a lost watch, naively
she'd removed her watch for gym class and shut it in her (unlocked)
locker and it was gone when she'd returned—as I might have warned
her, if I'd thought it was my business. And why she imagined the watch
might be reported as *lost* and waiting for her in the *lost-and-found* when
clearly it had been stolen was a mystery to me—but again, commenting
on my friend's judgment was not my business.

How strange it always seemed to me, people can lose so much,
people are so careless.

We—my younger brother and I—had been brought up *not to
be careless*. We did not have *money to throw around* as my excitable
mother liked to say with an airy gesture of her hand that seemed
to belie what she was saying, for you had a sense of how much my
mother would have liked to *throw money around* if she'd had money
for that purpose.

Nor did we squander emotions, or opinions. My opinions of others,
including my closest friends, were kept private, unuttered, which was
why, among girls who knew me in high school, and now in college, I was
very *well liked* as one *to be trusted*.

I did not share secrets with others. If told secrets, I did not betray
the teller.

Guiltily I glanced up—but no one seemed to be watching. Even a middle-aged man who'd stared rudely at me as I'd made my way along the aisle had lost interest and was reading a newspaper. The childish thought came to me—*It's a trick. A test.*

Maybe a conductor had seen me. Maybe he would loom over me and claim the wallet as *lost property.*

But the conductor was at the far end of the car. He hadn't seen, of course. If I'd wanted to shove it into my bag, the wallet was mine.

The wallet was promising: it looked stylish, expensive. Except the "leather" was synthetic and the brass-like trim was beginning to tarnish.

On the back were tarnished-brass initials—*AMN.*

Inside, the wallet was like any other wallet—a compartment for change, a compartment for cards including a Visa card, an AAA card, medical and dental health-management cards, as well as a few snapshots, and a driver's license made out to *Anna-Marie Nivecca, 2117 Pitcairn St., Carthage, NY.*

The little photo on the driver's license showed a smiling young woman with streaked-blond hair spilling over her shoulders, dark eyebrows, dark lips. She was not a natural blond, you could see—the hair was dark at the roots. The camera's flash was mirrored, in miniature, in her eyes.

Born 5/19/74, Carthage, New York. Only seven years older than I was but a mature *woman.*

Anna-Marie Nivecca was very attractive, I thought. Men would turn to glance at her in the street. Women, too.

I might have felt a pang of envy, jealousy—not exactly resentment but a sort of self-lacerating admiration for one so clearly more attractive—"sexy"—than I was, or could imagine being.

Except, in other photos, by herself or with others, *Anna-Marie Nivecca* looked somehow plaintive, vulnerable—even when smiling.

Like a glamour-girl of another era, one of those Hollywood starlets about whom you learned that despite her beauty she'd had an unhappy life, divorce, alcoholism, an early death.

There were just four snapshots in the wallet, trimmed to size: a young, busty *Anna-Marie* in a bridal gown with a strikingly good-looking, pale-olive-skinned young man clutching her around the waist, his smiling face pressed cheek to cheek with hers in a pose that must have been a strain to both; *Anna-Marie* with an older, heavy-set couple who might have been her parents, all in dressy attire, and smiling broadly at the camera; *Anna-Marie* with a baby on her lap, and the handsome young groom now in T-shirt and shorts, sitting on the grass beside her chair with his hand loosely closed around her bare, shapely leg; *Anna-Marie* with several other very festive young women with eye-catching hair, celebrating someone's birthday in a restaurant.

I felt a wave of something like dismay—*This is the life of a woman—a real woman. Wife and mother, loving daughter, girlfriend.*

In my plain utilitarian wallet there were no snapshots, only just tight little pockets for cards. And not so many of these, either.

It seemed probable to me, the wallet with its initials had been a gift to Anna-Marie from someone who loved her. And many people loved her.

Having initials put on the wallet, in what would have been, at the time of purchase, shiny brass—was this expensive?

At last, having looked through the wallet, now I checked the bills—as if, until this moment, I hadn't been thinking of the bills in the wallet at all.

As if the amount of money in a "lost" wallet isn't the most crucial feature of that wallet.

As if the money hadn't been the first, the *absolute first* thing I'd thought of, even before I'd tugged the wallet out of its niche against the wall. As soon as I'd felt the edge of the wallet nudging my hip, my instinctive thought had been—*Something valuable, left behind!*

The crude jeering singsong of childhood—*Finders keepers losers weepers.*

(Was I really so poor? My family so anxious about money? From earliest childhood I'd absorbed my parents' worries—they'd been born during the Depression, and could not ever forget it. We lived with my father's widowed mother in her clapboard house in Carthage and my father worked at a variety of jobs that seemed always to be evaporating through no fault of his; young, I'd learned that you can work, work, and work and yet be "poor" and the stigma of poverty is more painful for you than for those who chose scarcely to work at all. At the small liberal arts college to which I had a music scholarship I would have been mortified if my classmates had known how desperate I was for money—how anxious, that even my scholarship might not be enough to keep me in school. I worked part-time for food services, at the minimum wage, and hadn't even the satisfaction of complaining bitterly and funnily about my job since I couldn't risk others guessing how desperate I had to be for money, to work at such a job.)

Slowly I counted—and recounted—the bills in the wallet: a rumpled twenty, a five, a few dollar bills—not quite thirty dollars.

Thirty dollars! This wasn't insignificant to me, whose wallet contained about eighteen dollars and change after the purchase of a round-trip train ticket to Carthage.

I understood, the wallet's owner Anna-Marie didn't have *money to throw around*, either.

You could tell by the snapshots. The hairstyles of the young women, their "dress-up" clothes, lavish makeup and jewelry.

In one of the little pockets was a card—*In Case of Emergency Please Contact Next of Kin Jalel Nivecca, 2117 Pitcairn St, Carthage, NY.*

"Jalel"—this had to be the husband, olive-dark-skinned, eerily handsome like a Romantic painting of a gypsy lover, a Byronic hero, a Heathcliff.

The name "Jalel" was new to me. I wondered if Anna-Marie's husband was of Mediterranean descent, maybe Greek, Tunisian—Middle Eastern. I wondered what it would be like to be married to such a face, for even an attractive woman like Anna-Marie Nivecca.

Outside the train window, that looked just perceptibly foggy, or greasy, as if it hadn't been washed in a very long time, a desolate late-autumn landscape rumbled past. The train moved along the Mohawk River but I was sitting on the side opposite the river—just hills, pine woods, a chill pale late-morning sun. I sniffed at the wallet—there was a faint fragrance, a woman's perfume maybe.

A powerful sensation swept over me, to which I could have given no name.

Next to the name "Jalel Nivecca" was a telephone number.

I thought—*I should call this number.*

Except—I hated telephone calls. It was an obstinate sort of shyness, that made me stammer. I could not stop myself from imagining, at the other end of the line, someone frowning in impatience.

Yes Who is this? What do you want?

I did not like calling my parents, even. I did not ever like to call strangers.

It was not my choice to be returning home for the weekend from college, where I studied piano and composition; my mother wanted me to help her with the care of my grandmother, who was now more or less bedridden with severe rheumatoid arthritis and what was called—the words filled me with horror—congestive heart failure. (And there were other family problems, too boring and heartrending to enumerate! "Just come home. Help me, for once"—my mother's plea.) It was generally believed in the family that I was studying to be a public school music teacher but much of my time was spent on music composition, and much of my life—the intense, secret life in my head—was filled with music and poetry: poetry-set-to-music.

Strands of music, strands of things I'd read or heard were always weaving in and out of my thoughts. Alone, I was engaged with this other world, and did not feel lonely; I felt most lonely when I was with other people, with whom I struggled to feel a meaningful connection, or suffered wondering what they felt for me. *Such a plain, earnest girl—but why does she take herself so seriously? No one else would!*

Traveling to and from Carthage on the train, I loved to sit alone and work on my music. Sketchy compositions that were inspired by—though I would not have wished to acknowledge this—such American composers as Henry Cowell, Charles Ives, George Crumb, Daniel Pinkham who were the first composers I'd encountered who were not household names. (Pinkham had been composer-in-residence at the small liberal arts college in Utica for just one year, sixty years ago. Yet his influence persisted.) And I worked on my poetry, which was inspired by such Romantics as Shelley, Keats, Emily Brontë but also Emily Dickinson—whose work most intrigued me when I felt that it was beyond my comprehension. When I opened my manila folder, I felt a charge of excitement and hope.

My professors encouraged me—of course. Effusive with praise, uncertain of their own talent, our professors knew that it was in their interest to encourage as many of us as possible.

My roommates might have been twins: big brusque jovial girls who campaigned for class offices, excelled at sports and took it as a personal challenge to "draw out" people like me. One of them, Lolly O'Brien, told me, memorably: "Y'know, Nadia—a person could spend a lifetime—*two* lifetimes!—listening to the great music that has already been composed." Lolly wore the navy-blue nylon parka issued by the college crew team. Her forehead furrowed as she regarded me with pitying eyes. "Mozart, Beethoven, what's-his-name—the opera-writer—the German . . . Just the operas of Wagner—the one with the flying horses in it, the 'Val-ker-ie' . . . You could spend a lifetime just listening to *that*."

I tried not to laugh. Or maybe I just laughed. It was very funny, and it was very good advice.

I told Lolly that I wasn't trying to write Wagnerian operas. And I wasn't trying to listen to them, either.

Later, I overheard Lolly complaining to our roommate—*She's weird! She'd be better off with a single room.*

IN CARTHAGE, I left the train with the wallet in my bag. It was not my intention to carry the wallet away with me but to turn it in to the lost-and-found in the depot but when I approached the clerk at the counter—a young woman with a sty prominent on her eyelid who called to me sharply, "Yes? Next?" as if I were waiting in line and not just standing a few feet away indecisively—I realized that I couldn't entrust Anna-Marie Nivecca's wallet to her.

She will steal the money.

She will steal the snapshots.

Nor did I call the telephone number listed for *Jalel Nivecca*.

Instead, I thought that I would return the wallet to the Pitcairn address: the street wasn't far from the train station, in south Carthage. This was a part of the city in which I didn't think I knew anyone.

It wasn't like me to behave so impulsively. Recklessly!

Vaguely I knew that my mother would be waiting for me—though cell phones were beginning to be in use they weren't yet common, and it would not have been expected that I should call my mother to say that I'd be a few minutes late.

Just a few minutes! Well—maybe a half hour.

The train might have been delayed. Yes in fact—I would tell my mother that.

Pitcairn was one of the narrow residential streets of south Carthage, that led down to the riverfront—the Black Snake River that bordered the city on its eastern edge. Much of this part of the city was loading docks, warehouses and small businesses, but the Nivecca address was in a residential neighborhood of brownstone row houses built almost to the curb.

It was a neighborhood not so different from my own, except just a little older, shabbier—there were no driveways, and so vehicles were parked on the street; there were virtually no front yards, so children's toys, even bicycles, lay on the edge of the sidewalk where they'd been allowed to fall.

The row house at 2117 Pitcairn resembled its neighbors: two-storey brownstone with a steep shingled roof, a small front stoop, a small grassless front yard. On the sidewalk I stood uncertainly, wondering what I would say. Would glamorous Anna-Marie Nivecca answer the door? Would I thrust her wallet at her and stammer—what?

How surprised she would be! I would say *I thought I had better bring this over in person. Otherwise—it might have been appropriated.*

But was *appropriated* too ostentatious a word? Maybe better to say—*stolen?*

I saw a movement at a window beside the door. Someone had been watching me.

"Hello?"—the door was opened, a man stood in the doorway.

It was Jalel Nivecca: I knew him.

Except, the man looked older than I would have expected. His hair straggled in his face, very dark, but laced with gray. His face was still gypsy-handsome but ravaged with worry or tiredness and his clothes—shirt, trousers—looked as if he'd been sleeping in them. And he was barefoot.

I told him hello and explained that I had a wallet belonging to Anna-Marie Nivecca.

"A wallet? *Her* wallet?"

He took the wallet from me and looked through it eagerly.

"Where did you find this?"

I told him: on the train from Utica to Carthage, just this morning.

"On the *train*? From—?"

"From Utica."

Of course, the train had come from Albany, or New York City. It was misleading to say Utica, which happened to be where I'd gotten on.

And the wallet might have been lost at another time, the previous day perhaps. On a train from Carthage to Utica and beyond.

The man who had to be Jalel Nivecca, Anna-Marie's husband, was looking stunned, as if he'd been hit by a blow on the head not quite powerful enough to knock him out—he was still standing. But the more I tried to explain the circumstances of my finding the wallet, the less he seemed to be listening. He was staring at the snapshots—his eyes filled with moisture.

He hadn't checked the bills. Or the credit card.

"You say you found this on the *train*? This morning?"

Carefully I repeated what I'd said. I had not ever been so close— physically—to a stranger, in such an emotional state; I could not help but feel responsible. I tried to assume the brisk no-nonsense but friendly manner of my college roommates, who would excel in such a minor emergency.

"Yes. I thought I'd better—bring it to you in person . . . There's a card in the wallet—'In Case of Emergency Please Notify . . .'" My voice faltered. "You are—'Jalel Nivecca'?—next of kin?"

"Yes. I am—'Jalel Nivecca.'" He was staring at me, holding the wallet in his hand like something wounded he had no idea how to deal with. I thought—*She has left him. She has run away. He doesn't know, yet—not just yet.*

Slow-witted in grief, or in a kind of panic resembling grief, Jalel Nivecca asked me again about where and when I'd found the wallet:

"On the train, coming to Carthage? This morning?"

"Yes. I sat down in an empty seat, and the wallet was wedged between the seat and the wall. That's why no one else found it, I guess—it was sort of hidden." Nervously I spoke, as if hoping to placate the agitated man. "I thought, instead of turning it in at the depot, it would be safer, it would be quicker, to bring it to you—to bring it here—in person."

Now that I had delivered the missing wallet, it was time for me to leave. Yet how strange, this simple fact, that would have been screamingly obvious to my mother, for instance, seemed to have no effect upon me at all.

Mr. Nivecca suddenly realized: I'd done him a favor.

Belatedly, he thanked me. He fumbled to remove a bill from the wallet, to offer me.

" 'Good Samaratin'—'Samaritan'—" His smile was a fumbling sort of smile, in his ashy unshaven face.

Quickly I declined—"Oh no, thank you, Mr. Nivecca, I—I couldn't . . ."

It seemed strange to me, faintly unbelievable, that this bizarrely handsome straggly-haired man seemed unaware of his handsomeness—the way he would look to a stranger, like me. If he'd been aware perhaps he would have been ironic, self-conscious; even scornful and bitter. To those who are not-beautiful, the fact that beauty doesn't protect an individual from upset and injury always seems startling, though common sense should tell us otherwise.

At close quarters, the man's physical beauty was not discernible, like an image seen too close, dissolving into pixels, molecules. His skin looked unhealthy and his large but deep-socketed eyes were threaded with tiny broken capillaries. His voice was hoarse, straining to sound exuberant: "Miss, thanks! My wife would want you to have this—a little 'reward.'"

He mumbled something further—*reward, Samaritan. Good Samaritan.* There was a drunken sort of almost-jovial persistence in his speech as if he were speaking not to me primarily but to someone else, an invisible listener.

Weakly I said: "I don't need a reward, really."

It was strange, how I insisted. When I could certainly have used the money.

(Was it a five-dollar bill he clutched in his hand? *Ten?* I couldn't imagine that Mr. Nivecca's reward was any more than that.)

Barefoot Mr. Nivecca continued to stand on the front stoop of his house, wallet in hand. He didn't seem to want the Good Samaritan to leave, just yet.

"*She'd* want you to have—something. For coming all this way . . ."

"I didn't come far. From the train station."

"You could have called. That would've been easier. No, you're a *Good Sam'tan.* There's not many like you . . ."

This vision of myself was embarrassing! I could not think of myself as other than conniving and opportunistic. For what I'd wanted—I think this was so—was to hand back the wallet to Anna-Marie herself, and see her striking face "light up" with gratitude.

I dared to ask Mr. Nivecca if he had any idea where his wife might be.

"No. I guess—I'm afraid—I'm ashamed as hell—I don't." He laughed, mirthlessly. The bloodshot eyes were pleading. "I'm trying to calculate—if you found this wallet on the train this morning, coming to Carthage from Utica, it's possible that my wife took the train from

Carthage yesterday to Utica, or beyond—Albany, New York City. And she left the wallet on the train then, but it was hidden, and the same train returned the next day—today. But it isn't like Anna to be careless about money—it's a bad sign the wallet was 'lost.'"

"Did you notify the police?"

"The police! N-No."

Mr. Nivecca was looking lost and forlorn and now frightened.

"My wife hasn't been missing that long—only about sixteen hours. The police won't look for a 'missing' adult unless she's been gone for weeks. The assholes will say *An adult has the right to walk away. This is a free country and your wife can go anywhere she fucking wants to go and you can't stop her.*"

Such bitterness and scorn for the police was very like the bitterness and scorn certain of my relatives, my father's people, felt for law enforcement officers.

I felt very sorry for the man. I felt very sorry that I'd been the one to bring him the wallet, that seemed to indicate bad news.

"Would you like me to help you, Mr. Nivecca—somehow?"

"Would you? Y-Yes, I guess so . . ." He ran his fingers through his already disheveled hair. The bloodshot eyes moved onto me, appealing.

Here was an adult man, a husband. Anna-Marie Nivecca's husband. He had to be in his early thirties—more than ten years older than I was. Yet, he seemed so stricken; so in need of sympathy, advice. He seemed so *lonely.*

"Yes. I could use some help. Like, moral support . . . Please come inside. I—I haven't been—guess I haven't been thinking straight, since . . ."

He opened the door wider and stepped aside, to allow me in.

I hesitated—then stepped inside.

Passing close beside him, as I stepped inside.

And Jalel Nivecca shut the door behind me.

———

"YOU KNOW MY NAME, I guess, but—what's yours?"

And when I told him he repeated just my first name—"Nadia"—as if he'd never heard such a beautiful name before.

He shook my hand, vigorously. His fingers gripped mine in a way no one had ever gripped my fingers before.

My heart was beating very hard. And I swallowed hard.

He was saying that he'd taken "the little girl" to his mother's house, until Anna-Marie returned. "I've been so kind of crazy-upset, all last night. Making telephone calls and waiting to hear back. And waiting out front—watching for headlights . . . Though Anna-Marie didn't take the car, I have the car." He paused, breathing audibly. "It's better for the girl not to see her father so upset."

"How old is she? Your daughter?"

"How old? Three, I think . . . Four. Her name is Isabelle."

His voice quavered with tenderness. His hand shook as he lifted a framed photograph of a little girl: blond hair, a sweet but pouty little face, rosebud mouth like a doll's. Framed photos crowded the tabletop and prominent among these were photos of Anna-Marie, invariably photographed smiling in the posed-seeming incandescent way of a celebrity. In one, Anna-Marie seemed almost to be leaning out of the frame, jutting breasts in a gold lamé V-neck sweater.

"Your wife is very beautiful."

"Is she!"

He sounded aggrieved, staring at this photo. If I hadn't been there he might have slammed it flat on the tabletop.

We were in a small cluttered living room. The ceiling seemed low. The carpet was patterned in a way to distract the eye. The furniture was nondescript, the sort of things you might buy at an outlet store, but someone had taken care to drape colorful shawls and scarves over the backs of chairs and a sofa; there was even a gaily patterned silk scarf wound around a lamp shade. In vases there were dried flowers—some of them large tall bouquets of the kind you'd see in a florist's display window.

All this *showiness* contrasted with articles of clothing—a child's clothing?—carelessly flung about. And dirty dishes in a small stack on a badly stained glass-top coffee table. And the TV, muted, bluish flickering images at which no one was looking, in a corner of the room.

There was a smell of candles, or incense—the odor I'd inhaled from the wallet.

Seeing the gaily colored scarf tied around the lamp shade reminded me of something I'd forgotten—how I had brought a birthday present, a little silk scarf, for the pretty, popular girl whose locker was beside mine in eighth grade homeroom. Crystal Donovan was the girl's melodic, wonderful name, a name I'd often whispered to myself, or wrote in my notebook. Around the gift box I'd wrapped a red velvet ribbon. The birthday card was one I'd taken time to choose, and it had been, like the little scarf, far more expensive than I would have expected. Crystal had been delighted with the gift, or had seemed so: she'd thanked me, and kissed me, and told others about it, and meant to tie it around her neck except someone came along, one of her closer girlfriends, or a boy, and so she'd absentmindedly set the box on her locker shelf, and forgot it.

Mr. Nivecca was talking about his wife—and their little daughter—in a rapid nervous voice. I couldn't follow the thread of his remarks—I was thinking, just a little, of Crystal Donovan, and wondering what had become of *her*.

Like Anna-Marie, she'd gotten married young, I was sure. Had a baby, or babies. Young.

Meanly I thought—*It doesn't mean so much, then. Having a man's baby. You can lose him—he can lose you.*

The aggrieved husband was telling me how he'd first met Anna-Marie in a local park—(of course, it was a park familiar to me, overlooking the river)—when she'd just graduated from high school, though he hadn't known she was so young; she'd been at a picnic with friends and she'd run toward him, out of nowhere, laughing, and touched his wrist, and said something about a game of tag— "And you're *it*." It would turn out, Anna-Marie was engaged at the time, and Jalel hadn't known. He'd driven her in his car to Lake Ontario, a half-hour's drive, and they'd walked on the beach, and waded in the water: "And I asked, 'Who is it you're engaged to, if you're out here with me?' And Anna-Marie said, 'It's an experiment. If I'm here with you, that means—I'm not with *him*.'"

She'd broken off that engagement. They were married a year later. They'd always had a "pretty emotional" relationship—breaking up, getting together again—breaking up . . . Except, once you are married, Jalel said, you can't *break up*.

"Anna-Marie was always a happy person—except when she wasn't. I don't mean that she's crazy—she is not crazy. She's been a good mother, most of the time. But after Isabelle, she's been more unpredictable. She cries a lot, and she drinks. And more than wine. There's this secret side to her. Sometimes when I'd return home, from work, she wasn't here—she'd come home hours later and say she'd been 'just walking'—'just driving.' She'd have left the baby with her mother or the girl next-door. Once, she said she'd been 'in the cemetery.'

"(I even followed her once—and she did drive over into the cemetery. Her father had been buried there a few months before.) She likes to sing—loud—when she's alone in the house with just Isabelle—or driving her car—but if I hear her, if she knows I'm nearby, she'll stop. And she gets angry with me saying I'm spying on her. Christ!" Jalel paused, lowering his quivering voice. "I think Anna-Marie has a life I don't know anything about—nobody does. When we got married her sister told me, 'You think you can get to know Anna, but you can't. You can never trust Anna.' I thought it was bitchy of her, at the time."

We were standing in the living room, in front of the muted TV, of which the aggrieved man took no notice. What was strange was that it seemed altogether natural that Jalel Nivecca should speak to me in this intimate way—as if we knew each other, and he needed me to listen.

Even before entering the Nivecca house, I'd begun to feel a stir of emotion that was new to me, weirdly new, unsettling. If anyone should ever love me in the way that Jalel loved Anna-Marie—not a calm placid marital love but this other, passionate, operatic love—if anyone should ever desire me in such a way, yearn for me, brood over me—how romantic this would be! I had not known many boys or young men well—I had not yet had what was delicately called a *steady boyfriend*—(meaning a guy with whom one had sex, and was expected to have sex)—and so my experience was very limited. Boys I'd known were down-to-earth and practical: if I'd begun to behave oddly, like Anna-Marie, if I'd exhibited "emotional" tendencies, they would simply have stopped seeing me, and kept their distance.

I understood: I wouldn't have blamed them. We don't want to— we can't afford to—expend our love on someone we can't trust, who will squander our love, and leave us abandoned.

Still, music celebrated this other sort of passionate, unbridled and unpredictable love. Wagner's *Tristan und Isolde* . . .

Music that had the power to unsettle, disturb. The power to burrow beneath the skin.

"Anna-Marie is a good, loving mother, when she's *here*. I mean when, in her mind, she's in this place . . . with us. She said she'd wanted to have a baby 'to wake me up—to make me responsible.' But it hasn't seemed to make any difference. And sometimes I think—I have reason to think—she's seeing other men . . ."

For a man, nothing could be more upsetting or shameful. Jalel spoke bitterly yet matter-of-factly.

I wanted badly to help him. Impulsively I said, "Maybe I could look at your wife's things?"

I'd seen programs on TV about psychics. I'd read, in the local paper, that a "psychic" had been consulted by police, in their search for a missing child.

"Yes, Nadia! Maybe—who knows?—you will think of something."

Far from being offended by my naïve suggestion, in his distracted and distraught state Jalel Nivecca seemed to think it was an excellent idea.

"Good! Yes! 'Look at her things'—upstairs."

JALEL HAD ME proceed him, up the stairs.

Which made me uncomfortable. Though it was only good manners—I supposed.

Thoughts flew at me like panicked hornets—*Why am I here, what is this place? Who is this man I've never seen before?*

Yet it had seemed to me, from the first, seeing Jalel Nivecca's face in the snapshots in his wife's wallet, that I had seen him before, and in some way knew him.

Unless this was delusion.

(*Was* this delusion? I could not think so, my feeling for Jalel seemed matched by his for me, and it came very strong.)

Close behind me on the stairs he was breathing audibly, as if out of condition, for a youngish man who looked fit. A faint scent of something like wine or whiskey wafted to my nostrils and I wondered if he'd been drinking.

The stairway was narrow and unusually steep. The brownstone row houses of south Carthage are old, built in the late nineteenth century, places where mill- and dockworkers once lived.

Upstairs there was a smell of unlaundered clothes, towels and bedding. I recognized the smell from my college dorm in which undergraduate girls lived happily slovenly lives out of sight of their elders. Though the bedroom into which Jalel guided me wasn't unusually messy—just lived-in; a satin bedspread pulled up over a probably unmade bed, a few articles of clothing scattered about. And an ordinary lamp shade about which a colorful scarf had been tied, now badly askew.

"This is our bed. This is Anna-Marie's side."

Jalel guided me, his hands on my shoulders. As if I were a blind girl, gifted with "second sight."

He was taller than I was, by several inches. And I was a tall girl, five feet nine inches.

His hands were warm, just slightly heavy. I could not recall any man—anyone—placing hands on my shoulders like this, both leaning on me just a little and guiding me in such a way that I could not have turned aside if I'd wished.

"D'you 'see' anything, Nadja? D'you 'smell' anything?"

My heart was beating rapidly. I could not see very clearly, and I could not "smell" anything except the incense-fragrance, unwashed laundry, Jalel Nivecca's faint-alcohol-breath.

"No. Not yet."

"Her pillow. Here. Nadja."

Jalel lifted the pillow fumblingly. Jalel held it to my face—not hard, not uncomfortably close—but in a way I found awkward, for I could not breathe except to breathe in the intimate odors of the woman—I think this is what I was smelling. A reflexive panic made me pull away, and Jalel, laughing irritably, replaced the pillow on the bed, beside the other, matching pillow: his.

He'd begun to call me, not "Nadia" but "Nadja." I couldn't determine—had he forgotten my name, or was this a very subtle, just perceptible sort of jeering, mockery of a female name?

On the cluttered top of a bureau with a large oval mirror there was a tortoiseshell hairbrush, and in the hairbrush were dozens of long, tangled blond hairs. This hairbrush I lifted as if to study. The bristles were not very clean.

"D'you see where she might be? Eh?"

The bureau top was covered with an embroidered cloth, soiled with spilled powder. Lipsticks, earrings, wadded tissues, a plastic comb with broken teeth. More framed snapshots crowding one another.

In the mirror, I saw a man watching me with an unreadable expression. One of his eyelids was drooping just discernibly. His mouth twitched into a dreamy smile.

Absurdly I thought—*This is how we have met. This is our fate. I will help him put together his life.*

I examined Anna-Marie's earrings, inexpensive but attractive costume jewelry, miniature green "gems" meant to be emeralds set in *faux*-gold. I shut my eyes—my eyelids were quivering with strain—hoping to "see"—exactly what, I had no idea.

Next, Jalel opened a bureau drawer and placed in my hand something silky-soft—the lacy top of a half-slip which I pressed against my face with a little shiver of dread.

"Is she in—daylight? Or is it dark where she is?"

My eyes remained shut. Badly I was wishing that a vision would come to me—any vision.

"Is she—breathing? Is she *alive*?"

Jalel Nivecca stood close beside me. I knew that he was regarding me in the mirror but I did not dare open my eyes, to see.

A sensation like smothering, smothering-mud, very dark, glutinous, hideous, came over me, and I shuddered.

"What is it, Nadja? Some kind of—sign? Eh?"

"No. Nothing."

"Nothing?"

He seemed both agitated and oddly jocular. As if he knew that what we were doing was ridiculous, and yet—!

One of his hands fell casually onto my left shoulder, but did not take hold; I felt his fingers, hard but harmless, trailing down my back, lightly on my hips, and away, as you might stroke a cat or a dog, mildly affectionately but not very seriously.

"There's her towels and things, in here. Nadja."

The bathroom was a small cramped dispirited room with a water-stained ceiling. Again it seemed that the ceiling was low—lower than the bedroom ceiling. On the medicine cabinet mirror was a patina of dried water-splotches and fingerprints. Hair and scummy-dried soap in the sink. The toilet was comparatively new, with a swanky plastic seat and a lid covered in bright green shag.

Jalel handed me a rumpled towel, wordlessly. I pretended to inhale its odor—my eyelids fluttered shut, in terror of what I might see.

"No luck? Nothing? She's off our radar—y'think?"

Jalel drew back the shower curtain which, too, was comparatively new, and not yet stained or ragged. In fact there were two curtains: the inner, which was utilitarian plastic, and transparent; and the outer, which was ruffled white and red organdy.

The tub was old, but clean; the bathroom smelled of cleanser. I thought—*She cleaned this part of the house, before she left.*

Or—*He has cleaned this part of the house, to remove the memory of her.*

"I found this, here. I wasn't sure if I should—what I should do— if . . ."

Jalel was pointing to an unfolded piece of paper, which had been placed beneath a pearl-like seashell, on the back of the toilet. It was a strange place for a note to be left—something about it filled me with dread.

"Did you read it? What it said?"

"I read it, and I—put it back where it was. She never did anything like this before, I mean—leaving a note. Any kind of explanation, that wasn't like her. I found it when I came home from work last night. Isabelle was in bed. I hunted for Anna-Marie all over the God-damned house, up and down and in the basement, and I found this here— *Don't worry. I know you won't. I will be back before you miss me.*"

Jalel showed me the note which was written in pencil, and so shakily written, as if on an inadequately hard surface, the point had pierced the paper many times and the message was all but indecipherable.

"You can't help me, Nad-ja? Even reading this? She'd have had to think about it, writing something like this. See, there's an insult in it. *Will be back before you miss me.*"

I held the sheet of paper in both hands. I didn't think that I could have read the message, if Jalel hadn't read it for me. When I shut my eyes, I felt dizzy. The smell of the man, his breath, his body, and his unwashed hair made my nostrils pinch.

"N-No. I'm afraid that I . . . I can't help you."

"You can't help me? Why'd you say you could?"

"I didn't s-say that I could. I don't think I said that."

"You said that, Nad-ja. You were boasting."

"I don't think so, Mr. Nivecca. I'm sorry to disappoint you."

"You haven't disappointed me. You just haven't helped me. Are you saying that I should call the police?"

"I—don't know. Maybe—if she doesn't come back by tonight."

"If she doesn't call. You'd think, the mother of a four-year-old little girl, she'd call—but you'd be wrong. She didn't call."

"She might call, yet. You said it hasn't been so long . . ."

"I'd have to show the police this note. They would want to take it. I want to keep it."

We left the bathroom. The dizziness began to lighten. I saw the doorway: the stairs was just beyond. If necessary, I could run—I could run to the stairs.

The man would outrun me, I knew. My shoulders throbbed still with the grip of his fingers and he had not gripped my shoulders nearly so hard as he might have.

We were leaving the bedroom. We descended the stairs. I was ahead of the man, my heart kicking and thumping like a big clumsy drunken bird. Almost disbelieving I heard myself offer to make a meal for him—"You must be hungry, Mr. Nivecca?"

If she has left him. If he is lonely.

He thanked me, gratefully. He guessed he was hungry, yes—he couldn't remember when he'd eaten last.

"You are—like an angel. Sent to me in my hour of need."

He laughed, he was speaking playfully. I tried to laugh, to fall in with his ever-shifting mood.

You will say that I was naïve, stupid. You will say that I was reckless. But I think that I was only just desperate. A girl who had not—yet—been in love, and whose parents' marriage seemed to have bled dry of love. Only responsibility remained, an atmosphere of angry duty in my parents' household.

Badly I yearned to be put to the test—I wasn't sure what *the test* would be.

I wanted to be unafraid. Or, if afraid, I wanted not to succumb to fear.

As I moved about Anna-Marie Nivecca's kitchen I was shivering with excitement, apprehension. I could not bring myself to check the time—I'd spent nearly an hour in the Nivecca house, I knew; all this while, my mother had been waiting for me.

There was a matter of taking my grandmother to the clinic for tests. And while she was away, her room—her bedroom at the rear of her house with its melancholy unspeakable odors—had to be cleaned; the stained bedding "aired"; the stained floor scrubbed and polished. Hours of work, manual work, set beside which my boring job in the college library was a lark on a summer's day. I thought—*There is joy in life, a terrible joy. There is joy for the taking if you are not afraid.*

Jalel Nivecca leaned in the doorway watching me, brooding. I smiled to think that the man, the husband, wasn't in the habit of helping Anna-Marie prepare a meal even when the meal was for him.

"Even if she does come back—can I trust her? What if she hurts Isabelle? Takes Isabelle with her—wherever she goes? Like, the cemetery? Jesus!"

I opened a can of soup—"Italian Wedding"—to heat on the stove. In the refrigerator—that smelled of old, stale, slightly rancid food—I discovered a half-loaf of whole grain bread, a chunk of Swiss cheese, several soft tangerines and a jar of apricot jam. Jalel sat at his place at the kitchen table—unmistakably, that chair was his; I sat nearer the stove and the sink. He ate hungrily. The sight of the man eating the food I'd prepared was immensely satisfying. I thought—*I will remember this, all my life.*

"Last night was hell. I'm not going through that again. I got in the car and drove—after my mother took Isabelle home with her—I drove in places where I thought Anna might be—past houses—people we knew—her women friends—places we used to go: restaurants, bars—everything was shut up and dark. I guess I was kind of crazy—I couldn't sleep anyway. Can't sleep now. It's like—now—I'm asleep with my eyes open. I'm 'eating'—but it isn't real. I was thinking—*She wouldn't go outside the marriage, no matter how she felt. No matter who was telling her he was crazy for her, he'd be better for her than me. She would not go outside the marriage—would she?* There's been men before I met her, not just the 'fiancé.' There's one—or two—would've liked to kill her, she said. She'd laughed . . ."

Near the end of our meal, the phone rang.

Jalel leapt up from the table, his chair overturned.

Ashen-faced he lunged for the phone, that was on the kitchen wall. "H'lo? H'lo?"

I felt a pang of hurt, loss. I could not help but know—*He will never love another woman, like this. She will never let him go.*

But it was just Jalel's mother on the phone. She had no news of Anna-Marie. Eagerly Jalel told her about Anna-Marie's wallet being found on the train, when it was found and by whom, but he said little about me, he did not mention my name or the fact that I was sitting three feet away from him; in the terse recapitulation of the morning's events, it had been a "nice college girl" who'd found the wallet and brought it to him.

"Just—on the train. Like she'd traveled somewhere—yesterday, maybe—and lost the wallet, and . . . She could be in New York, or— who the hell knows—Miami. She could be with somebody—I'll find out who."

His mother had questions to ask, Jalel answered tersely: "No. Any-body who called me back, they didn't know any damn thing. They hadn't seen her—they said." He paused, running a hand through his hair, fingers like angry claws through his greasy hair. "No! Fuck we 'had words.' What kind of—fucking kind of—asshole thing to say to me—*we did not.* Go to hell!"

Violently he hung up the phone. In an instant he'd become furious, glaring.

He had not asked about his daughter. I understood that he would regret this and regret his angry outburst and if I hadn't been there, he would have called back his mother immediately.

He'd hung up the phone so hard, the receiver slipped off the hook. Panting and muttering to himself he replaced it, with care.

"Nobody *knows*. Bullshit anybody can 'read anybody's mind' . . . *She* left *me*."

Jalel wasn't speaking to me but he saw me now—a strange tender smile rayed across his face. He came stumbling to me—collided with a kitchen chair, pushed it aside—took my hands in his hands—both my frightened hands, in his hands. Still panting, reeking of his body, he leaned down to kiss my forehead.

"Nad-ja! It has to be something special—why you came here to me. Why you brought the wallet to me . . ."

Something in his voice, in the way he stared at me, made me draw back now, abruptly.

"No. I don't think so—no."

I managed to stand. He was slow to release my hands.

"Yes. You came *to me*. There is a reason to all things."

He was smiling. He wasn't altogether serious. He'd want you to think this was so: the speculations of a man who'd been drinking but wasn't, you had to know, *drunk*.

" 'Good Sam'tan.' Yes, there's a reason God sent you."

Long I would remember the kiss on my forehead—wet, forceful—a man's kiss, deflected.

Before I left, Jalel took down my name, my address, my telephone number in Carthage. I wanted to think—*He will call me. He will want to see me again, if she doesn't come back.*

*

Whenever I return to Carthage, which is at least once a year, I drive past the brownstone row house at 2117 Pitcairn Street. I park my car, and I walk past the house—though it has been thirty years now, and no Niveccas live there any longer, I'm sure.

Yes, I have checked the Carthage telephone directory. There are a number of *Niveccas* listed, but none with the initial *J*.

A few days after I'd brought the wallet to Jalel Nivecca, a call came for me—not from Jalel but from a Carthage police officer.

He was checking information that Jalel had given them. That I'd found the wallet on the train, and when; and that I'd brought it to him.

Carthage police were investigating the "missing" woman now—Jalel had had to notify them, finally.

Though I was feeling shaky and uncertain I answered the police officer's questions in a firm friendly voice, borrowed from Lolly O'Brien for the purpose.

I did not tell the detective—I did not tell anyone—that, a few days after I'd brought the wallet to Jalel, I'd called the number I had for him, the *next-of-kin* number. Wanting just to know if Anna-Marie had returned home yet. Wanting just to know—how he was. But no one had answered, the phone had rung and rung.

When finally I'd arrived at our house on that day, an hour and a half late, my mother hadn't been furious with me but anxious—she'd thought that something must have happened to me on the train. Quickly I told her that yes, there'd been an emergency on the train, a woman had fainted in the seat beside me and I'd been involved in trying to help her.

Seeing that I was all right, and grateful that I'd arrived, and with so much to do in our beleaguered household, my mother didn't question my story.

I returned to school. I tried not to think of Jalel Nivecca.

I tried not to think of Anna-Marie Nivecca.

The pressure of the man's hands on my shoulders. The pressure of the man's lips on my forehead. The smell of the household—the smell of the man. The conscientious way in which, taking down my name, address, telephone number, Jalel Nivecca had gripped the pencil in his left hand, like one not accustomed to writing; the way in which the pencil point had pierced the scrap of paper.

Often alone I walk quickly and with a sensation that someone is looking after me, or following me. Usually, there is no one.

I would never meet any man like Jalel Nivecca. I mean—any man whom I seemed to know, and who seemed to know *me*.

I would meet many men, and most of them were friendly—civil, kindly, dependable, predictable in good ways. And one of them, I would marry at the age of thirty-seven. But none of them was Jalel Nivecca.

The Carthage police called me several times in the fall and winter of 1981, at college. Each time a detective asked me the same thing: where I'd found the wallet belonging to *Anna-Marie Nivecca*, when and how; and who was I, and had I known *Anna-Marie Nivecca* or *Jalel Nivecca* or anyone in the *Nivecca* family, previously.

Once, I asked the detective if police believed that something had happened to Mrs. Nivecca but the detective cut me off abruptly saying the investigation was "under way."

Another time, I heard myself say that I'd had the impression at the time that Mr. Nivecca was genuinely surprised when I brought the wallet to him but that, later, when I considered it, I had to wonder— "Maybe he'd left the wallet on the train, himself."

For a moment, the detective was silent. My old, chronic unease with speaking over the phone, particularly to strangers, returned with force—I felt sweat break out on my body. I wanted to retract my impulsive words but could not.

"Why do you say that, ma'am? Any reason for you to say that, that Mr. Nivecca gave you?"

"I—I don't think so. No."

"Your impression was, he hadn't expected to see the wallet?"

"Yes. That was my impression, at the time."

"But now you say—maybe he'd planted the wallet on the train, himself? Why would you think that?"

A rivulet of sweat ran down my side, inside my clothes. I felt sick with regret, I had said such a thing about Jalel Nivecca.

I stammered a reply—I didn't know.

The detective thanked me for my "assistance" and told me that I would be hearing from him again, very likely.

When I could, I read the Carthage newspaper. Headlines became familiar—POLICE SEARCH FOR MISSING LOCAL WOMAN CONTINUES; POLICE SAY NO LEADS IN SEARCH FOR MISSING LOCAL WOMAN.

In the summer, when I was home and working at the downtown Carthage library, I had the opportunity to look through back issues of the newspaper and so discovered, belatedly, that Jalel Nivecca had been "interviewed" in the matter of his wife's disappearance, and that Jalel Nivecca was a "suspect" in the matter of his wife's disappearance; I discovered his picture in the paper, and felt a stab of recognition—*Him!*

But I did not discover that Jalel Nivecca had ever been arrested, still less indicted for any crime, and tried.

Jalel Nivecca insisted that he knew nothing about his missing wife and that he "loved" her—"wanted her back"—"could not imagine where she was."

There was no evidence that Anna-Marie Nivecca had been harmed. There was no evidence that Anna-Marie Nivecca was not alive somewhere, and in hiding.

Only the missing woman's family and friends protested that Anna-Marie would never have disappeared in such a way, without telling anyone—without taking her little girl with her.

The house at 2117 Pitcairn was thoroughly searched. Not once but several times, according to the Carthage newspaper. The basement floor had been "dug up."

Eventually, police officers ceased calling me. In the spring of 1983, I graduated with honors from the small liberal arts college, I went on to study at the Indiana School of Music, I did not ever speak with Jalel Nivecca again and never learned what became of him and his daughter Isabelle. Now in the era of personal computers it isn't difficult for me to check *Carthage 1981 Anna-Marie Nivecca police investigation* and to learn that the investigation is still, officially, "ongoing" though nothing new seems to have come to light in decades.

He would be an old man now, or nearly—though probably not much changed. In his soul, he would not be much changed. If we saw each other, we would recognize each other. I am sure of this, as I am sure of very little otherwise in my life.

My college roommate wasn't entirely correct about me. I have had a professional career of some achievement—modest, moderate. Of course, I am hardly Richard Wagner.

I am hardly Daniel Pinkham.

But if you search my name you will discover that I am listed as *an American composer, born 1981*; I am a recipient of awards, professional fellowships, and commissions; my work has been performed at Tanglewood and the Kennedy Center in D.C. and I am currently composer-in-residence at William and Mary College.

I have been married now for thirteen years. My husband and I have two young, adopted children. At times, I am so overwhelmed by the happiness of my life, the sensation I feel is purely visceral, musical—the way Mozart must have felt on an ordinary day. Unlike Mozart, I can't translate this sensation into musical notes—my compositions are very different, darker and, as critics have complained, "gnarly"—"unresolved." But that does not invalidate the power and the authenticity of my feelings.

On Pitcairn Street, Carthage, I park my car, and I walk past the brownstone at 2117. It is an utterly ordinary row house—

indistinguishable from its neighbors—in a neighborhood that seems to have become Hispanic and Asian. I know no one here, no one knows me, no one glances after me, it's as if I am invisible here, and so I feel strangely safe, consoled. For I feel his hands on my shoulders guiding me and I hear him say again in his hoarse intimate voice—*It has to be something special, why you came to me. Some reason God sent you.*

And this time I hear myself say—*Yes. I think that you must be right.*

III

A BRUTAL MURDER IN
A PUBLIC PLACE

At Gate C33 of Newark International Airport in a waiting area of seats facing curved glass windows and a heavily occluded sky beyond the windows, a sudden frantic chirping!

Everyone looks around—upward—the frantic chirping continues—the bird—(if it is a bird)—is hidden from view.

A bird? Is that a—bird? Here? How—*here?*

In these rows of seats, strangers. Directly in front of the curved-glass windows facing the runway outside and the overcast New Jersey sky are three sections of seats of ten seats each, with six plate-glass windows facing each section of seats: in all, eighteen windows.

On the other side of the walkway, which is not wide, no more than a few yards, are rows of seats arranged in the usual utilitarian way: back to back and, across a narrow aisle, facing one another.

Barely, there is room for people to make their way through this narrow aisle, pulling suitcases.

You might guess fifteen seats in each row. Ten such rows of seats at Gate C33.

This place of utter anonymity, impersonality.

This place of *randomness.*

Emptiness.

And suddenly—the tiny bird-chirping!

An improbable and heartrending little musical trill like an old-fashioned music box!

A sound to make you glance upward, smiling—in expectation of seeing—what?

At the ceiling above the closest row of seats facing the window there appears to be a ledge of some kind, probably containing air vents—(from my seat about fifteen feet from the outer row of seats by the window, I am not able to see the front of the ledge)—and very likely the trapped little bird—(if it is a bird, it must be "trapped" in this place, and if it is between the ledge and the ceiling, it must be little)—is perched there.

The seated travelers continue to look around, quizzical and bemused.

A white-haired woman in a wheelchair squints upward, with an expression of mild anxiety. A contingent of soldiers—mostly young, mostly male—mostly dark-skinned—in casual-camouflage uniform like mud-splotched pajamas—squint upward frowning as if the bird's chirping might be a warning, or an alarm.

How is it possible, a bird *here?*

Though the chirping is fairly loud, rapid-fire and somewhere close by, yet no one has sighted the bird. A lanky young man with a backpack stands, to squint toward the ceiling, with the air of an alert bird-watcher, but the bird remains invisible.

Another possible place (I see now) in which the little bird might be hidden is in the leaves of a stunted little tree near the windows.

This is a melancholy tree of no discernible species in a plastic pot meant to resemble a clay pot. At first you assume that the tree must be artificial then, when you look more closely, you see to your surprise that the stunted little tree is a *living thing*.

The tree is a well-intentioned "decorative touch" in Newark International Airport. Intended to soften the harsh utilitarian anonymity of the place.

And the horror of *randomness*—of strangers gathered together to no purpose other than to depart from one another as swiftly and expeditiously as possible.

But the little tree has not fared well in this mostly fluorescent-lit environment. Coaxed out of a seed, nurtured into life, it is now a *thing* scarcely living: its large spade-shaped leaves are no longer green but threaded with what looks like rust. Still, the little bird might yet be hidden among these leaves . . .

I've noticed another tree of the same indistinct species in the same plastic pot about thirty feet away, at (unoccupied) Gate C34. Very likely at other gates in the terminal, in all the terminals of the airport, there are other trees similarly potted, of a near-identical type, height and condition, their once-glossy green leaves grown shabby, desiccated. You can tell that these trees are *not artificial* because they are *shabby, desiccated*.

The *artificial* endures. *Living* wears out.

Invisibly, almost teasingly, the tiny chirping continues.

Like tiny bits of glass being shaken together in a great fist.

The chirping is drowned out by an announcement—a particularly shrill-voiced woman—and when the announcement ends, the chirping has ceased.

Everyone has turned back to their preoccupations of a moment before—desultory conversations, laptops and books, the high-perched TV news of far-flung and domestic tragedies that never ceases whether anyone is watching or not.

Even the soldiers who'd appeared vigilant a moment before have turned away. Even the lanky young man with the backpack, who is hunched in his seat speaking on a cell phone.

Am I the only traveler thinking—The little bird is still here somewhere, it could not have flown away without our seeing?

Stubbornly, I listen for the little bird. Scarcely daring to breathe I listen for the little bird. As if its tiny heartbeat had aligned itself with my heartbeat and acutely it is aware of me, as I am aware of it.

A living thing. Somewhere close by, invisible.

How loud and intrusive are the announcements—flights boarding, flights departing—flights delayed. How grating, the human voice.

For it seems that, at Gate C33, an incoming flight has been delayed (weather, Chicago) and an outgoing flight has been delayed (weather, Minneapolis).

But at last, a few minutes later, the frantic little chirping resumes, with greater urgency.

Already I am on my feet, restless and alert. Where I'd been annoyed and mildly anxious that my flight has been delayed—(another forty minutes)—yet I am more intrigued by the mysterious little bird, that has drawn my attention. Pages of the *New York Times* lay scattered on the seat beside mine, and on the floor.

I know—you are advised not to leave your luggage unattended in this public place, but I intend only to walk—to stretch my legs—for a short distance.

Unlike the others who've turned their attentions away from the mysterious chirping overhead, I'm consumed with curiosity about the little bird in our midst who is not only hypothetical but also invisible. For the fact remains: *there is a bird here at Gate C33 of Newark International Airport.*

It's probable that the bird entered the terminal through an opened door in this area when passengers boarded one of the smaller, propeller planes. At such times passengers are not shunted directly onto the plane through a covered chute but are obliged to walk across the pavement—(invariably in windy, wet weather)—to steep metal steps ascending to the prop-plane that, when entered, exudes the cramped, airless, and claustrophobic air of a straining intestine.

And yet—think of the odds against this! A luckless bird blown by the wind, unable to prevent itself from being sucked into the terminal through the opened door . . . Unless, confused by plate-glass reflections, the poor bird had blundered into the opened doorway of its own volition.

Now there's a sudden blur of wings! Small wings! My vigilance has paid off since I am almost directly below the bird—it was hidden, as I'd surmised, between the ledge and the ceiling—it's a small sparrow—beating its wings madly, careening in the air—striking the rows of plate-glass windows looking out onto the runway—making its way dazed and confused into a high, windowless corner of the waiting area. By this time everyone has glanced up again and several people smile—(why does the panicked fluttering of a small bird, trapped in such a place, provoke people to smile?).

After a few minutes of wing-beating, chirping, blundering along the row of windows, the little bird—(it's a beautifully patterned sparrow)—has positioned itself back on the ledge, but near the edge where it's visible. I have followed it here, in this relatively quiet space near the (unmanned, unlighted) Gate C34; beyond the window here is an empty runway, and close by is another stunted little potted tree— glamorous poster-ads for Costa Rica, Tampa Bay, Rio. Poor little bird! How did it get into this terrible place, and what can I do to help it?

Gazing up at the tiny damp eyes, the tiny beak moving soundlessly, as if its terror has made it mute—and my heart begins to beat rapidly, and my wings—(wings! suddenly I realize what is sprouting from my shoulders)—and now I see a fattish woman standing about twelve feet below me and peering up at me, quizzical and curious rather than concerned—I am crying *Oh please help me! I am one of you! I don't know what this terrible thing is, that has happened to me but—I am a living thing, I am one of you . . .*

Unable to stop the agitation of my wings, I am flying about in terror—striking the ugly, unyielding ceiling—ricocheting against the windows—and the ledge—there is a ventilator humming within, a ghastly grinding sound—in the midst of my terror another woman comes to observe, eating an apple—so acute is my eyesight, I can see saliva gleaming on this woman's lips—in her eyes a reflection of mild concern—so very mild, it's like a flickering candle seen at a distance; beyond this woman are rows of seats of which most are occupied—there are the U.S. soldiers in their bizarre jungle-uniforms—some glance up frowning, or smiling—faint distracted smiles; a few have seen me, or the blurred beating of wings that I have become. *Help me! I want to go home! I don't belong here, I live in*—but my tiny trilling voice can't accommodate multisyllabic words. *I am one of you—I am a living creature—help me out of this terrible place—I was a traveler like you—a human being like you—my flight to Chicago was delayed for forty minutes—and then for another forty minutes—and then—somehow—this has happened—this, to which I can give no name—this curse! Please hear me! Please help me! I have done nothing to deserve this punishment—I am innocent—I cannot even remember my "sins"—my "crimes"—I may have believed that I was an extraordinary individual but the fact is, I was utterly ordinary—I am utterly ordinary—I am blameless—it is a terrible injustice that I have been singled out like this—please, you must help me! Don't just smile inanely at me or look away, bored—help me! It is a mistake that I am here trapped against plate-glass windows—flinging myself against plate-glass windows—so yearning to escape into the open air, to freedom, my tiny heart is near to bursting! Take me to my home—when they see me, they will recognize me—there are those who love me—they will know who I am—I must consume food at once, I am starving—my little sparrow-wings, my tiny organs, my heart, my teaspoon of blood must be nourished—I am so very cold, I am shivering convulsively—if I don't consume food—just a few crumbs—please, just a few crumbs—I will begin to die within a few minutes—my organs will begin to shut down—my panicked-darting eyes will begin to close over, and my vision will become occluded—my wings which I had believed would beat forever, will slow—not one of you is starving—not one of you is beginning to shut down, and die—you have no right to smile at the suffering of a bird in the final minutes of its life—you have no right to ignore me for I am a very beautiful white-crowned sparrow with elaborately patterned wings of white, brown, black and rust-colored curved feathers—*

—I am more beautiful than any of you crude, wingless, earthbound creatures—I am as deserving of life as you!—more deserving than you!—I deserve better than this nightmare-curse: a random death among strangers.

Except—am I going to be rescued? Has someone called for help, and help has come? Eagerly my eyes take in an unexpected sight below: two men in work-uniforms—quick-striding, efficient and seemingly well-practiced—are approaching, at last. One has a stepladder and a small net with a three-foot handle, the other a wicked-looking broom.

ROMA!

The Hotel Bellevesta glittered by night like a multi-
tiered wedding cake and by day gleamed in the sun—
dazzling-white stucco, marble, and stained glass framed, on its ground
floor, by banks of gorgeous crimson and purple bougainvillea. The
original building had been the private residence—the "palazzo"—of
a seventeenth-century cardinal of the Roman Catholic Church but
in more recent centuries had been allowed to deteriorate; now totally
renovated, and refurbished, as a smart new five-star tourist-hotel, it
was an architectural gem amid the mixture of staid old historic buildings and expensive boutiques, designer shops, and beauty salons on the
fashionable Via di Ripetta.

Their suite was on the seventh floor, at the rear of the hotel as
they'd requested. From one of the windows they could see, across the
Piazza del Popolo, the tall stark beautifully silhouetted cypresses of
the Borghese Gardens less than a quarter-mile away.

Alexis shivered with an emotion she could not have named—
anticipation, apprehension. She'd seen—she was sure she'd seen—
these heraldic-seeming trees in a premonitory dream of the previous

night, as she'd seen an archaic obelisk resembling the monument at the center of the piazza, not clearly, but with a powerful stab of nostalgia.

"This is wonderful, David! We'll be happy here."

In other hotels, in other Italian cities, they had not always been so happy. But this was Rome, and this was the five-star Hotel Bellevesta. It would be the final hotel of their Italian trip.

Their room was elegantly furnished, much larger than they'd expected—with dusty-rose silk wallpaper, an astonishing twelve-foot ceiling and a marble floor that exuded the coolness of centuries; a crystal chandelier, of a size disproportionate even to this large space, and not one but two French doors. Framing the wide windows were draperies of white silk and a thinner, gossamer fabric, over a dark blind designed to keep out both sunshine and the noise of street traffic; the effect, even at midday, was secluded, cave-like—a space in which one could sleep, undisturbed, or reasonably undisturbed, in the midst of the thrumming city.

"Come look! It's like—Venice . . ."

The larger of the French doors opened onto a small balcony and from the balcony you could see, six floors below, a quaint cobblestone street, narrow as a lane, and the rear—fascinating in its detail, like a weatherworn topographical map—of a block of apartment buildings joined together like row houses but dissimilar in size and height and condition; one or two appeared to be vacated and shuttered, as if abandoned, while the others—so far as Alexis could see, without leaning too far over the balcony railing—were clearly lived-in, populated. The rooftops, too, were remarkably heterogeneous—some were made of ceramic tiles, of that lovely earthen-orange hue reminiscent of rooftops in Venice, while others were more rough-hewn, of some crude material like tar paper; still others had been converted into rooftop gardens with lemon trees, rosebushes, and small plants in cultivated rows, resembling a setting in a doll's house, in miniature. There were chairs and tables precariously positioned, it seemed, at the edge of rooftops as at the edge of an abyss; there were drooping clotheslines and laundry hanging like swabs of paint in an Impressionist painting; over all hovered clusters of TV antennae like antic grave markers. Here and there were stucco huts silhouetted dramatically against the sky—and the sky above Rome, on these warm summer evenings, like the sky above Venice, resembled an El Greco sky of bruised clouds, subtly fading and melting colors. On many of the older roofs moss grew as well as grasses and even a scattering of a bluish-purple wildflower Alexis had been noticing throughout Italy, for which she knew no name—a bell-shaped cluster-flower that appeared exquisite to the eye but was in fact tough and sinewy, with surprisingly sharp thorns, as she'd discovered in the ruins of the Roman Forum on their first day of sightseeing in the city.

So strange! Like a pueblo dwelling, in the American Southwest: many individuals crammed together in a relatively small and primitive space. The busyness of Rome, the startling modernity of Rome, seemed remote here; the alley was too narrow for traffic other than motor scooters, and there weren't many of these, at least not that Alexis had noticed. Yet she didn't doubt, this was truly Rome: this was the Rome in which ordinary citizens lived, oblivious to the glittery Hotel Bellevesta as the Hotel Bellevesta was oblivious to them.

"David? Come look. The backs of these buildings—like a painting, or a fresco—fascinating . . ."

David stepped out onto the balcony but didn't speak for some time. It was like him to withhold comment; he would see for himself what Alexis wanted to show him, for he wasn't readily susceptible to others' enthusiasms. Just as he didn't often reply to Alexis's remarks if he thought them naïve, banal, or self-evident—in their travels together, as in their marriage, it had come to be David's role to hold back, to express doubt, or even skepticism, or cynicism, while Alexis maintained her girlish manner of openness, curiosity. The wife plunging head-on, hopeful; the husband thoughtful, inclined to hesitate.

Like figures on a teeter-totter: the one who is elevated is dependent upon the one who is heavier, and grounded.

So many ancient, heraldic and lapidary figures they'd been seeing, in the tourist-world of classical antiquity, almost Alexis could think that she had seen just this figure, carved in stone.

"Isn't it? The peeling walls, the beautiful fading colors? Like Venice?"

David leaned out over the balcony railing, just conspicuously farther than Alexis. His forehead creased in the effort to discern what there was here to be seen, if it was so very exceptional. The strange heterogeneity of stucco dwellings, the jumble of rooftops, TV antennae, part-opened windows and shuttered windows—yes, there was something beautiful about the scene, David conceded, or anyway intriguing: "Not quite like Venice since there is only one Venice but yes—very intriguing."

How happy it made Alexis, when her husband agreed with her! She had always deferred to him, as she had always adored him; his feeling for her was more modulated yet she didn't doubt that he loved her, or would have said that he loved her—this was all that mattered. In their daily lives, which, in the enforced intimacy of travel, became yet more intense, no matter was too small, trivial or domestic to Alexis, to be proffered to David's judgment; all matters seemed to her about equally crucial as if their marriage, though an established fact, was nonetheless always in doubt, depending upon her husband's ever-shifting, ever-unpredictable assessment of her worth.

"'ROMA.'"

The word seemed magical to her, a floating sort of word, unlike the dour-sounding "Rome."

Through the city there pulsed a heightened energy so palpable you could nearly see, taste, touch it—but this energy, Alexis thought, was only just on the surface: beneath was a hidden subterranean world, a kind of vast cave, or catacomb, brooding and impersonal, with a far slower pulse, like the movements of glaciers, or continents. In the visible Rome, a place of elaborated encoded maps, tourist-pilgrims by the thousands drifted each day—each hour—in quest of some sort of profound, secular miracle: a succession of visions to photograph, to appropriate as *experience*. For the life of the senses is a continuous depthless stream—it has no accumulation, it has not even a destination; the conclusion of a life in time is of no more consequence than any preceding moment; so there is the yearning for *experience*—if not personal, the collective and impersonal will do.

But this deeper Rome, this secret, dark-brooding, inward and subterranean Rome was inaccessible to the outsider, and could not be appropriated. So each evening when they returned to the Hotel Bellevesta after a long day of sightseeing they were made to feel dissatisfied, incomplete; particularly, David felt this, the suspicion of being cheated, or missing something; as if an entire page in their Rome guidebook had been torn out, to mock him despite his Nikon D300—newly purchased for this trip to Italy, after considerable research.

" 'Rome.' Not 'Roma'—to us."

Alexis laughed, though David might have meant this as a rebuke. For he, too, was smiling—in his ironic way.

On the first heady days of their trip, which began in Venice, David had taken hundreds of photographs, rapidly, his fingers moving as swiftly as his eye; there had been a grim efficiency to his picture-taking, Alexis had thought, for, with the new digital technology, in contrast to older, more calculated photography, one scarcely needed to "see," still less to think—in theory, the photographer could photograph virtually every moment of his presence in a place, of which, later, in solitude, he could select just those few moments of worth. In this way, the photographer was postponing the very experience of his trip—by snapping pictures, he was deferring the effort of evaluation. When David showed Alexis the multiple images he'd taken on the LCD display, some of them including her, she'd been struck by how closely the pictures resembled one another, with only minute differences between them; in multiples, none had appeared particularly distinctive. "But which do you prefer?" David asked. "Which would you like me to print?" His tone was just slightly coercive, for he liked to present "choices" to Alexis as if testing her.

Which images to print? When they were so much alike? Alexis had no idea. Yet she could not say *But you're the photographer!—you must judge.* And so with a bright smile she told her husband x, y, z— reasonable choices which seemed to placate him, at least temporarily.

Back home, in their hilltop suburban home in Beverly Farms, north of Boston, David had had little interest in photography—he hadn't time for such an interest, or patience; on this trip, Alexis had begun to see a side of her husband she scarcely knew, that had been hidden from her until now.

He was fifty-seven years old, Alexis was several years younger. The gap in their ages—though not considerable—had always been a determining factor in their relationship as, it is said, just a few minutes' seniority makes a considerable difference in the intimate lives of identical twins.

Of course in any relationship there is the more dominant individual—the one who is loved more than he can love in return. But the love of the weaker for the stronger is not inevitably a weak love. Alexis had always thought *He will see, someday. He will understand how I love him.*

Ostensibly, the Italian trip was to celebrate their thirtieth wedding anniversary. But there was some other motive on David's part,

Alexis thought. He was a reticent man, you could not know what he was thinking and so often in their lives together Alexis had been quite mistaken, trying to imagine what her husband was thinking, but she felt now, in him, an almost panicked need to *get away*—the place to *get away to* only just happened to be Italy.

Rarely had they traveled together in any ambitious way, in the years of their marriage. For David had had to travel frequently for business reasons and always he'd traveled alone, bringing his work. This trip, David had made it a point not to bring work—nor would he speak to Alexis about his work. He had wanted a new, different experience—clearly. And in the early days of their trip (of three weeks) he'd seemed happy, engaged. For travel is in essence problem-solving and David was one who liked the challenge of problem-solving even if, in travel, the problems to be solved are both transient and trivial; as, in David's profession, he'd built a career of considerable success out of a pains-taking relish for problem-solving in matters of "tax law"—a body of information continuously shifting, and requiring re-interpretation. What dismayed him about their trip was the *crowdedness* everywhere, that seemed to diminish the significance of travel, and the individual traveler; particularly in Rome, David was annoyed by the constant traffic—taxis, motorcycles and scooters, buses and trucks emitting clouds of exhaust—those small European automobiles that appear, to the American eye, almost like toys—"And so many tourists! And American pop culture—brainless and ubiquitous."

He spoke vehemently, seriously. Alexis supposed it must be a tru-ism of travel: you are most appalled by what most resembles what you are. But she couldn't suggest this to David, he would be hurt, or angry at her. Like all tourists, David imagined himself a traveler. *He* was not a mere tourist, *he* was not brainless for he was himself—*different.*

At night, enervated from another of their late, protracted, expensive dinners, as from a carefully calibrated day of sightseeing in the mid-summer heat—(mostly by taxi, though often, inescapably, on foot—up steep stone steps, and down steep stone steps—amid packs of fellow tourists)—they were yet too over-stimulated to go to bed, despite their exhaustion; a final drink, and then—maybe—another drink, from the minibar, brought outside onto the balcony where in the cooling night air they found themselves gazing at the row of apartment buildings across the alley—now mostly darkened, and shuttered; above, the nighttime sky of Rome, lights reflected against a lowered cloud-ceiling; immediately below, the cobblestone street like a dark stream. From time to time they heard snatches of voices, music, laughter—shouted words, presumably in Italian—unintelligible.

Was the language beautiful, Alexis wondered. Or was it just—foreign. Like so much of what they'd been experiencing since leaving home.

"Another drink? Or—more ice?"

"Both."

Eventually, Alexis thought, David might tell her what had propelled him to Italy—what problem in his corporate-tax-law work had proved insoluble, or whether in fact—(she did not want to think this, and had no real reason to think this)—his employer, allegedly the third-largest pharmaceutical company in the world, was suggesting early retirement for him, as for others in his division, in the wake of financial losses. In the man's eyes the unspoken command *Don't ask! Don't even imagine you want to know.*

It would have been a daunting task to count the rickety-looking little outdoor stairs that ascended to the multilevel rooftops across the way, or the numerous windows overlooking the alley; at first you thought that the windows were uniform, of the same general proportions, but a second glance suggested that each window was distinct from its neighbors in some small, subtle way. All of the windows were outfitted with shutters that were closed at night, and against the heat of the afternoon sun; one or two of the windows seemed always to be shuttered, Alexis had come to notice, as if no one lived inside, or harbored a secret so terrible it could not withstand the light of day. Most of the shutters were black, but some were dark brown, and a few were beige; some appeared to be recently painted, and in good repair, while others were faded and weatherworn, peeling, leprous-looking; yet, like Venice, exuding a curious quaint heartrending charm, the particular beauty of decay.

The particular beauty, Alexis thought, of another's decay—not our own.

She'd been staring at a lighted window across the alley, on the fourth floor of one of the older buildings: inside, at what appeared to be a table, a man was sitting, eating—of his face, only his jaws were visible—and of his solid muscled body, only his torso and upper arms; the man might have been in his early or mid-thirties; he was dark-skinned, swarthy; he seemed to be speaking to another person, or persons, at the table, but Alexis couldn't see anyone else; he was gesturing as he ate, with abrupt, jerky motions of his beefy arm, like a puppet—for how like puppet-movements our motions are, detached from speech and from the more subtle expressions of our faces. Alexis thought how odd this was—or maybe not so odd, since most people adhere strictly to their domestic schedules—that the dark-skinned man had been seated at the table the previous night, more or less in the same position, at about the same time, when she and David had been sitting outside on their balcony with glasses of wine. And, a flight up, in an adjoining building, almost directly across from the balcony, at one of the windows that had been shuttered through most of the day, a woman lay on a couch watching TV, as she'd watched TV the previous night; as it had been the previous night, the light in the room was an eerie pale blue that flickered and quivered. The woman was middle-aged, and full-bodied; Alexis was embarrassed to see that she wore something like a negligee, carelessly wrapped about her soft slack naked breasts, and her hair was blond, and disheveled; clearly, the TV-entranced woman had no idea that strangers were observing her in so intimate a way—(or did she?)—or that the sidelong sprawl of her body on what appeared to be an old, heavy piece of furniture suggested Rousseau's iconic, final painting *The Dream*. As in the famous painting the framed image of the voluptuous-bodied woman in pale-bluish light exerted a powerful nostalgic aura—Alexis stared, and stared. (Was this voyeurism? Was she intruding, unconscionably, on another's privacy? Or did the fact of the woman's anonymity—and Alexis's anonymity—somehow render the act innocent, as it could have no consequences for either individual?) "So strange! That woman, I mean—watching TV—you'd think she'd pull her blinds, or close her shutters, wouldn't you? After all she must know—there's a hotel here, people in many rooms, here . . ."

Though there must have been at least thirty feet separating the balcony and the window, and, if the woman had glanced up, to peer out her window, she'd have had difficulty making out the couple sitting so very still on the darkened balcony two storeys above her, Alexis spoke in a lowered voice as if fearing the woman might hear her, and take offense.

"What? Who? Oh—*her* . . ."

It was a vague reply, coolly courteous. As often David replied to Alexis when she said something self-evident, banal, or of little interest to him.

Hesitantly Alexis said: "I suppose we shouldn't watch. It's like that Hitchcock film, *Rear Window*—you don't want to look, but . . ." Had she made the same remark, the previous night? Her words sounded familiar to her, unsettling.

Carefully pouring the last of a miniature bottle of red wine into his glass—for Alexis had barely touched hers—David didn't reply. If he'd been aware of the voluptuous sprawling woman on the couch and the dark-skinned man at the table he gave no sign as several times that day, in the art and archaeology museums they'd visited, he hadn't appeared to be very much engaged in the exhibits though, dutifully, when not expressly forbidden by signs, he'd taken photographs of major artworks, the facades and interiors of churches, astonishing Roman views from windows and hillsides. For much of the evening he'd been in a distracted mood: he'd had too much to drink, which wasn't like him, and at dinner, in a three-star Tuscan restaurant above the Spanish Steps that was highly recommended by his much-thumbed *Michelin* guide, he'd been upset by something on the bill—some ambiguity about the price of the wine, or the number of bottles of sparkling water they'd consumed, or the bill itself, which translated into U.S. currency was considerable.

By degrees, as if bemused by Alexis's interest in the anonymous individuals across the way, David began to observe them, too. Though, if he'd been alone—(he allowed Alexis to know this, obliquely)—he would scarcely have noticed them.

"If this is an intimate look into the lives of ordinary Romans—it certainly isn't very revealing, or significant."

"Oh but I think it is 'revealing'—'significant.' We can't judge people by just seeing them, outwardly."

"We can't? How do you think they judge us?"

"I don't see why we should judge other people at all. Just to see them, to acknowledge them as different from ourselves . . ." Alexis's voice trailed off, she'd lost the thread of what she meant to say. Now another window had lighted up, like a stage set, on the fifth floor of a stucco building to the right of their balcony; this building, the width of two windows of ordinary size, was so narrow as to resemble a tower, that had faded to a faint sepia color like an old photograph. The roof of the building was partly ceramic tile, cracked and broken, and partly the ruins of an abandoned roof garden in which tall grasses and wild-flowers grew. Alexis had noticed this garden before, and had wished that someone, a child perhaps, might have climbed the outdoor stairs to it, but no one had come. There was something both slovenly and exquisite about the narrow building, that reminded Alexis of an illustration in a child's storybook.

Inside the newly illuminated room, through a scrim of tissue-thin curtains, a figure was moving, indistinctly. Alexis couldn't see if it was a woman or a man who'd switched on a dim light, or had lighted just a candle. Alexis said, in her conspiratorial lowered voice: "It seems wrong to watch them somehow, but—I suppose—it's harmless. They aren't actually *doing* anything—like the characters in *Rear Window*."

David said, with a snort of derision: "They certainly aren't doing anything of interest! And it isn't as if, their windows open to the world as they are, they can have any expectation of privacy."

"Well—we can't see their faces, anyway. We have no way of knowing who they are."

Alexis spoke uncertainly. She was beginning to feel ashamed, so openly staring into a stranger's window.

But now, in the newly illuminated interior, the shadowy figure was moving briskly; unlike her neighbors who seemed inert as waxworks figures this one was intent upon an action, or a sequence of actions, of some precision, though it wasn't clear what she was doing—dressing? undressing? posing in front of a mirror? *dancing*? Alexis strained to hear—was it music?—jangling hard-rock pop-American *music*?

David, no longer indifferent, stared frankly at this new scene. It was soon clear that the shadowy figure was that of an attractive young woman, or girl, with swaths of shining black hair that fell to her waist—exposed white shoulders and upper arms, bare legs—(was she undressed? in a camisole top of some near-transparent material, or in night-wear?)—and she seemed to be alone; except that she was talking, or singing, to herself, as she moved her arms about provocatively, shifted and wriggled her breasts, her narrow hips, and shook her startlingly black hair, to the accelerated beat of not-quite-audible music; very like a seductive figure in a film who while solitary, glimpsed in isolation, is yet assured of being observed by countless staring strangers. How reckless of the girl, to leave her window unshuttered, or her blinds open, facing the Hotel Bellevesta with its seven floors of rooms! Alexis thought *She must know that we are watching. That someone is watching.* It was dismaying to her, alarming, that her husband would stare so openly at the partially undressed girl even as she, Alexis, was sitting close beside him, invisible to him as if he were alone on the balcony.

"I suppose—we should go to bed. It's past midnight."

"Is it!"

Unlike the others who scarcely moved, the girl with the waist-long black hair kept in motion, a sort of frenetic, continuous motion, like an animated doll. She was slender, agile—spirited. As David and Alexis stared she stopped abruptly, turned and hurried out of the room—like an actress unexpectedly leaving a stage, to the surprise and disappointment of her audience—but then returned, carrying something—a sort of stick, or wand; with quick steps she came to the window, as if to peer accusingly upward, at the American couple staring at her from their balcony above, but instead she disappeared behind the wall; a moment later reappearing, and then disappearing—were her movements deliberate? teasing?—or accidental? In the background, on what appeared to be steps in a doorway, a small creature appeared—a cat, or a dog— that brushed against the girl's bare ankles sensuously.

"No, a dog. One of those little yapping breeds."

Like the girl, the little animal disappeared, and reappeared; it followed the girl out of the room, and back into the room; approached the window, and disappeared beneath the windowsill, as if (perhaps) there was a food dish there. The girl paused to pet the animal, and to talk to it. (Or was someone else in the room, out of sight, to whom the girl was speaking?) Beside the attractive animated girl the other, older woman and man seemed very dull; they resembled those eerily bulb-headed, featureless and bandaged-looking mannequins in the early Surrealist paintings of Giorgio de Chirico, Alexis had seen the previous week in a museum exhibit in Florence.

David disliked the Surrealists. David disliked and distrusted any art—any way of life—that did not acknowledge what was *real*; and, to David, what was *real* was obvious and incontestable as looking into a mirror. Of course, the girl was young—much younger than the others. An aura like a flame seemed to glow about her slender limbs, and in the scintillate waves of her waist-long black hair. Her face was obscured to them, behind the gauzy curtain, but appeared to be heart-shaped, and the skin markedly white.

"See what she's doing now?"

"What? What is she doing now?"

"Vacuuming."

David was correct: the girl had dragged a small canister vacuum cleaner into the room, and was briskly vacuuming the floor, chairs and cushions. And so late, past midnight! There was something grimly frenetic about her movements as if she knew herself observed, and her hyperactivity was in some (reproachful) relation to her invisible audience, a rebuke to their voyeuristic passivity.

Alexis said, uneasily, "She should draw her blinds, or shutter her windows—anyone could be watching from the hotel. A man could try to figure out where she lived, and come to find her . . . She's old enough to know better. She isn't a *child*."

The girl seemed to have shed another article of clothing. For it was very warm in the mid-summer Roman night that was airless in this part of the city. Beneath the thin white camisole shift she was wearing just very brief white panties.

"It could be dangerous. Her behavior. Who knows who might be watching, if not tonight, some other night. In the United States . . ."

Alexis tried not to sound reproachful, resentful. It might have been the girl's very recklessness she envied.

David continued to stare frankly at the girl some thirty feet away, with a look of faint disdain, bemusement. His eyes were heavy-lidded, his forehead creased. He'd been tired out by the exertions of the long day and the long tourist-days had been accumulating since their departure from Logan Airport two weeks before. As he stared, the seductive-teasing girl vanished, again. It was impossible not to think—even as it was unlikely—that the girl was aware of her audience, and wanted to torment them. In her wake the little white creature rushed out of the room on short, clumsy legs. Abandoned on the carpet was the small canister vacuum cleaner with its hose like an outflung limb.

In the other windows, there began to be a minimal sort of movement. In the pale-blue-TV-lighted window, the woman on the couch roused herself, as if from a trance; she was sitting up, or partially sitting up; her negligee swung open even as, with a sort of mock alarm, her plump arms lifted shielding her breasts. Her broad heavy-jawed face was partway in shadow and had the look of a half-face—a kind of primitive mask. In the other, lower window, at last the dark-skinned man rose from his place at the table, and moved toward the window; still, his face wasn't visible—only just the lower part of his torso, cut off by the window frame. On the table behind him were plates, a glass and a wine bottle . . . You could see that there was a lighted candle on the table, that had burnt low.

"Well! We should go to bed, it's late . . ."

David said nothing. He made no move to rise. Alexis knew she shouldn't make this request more than once: though David frequently ignored her remarks, he did not like her to repeat them.

" . . . almost twelve-thirty. And tomorrow, the Sistine Chapel . . ."

This seemed funny, somehow. Tomorrow, the Sistine Chapel! The ancient ruins of the Roman Forum! The Colosseum! The Palatine! The Vatican, the Borghese Gallery, St. Peter's Basilica!

On the wrought-iron balcony outside their seventh-floor room in the Hotel Bellevesta they sat, the middle-aged American couple, as if unable to move; in a pleasurable trance gazing across the alley at a row of mostly darkened and shuttered apartment buildings. Above were rooftops obscured by shadow and farther above, the Roman sky, opaque with layered clouds, lightless, that resembled a cathedral ceiling, its fanatical detail softened by shadow.

JUST WHEN YOU THINK that your life is *run-down*.

Just when you think that your life is *frayed, worn. Done.*

If they'd had children, perhaps. But there had not been a time for children, not *the time*.

David had said, wait. We can wait. And Alexis had said—(what had Alexis said?)—Alexis had said yes. Of course we can wait.

Now, so many years later it could not ever be *the time*. What had been *the time* was now, irrevocably, past. And so they'd come to Italy, to a succession of beautiful Italian places—after Venice they'd gone to Padua, Verona, Milan—to Bologna, Florence, Sienna and San Gimignano—and at last Rome. In planning their trip, David had booked them longest in Rome.

Ostensibly, to celebrate their thirtieth wedding anniversary: this was the account they gave to others, that others were happy to hear.

For all journeys are journeys of desperation—the journey takes us *away.*

For most of the time that she'd known him, David had been a man driven and defined by his work: obsessed, ambitious. There was a particular sort of joy—Alexis didn't want to think that it was inevitably masculine, but she'd never seen it in any woman of her acquaintance—in ambition that has triumphed. (Triumph over a rival? Is there any other sort of triumph? In the Pitti Palace in Florence Alexis had stared appalled at a succession of over-life-sized sculpted figures by Michelangelo depicting Hercules in the quasi-heroic act of killing his opponent—Antaeus, an Amazon warrior, a centaur, among luckless others. *The Triumph of Victory* was the bombastic title. Tourists whose nerves would have been shattered by a poorly prepared restaurant meal or hotel rooms lacking adequate services stared solemnly at these ugly tributes to brute masculinity, knowing themselves in the presence of *serious art*. There was no female equivalent to such extravagant and excessive brutality nor even the general recognition that such an equivalent might be missing.)

Within their social circle, and certainly within their families, David was considered a highly successful man. To David himself, his success was marred by the fact that others were more successful, who did not seem deserving, as he knew himself deserving. Now, in recent years, these rivals were fading, disappearing; David's new rivals were of another generation entirely, young enough to be his children, though David didn't feel paternal toward them, any more than they felt filial toward him. Hired in a shrinking job market, these young rivals were yet more highly paid than David had been, at the same rank, after adjustments for inflation; he knew that they were unbeatable—time was on their side. He hadn't become embittered but only, as he often said, sharper, wiser. This sharpness showed in his face: beneath his smile of bemused or ironic well-being was an abiding wariness, the alertness of one who is anxious not to be disrespected, taken-less-seriously than he merits. David's once-abundant hair had thinned and his skull was prominent, like some implacable inorganic substance; almost, Alexis couldn't remember what he had looked like as a young man. His contemporary self, his middle-aged self, had seemed to have consumed his youth. Yet he seemed to her attractive, still—despite his ironic way of frowning while smiling as if the very act of smiling were a sign of weakness, vulnerability. He had not had patience with weakness in himself or in others and now that he was older, he was having to adjust his sense of manliness. As a man ages the Darwinian notion of natural selection shifts its meaning and other types of morality begin to exert their appeal.

"A barbaric world—but what art!"

Another time they'd gone to the ancient ruins for which the city was best known. The old, unspeakably cruel yet "noble" civilization that predated the modern, its acres of rubble set off by fluorescent-orange construction barriers—a jarring juxtaposition of ugly synthetic materials and the sun-baked stone of antiquity. Everywhere were decayed but yet beautiful carvings, monuments that seemed to Alexis's untrained eye a testament to the uses of futility—the uses one might make of futility.

The history of the great Roman empire was fraught with savage cruelty, violence, and delusion, yet a visionary self-assurance that seemed lost now, in the West. Who could believe that gods mated with mortals, to create a race of demigods? Who could believe that there was anything godly in even the stunning blue Mediterranean sky? Or that any "empire" was privileged over another?

Christian Rome, and Catholic Rome that followed—so many centuries!—another empire inflated and inspired by metaphysical delusion and the terrifying self-assurance of delusion. But these centuries, too, had waned, and could not be resuscitated.

"Though I suppose, we are not so much less 'barbaric' now. Our waning American empire, our mission of 'democratizing' the world for our own economic interests . . ."

David spoke with unusual vehemence. He was not by nature a political person, his political views were centrist, economically conservative. He had little trust in any politicians yet a sort of residue of wistfulness for the idealism of his youth—the generation that had come of age in the late 1960s and 1970s—the waning idealism of the great revolutionary decade of the American twentieth century, the bitter ashes of the end of the Vietnam War.

Strange for David to speak as if, for once, the impersonal were intensely, painfully personal. Alexis felt a stab of concern—or was it love?—for her husband, that he seemed to be losing his old, unexamined sense of himself as a man among men, a rival among rivals; in Rome, their destination city as well as the city of their imminent departure, more markedly than in any of the Italian places they'd visited, David had become oddly indifferent to news of home; he seemed to have stopped checking his e-mail; ever more, he was susceptible to the most superficial distractions—annoying fellow tourists in the Bellevesta, throngs of people in marketplaces and piazzas, boisterous young Italians on motorcycles—in a crowded side street he'd paused to stare at a young girl with long coarse-black hair like a horse's mane, a girl carrying a motorcycle helmet who was dressed provocatively in tight-fitting black leather, spike-heeled shoes and black net stockings, bizarre black-net gloves to the elbow, but fingerless; the underside of her jaw was defaced by a lurid birthmark, or a tattoo; poor David gaped, until Alexis tugged at his elbow.

He'd seemed dazed, smiling. A middle-aged sort of smile, as of one waking from a dream, uncertain of his surroundings. *He is a lonely man* Alexis thought. *My husband is a lonely, vulnerable man.*

By degrees, David had ceased taking photographs except of the most exceptional sights—postcard-sights. He'd taken many more photos on his digital camera than he would ever print—many more than he would ever examine. He'd left his expensive camera in a restaurant—a young waitress had run after them, to return it.

Like many other tourists he wore sandals, but David's sandals chafed his pale feet. His clothes were expensive sports clothes, short-sleeved linen shirts, pastel colors, stripes, limp from the heat, rumpled. His scalp, exposed by his thinning hair, had burnt in the sun, but David disliked wearing any sort of hat. Where in the past he'd insisted upon making travel arrangements, now he was more frequently depending upon Alexis to make them. The city's great public museums and galleries weren't air-conditioned—even their cool marble floors and high ceilings weren't sufficient to compensate for the heat of Rome. Fans blew languid air from room to room. There in the Borghese Gallery came David in a blue-striped shirt damp with the sweat of his solid compact body—shuffling in Alexis's wake like an undersea creature but dimly aware of its environment and pausing to stare, with a mild sort of astonishment, at the pale-marble Bernini *Apollo e Dafne*. While Alexis moved eagerly ahead consulting museum maps, David fell behind. In this exotic place, this beautiful city, he had but little sense of its geography, and little interest; he had not the slightest knowledge of the Italian language; Alexis had long ago taken French and Spanish, and so could recognize crucial words; she'd prepared for the trip, hastily, with language tapes, while David hadn't had time—of course.

In their marriage, he'd made Alexis the repository of such things—such airy and essentially useless activities. As he'd made Alexis the repository of emotions too raw, elemental and disorderly for a man to acknowledge: the deaths of his own parents he'd needed Alexis to register, that he might grieve for them. Without Alexis, would he have grieved at all?

Here in Rome—"Roma"—Alexis turned to look back at her husband trailing in her wake, or sitting in a café awaiting her; he'd lost interest in his guidebook, or was feeling just too tired. She tried to imagine life without him—his death, one day. She shivered as if a pit were opening at her feet. She felt—she didn't know what—a kind of numbness, nullity. She wondered if this was all that she would feel, one day, fully—or whether she was deceiving herself, in this mood of suspension, indefinition—in "Roma."

It was Alexis's idea to see an exhibit of Picasso pen-and-ink drawings in a private gallery near the Piazza di Spagna but the exhibit was disappointing to her, and unnerving: a succession of "erotic" drawings in which the same several images were repeated with tic-like compulsion, a leering/lascivious sort of glee; what pathos in this evidence of a once-great (male) artist reduced, as in a nightmare mimicry of senility, to so few visual ideas—fat voluptuous naked female, satyr-like younger man, elderly male voyeur. The sex-features of the female and the satyr were exaggerated, as in a caricature, or cartoon; the elderly voyeur was Picasso himself, a painful yet defiant self-portrait of sex-obsession. Staring at the walls of these drawings, each meticulously and strikingly rendered, yet, in the aggregate, numbly repetitive, Alexis felt the irony of the great artist's predicament: he had lost his imaginative capacity to invent new images but he had not lost or transcended his sex-obsession; as if, underpinning all of his art, the great variegated art of decades, there had been only this primary, primitive obsession, a juvenile fixation upon genitals. How much more profound—more "tragic"—the final, death-haunted work of Michelangelo, Goya, Magritte, Rousseau's *The Dream* . . . But David was shaking his head, smiling—"Well! These drawings are certainly . . ." letting his voice trail off suggestively, so that Alexis was prompted to say, "Pathetic. I think they are pathetic, demeaning." David laughed, amused by Alexis's reaction. "It's the subject that upsets you, Alexis. 'Erotica'—high-class pornography. Graphic sex makes women uneasy, they know themselves interchangeable." Alexis said, "And men? What do you think you are?—each of you unique?"

David turned to stare at Alexis, shocked as if she'd slapped him. It was totally out of character for her to speak so sharply and so coldly to him, or to anyone.

It felt good, Alexis thought. Her heart beat in elation, a kind of childlike thrill. Discovering that she could speak to her husband in such a way, and in this foreign city in which they knew no one else and had only each other for solace.

Now recklessly she said: "You can stay at the exhibit a little longer, if you'd like to see it again. I think I'll go out alone—I want to buy some things."

"Of course I don't want to see it again," David said, hurt. "I've seen enough—I've seen enough 'art' for a long time."

"I'll see you back at the hotel. In the café."

Alexis was walking away—she would leave him there in the chill interior of the art gallery, staring after her in amazement.

"But—Alexis—what time? We have a dinner reservation . . ."

"I don't know—six P.M.—or a little later. Good-bye!"

Desperate to leave the man, to be alone.

SHOPPING! In the elegant streets near the Piazza di Spagna she saw her blurred ghost-figure in the windows of designer shops and boutiques; she lingered longest in front of lavishly air-conditioned stores— *Armani, Prada, Dior, Dolce & Gabbana, Louis Vuitton*—whose doors were brazenly opened to the street in a display of a conspicuous wastefulness of energy. Her mood was near-euphoric—she smiled to see her ghost-figure merging briefly with the angular, sylphine figures of mannequins. She thought *But there is nothing I want. What is there in the world, anywhere—that I can want.*

Boldly she entered one of the chic designer shops. It was exciting to her, to be alone like this; exciting to be alone in the foreign city, without the man dragging at her, pulling her down. She was not by nature a "consumer"—if she'd taken pleasure in buying things in the past these were likely to be things for other people or for the household she and David shared, that Alexis almost single-handedly oversaw. Now she stared at flimsy little shifts on chrome racks, cobwebby sweaters, halter tops scarcely larger than handkerchiefs. Prices were outrageous, ludicrous: 350 euros for one of the cobwebby sweaters, that looked as if it was unraveling. Nonetheless she would purchase something—she would *shop*. She thought *If I can want something. Then*—

To extract pleasure from *consuming*! Almost it was a kind of erotic sensation, or might be—this sense that one must be worth a luxury item, if one can purchase it.

Alexis examined one of the shifts—an abbreviated "dress" designed to wrap around the body like a scarf, or a shroud; it was made of a beautifully rippling material that more resembled metal filings than fabric. Five hundred ninety euros! And another striking dress, sleek black silk with a "tattered" skirt that fell well below the knees, priced at seven hundred euros.

Alexis thought *If I could be the person who would want this! Who would be transformed by this . . .*

She would buy a present for her sister's daughter—a little *faux*-denim jacket, maybe—a leather belt with a gold buckle—an absurdly high-priced pullover in a delicate, near-translucent fabric like muslin—except she knew that her sixteen-year-old niece would probably not wear anything Alexis bought for her even once, and wouldn't be able to return it as she did in the U.S. She allowed herself to be cajoled into trying on one of the shifts, in a striking fuchsia color; it was certainly unlike anything she owned, or had ever worn. "*Bella!*"—the chic-black-clad salesgirls hovered about her, smiling in admiration.

She was thinking of her father, her poor public-school-super-intendent father in Ames, Iowa, whom she'd loved so much, who had saved money diligently, as the adults of his generation were conditioned to do; her father's chronic anxiety about medical and hospital insurance; his plan for long-time health care at home for her mother and for himself, and both had died fairly suddenly—both, in hospitals. Her father's concern, that had shaped much of his life, had turned out to be for nothing. The money he'd saved he left to Alexis and her sister, who had not needed his hard-earned "estate." Out of pity for this kindly, over-conscientious man, not wanting to emulate him, Alexis bought the fuchsia shift. She bought a patterned pullover for her niece, and a silk shawl for her sister. Daringly she bought a pair of open-backed leather sandals, salmon-colored, with a two-inch cork heel—she'd been seeing shoes like these on fashionably dressed women in Rome. She thought *Is this my Roman self? Is this me?*

She saw with surprise her youthful mirror-reflection, even her windblown ashy-blond hair with its gray streaks looked striking, attractive.

In another yet more elegant and expensive designer shop she made several more purchases, impulsively. A lightweight summer sweater with seed pearls scattered across its front—for herself. And a bizarre near-backless dress, sleek-dark-purple, with a single tight-fitting sleeve—her left arm remained bare. She smiled, the dress was utterly ravishing, very expensive. In a mirror she saw the stylish Italian sales-girls exchanging covert smiles—at the American shopper's expense? Yet their compliments were lavish, their voices were high-pitched little bird-voices—"*Bella!*"

She thought of David. He would be surprised! Maybe, he would be impressed.

She thought of her lost, beloved father, and she thought of David, her husband. She felt a wave of love for the man who was her husband—

who seemed to be distracted by something, some secret, he could not share with her, just yet; like a wounded creature that flares up in rage against anyone who comes too near, David would nurse his secret hurt. She would forgive him: she would buy him one of the gorgeous, ridiculously priced Italian neckties. She took some time deciding, before buying him a Dior tie in dark purple silk stripes, to match her Versace dress.

Alexis! Thank you. This is very beautiful . . .

He would look at her in surprise, yet he would be moved, she knew. Though he professed to scorn presents, he was grateful for a particular sort of attention, that suggested his own good taste, his distinction.

Bella!

It was 5:40 P.M. when she took a taxi to the Piazza del Popolo. Though burdened with packages she meant to walk back to the hotel by way of the block of apartment dwellings that had exerted such a fascination from their balcony—how curious she was, to see these dwellings close-up! She would have an advantage over David, she thought: and maybe she would tell him, what she saw. And maybe, not.

But, amid a deafening din of traffic, on foot, in her new-purchased open-backed sandals, which, in a rash moment she'd decided to wear out of the store, she couldn't seem to locate the street, nor even the cobblestone passageway behind the hotel. It was as if, as soon as she ventured out of the area of the Bellevesta, and its surrounding glittery stores, she was in an urban no-man's-land of narrow streets, treacherous motor scooters, delivery trucks exhaling waves of black smoke, littered sidewalks crowded with foreign-looking pedestrians—many of whom were clearly not Italian but Middle Eastern, Indian, African. Several times she was jostled—in a panic she gripped her shoulder bag, that it might not be torn from her. (Of course, their guidebook had warned of the folly of carrying shoulder bags in Rome.) When at last she located an alley between buildings just wide enough for a single vehicle to pass, it was desolate and littered, and smelled of garbage; from the front, the block of buildings was seen to be aged and derelict, abandoned and shuttered—seemingly slated for demolition. No one had lived in these decrepit quarters for some time.

"How strange! This is wrong . . ."

Fearful of getting lost, Alexis retracted her steps. Once on the busy Via di Ripetta she located the Hotel Bellevesta with no difficulty—its shining stained glass, stone and stucco facade was dazzlingly conspicuous. But she couldn't circle the hotel, of course—the way was blocked by a high wall; and when she made her way to what she believed might be the rear of the hotel, in a littered and foul-smelling alley near a Dumpster, she saw nothing familiar. In a doorway at the rear two hotel workers lounged smoking, and staring at her—dark-eyed, very foreign-looking, unsmiling. Alexis smiled nervously at them and backed away. She'd had no luck trying to determine where their beautiful hotel room was—on this side of the hotel, or another? In the enervating heat of late afternoon she was beginning to feel light-headed but she didn't want to give up the search for the mysterious block of apartment dwellings which she yearned desperately to see—but after another twenty minutes she found herself wandering aimlessly on a traffic-wracked street she was sure she'd never seen before—Via di Tiberio—and felt again a sensation of panic, that she was lost, or near-lost, in the very vicinity of her hotel. And it was strange to her, and unnerving, to be alone in this foreign place.

Crossing a particularly uneven cobblestone street, narrowly avoiding being struck by dark-helmeted motorcyclists rushing two abreast, Alexis lost her balance and tripped in her elegant new sandals—she turned her ankle, winced with pain—"Oh! Oh help me"—these words of childish appeal came unbidden—but luckily she hadn't sprained the ankle. Her heart beat as if she were in the presence of danger and her face smarted with perspiration. She thought *This is my punishment now. For who I am. But I won't give up!*

For another half hour in the fetid heat she continued her quixotic search—she was dogged, desperate—limping—but could not find, in these mostly commercial backstreets intersecting with the Via di Ripetta, anything resembling the block of apartment buildings with the wonderful jumble of rooftops and the quaint faded colors like peeling walls in Venice, that she and David had seen from their balcony. Another time she stumbled upon the first row of buildings she'd seen—on a nameless little street—an entire block of abandoned and shuttered dwellings, clearly slated for demolition. The dark-skinned man so slowly eating dinner, the disheveled woman sprawled on her sofa watching TV, the seductive girl with the waist-long scintillate-black hair—where were they?

"There has to be some explanation . . ."

She shivered, she was feeling sick. Seeing now to her dismay: she was carrying only three articles—her handbag, and two shopping bags. She must have left the third bag in the taxi, containing the Dior necktie. It had cost 190 euros . . .

Shaken and exhausted she returned limping to the hotel just before 7 P.M. The sky was bright as daylight though partly massed with malevolent-looking storm clouds. In the hotel courtyard café there was no one but a middle-aged German couple and, flirting awkwardly with a young waitress who was clearly trying to humor him, a stocky slump-shouldered older man in a blue-striped sport shirt—he turned, and it was David.

"Alexis. Back so soon."

SPOTTED HYENAS:
A ROMANCE

Hello? Is someone—there?"

Her voice quavered like a cello that has been crudely, clumsily struck. She was upstairs in the bedroom and gripping something—the back of an upholstered chair—tight. Through the doorway about fifteen feet away, in a mesh of light and shadow, a figure appeared to be standing, hesitantly—in a sort of crouch—not her husband, who wasn't home yet—(she'd just glanced down into the driveway, and her husband's car wasn't there)—but a less stolidly-built man, with an oddly-shaped angular head, and sandy-silvery hair bristling at the nape of his neck. The stranger's face was shadowed but his eyes gleamed like small bits of mica. In the shock of the moment Mariana had the impression that his legs were slightly stunted—just perceptibly short for the rest of his body.

She was too surprised to be frightened—she was too surprised to think *But this is not possible! No one is upstairs in this house except me.*

Though keenly aware of each other neither Mariana nor the intruder moved.

How many seconds, or minutes—Mariana would not afterward know.

In time, there are curious interludes of *pause*—an eerie suspension of the normal flow of clock-time—during which one is struck dumb, breathless and paralyzed—awaiting release.

When Mariana drew breath to speak again—*Excuse me? Who are you?*—the words choked in her throat. For now she was beginning to be frightened. She was alone in the house—her husband had not yet returned home from work. She was a small-boned woman, of forty-three—not strong, and not very aggressive. She'd been a high-school athlete but her days of competitive physical exertion, the contention of one body against others in the exigency of the moment, had long since ceased. Apart from her husband she had very little physical contact with anyone any longer—and her contact with her husband was likely to be routine, predictable, and brief.

If she could move fast enough she could—maybe—slam the bedroom door—this was a door with a lock—(she thought: she'd never tried to lock it)—to keep out the intruder; or, she could run into the bathroom that opened off the bedroom—(which certainly had a door with a lock)—but then, she'd be trapped in the bathroom—(but if she remained in the bedroom, where she was now, she would be trapped also). But—could she force herself to step forward, in the direction of the intruder, and seize the doorknob to shut the door? And—if the intruder grabbed the door, to prevent her? Or—grabbed her? Swiftly her brain was working with the desperation of a brain whose oxygen is being depleted; but she could not move—she could not breathe. As in the corridor so intimately close the shadowy male figure stood also unmoving—poised as if about to leap—his head turned to the side as if he were *listening at* her—*sniffing* her—though not yet confronting her. He appeared to be waiting—for what? Mariana's voice? Mariana's scream?

She couldn't see his face but she was beginning to be aware of his quickened breath—a harsh animal-panting.

And she could smell him—an acrid animal-smell, that made her feel faint.

This is no accident. He has come for me. But—who is he . . .

Outside, a vehicle approached the house—a flare of headlights lifted to the bedroom windows—for suddenly it was dusk. There came Mariana's husband in his steel-colored Land Rover elevated from the pavement like a military vehicle. In that instant, as if released from a spell, now alert and alarmed, the male figure in the corridor turned and hurried away—limping? The clear, curious thought came to Mariana—*Oh! something is wrong with his hind leg.*

Downstairs, her husband called to her—"Hello! I'm home."

It was a familiar pronouncement, and did not inevitably require a reply. Though often Mariana called down—"Hello!"—or, in a tone of wifely welcome—"Hi! I'll be right down." By the time Mariana descended the stairs, and entered the kitchen, Pearce might have left the room for another part of the house and on a bench by the side door his overcoat would have been flung, for Mariana to pick up and hang in the hall closet.

They had been married for nineteen years. Marital customs spontaneously created at the outset of the marriage prevailed in somewhat attenuated if not useless forms. In a voice of forced casualness Mariana said, "Pearce—did you see anyone outside? Leaving our house? In the driveway?"

"Who?"

Pearce was frowning at Mariana as if she'd interrupted his line of thinking. In his hands was the Italian leather attaché case she'd bought for him, for a recent birthday, to replace an identical attaché case she'd bought for him years before.

"Someone—a person—a stranger—no one we know . . . He was

just . . . I didn't . . ." Mariana paused, trying to catch her breath. By nature she was not an excitable woman, still less was she a woman inclined to hysteria; she did not imagine things, and took some pride, as a woman, in resisting extremes of emotion. Had she had a genuinely upsetting experience just a few minutes ago, or had it been wholly—imagined?

For now it seemed to her in the cheerily-lit kitchen that was like a glossy photograph of a kitchen, among pale-peach-colored counters, a dark-orange floor of Mexican tiles, a massive cook's stove and a massive Sub-Zero unit with *faux*-cherrywood doors, that she'd probably just imagined the intruder upstairs. Some trick of the meshed shadow and sunlight just outside the bedroom. Whatever the figure had been, it had vanished with no sound like a dream rudely awakened by a slamming door. The new, curious thought came to Mariana *The territory isn't large enough for two males of the identical sub-species.*

Pearce was regarding her with a commingled expression of concern and impatience.

"What do you mean—did I 'see' someone? Was someone here? At the door? I didn't see any car leave, if that's what you mean." Pearce paused in the smiling way of a seasoned lawyer about to deliver a *coup de grâce.* "Who did you expect me to see?"

Pearce was a lawyer by nature as well as by training: he carried with him a cloud of excited contentiousness like a concentration of stinging gnats. As a young man he'd been very attractive, with a sort of blond-Viking swagger—at least, Mariana seemed to recall being attracted to Pearce Shutt as a young man; now, in his early fifties, Pearce had become heavy-set, pear-shaped, with a sulky jowly face like a late Roman emperor and glaring deep-set eyes in which there gleamed a remnant of his boyish self, as in a slow-fading TV face. Pearce had been a competitive tennis player not so long ago—a trophy winner in the annual Crescent Lake Country Club tournament—an enthusiastic "sportsman"—deer-hunting in Michigan, trout-fishing in Colorado and bone-fishing in the Florida keys. After thirteen years at Extol Pharmaceuticals he'd recently been promoted to chief legal counsel—Pearce's particular expertise was defending the corporation against a flood of lawsuits involving the prescription antidepressant Excelsior, now the preeminent psychotropic drug on the American market.

Pearce's argument was that a certain percentage of depressed individuals will commit suicide whether they take medication or not. In courtrooms across the country he argued with faultless logic that deceased users of Excelsior were suicidal before beginning medication—otherwise, the medication would not have been prescribed for them. *Depressed individuals are by definition at risk for suicide, and only depressed individuals commit suicide; therefore, if Excelsior is prescribed for individuals who are severely depressed, and at risk for suicide, these individuals may commit suicide. But Excelsior is not the cause of the suicide, and Extol Pharmaceuticals cannot be liable.*

"Well? Who did you expect to see?"

Mariana had no idea what her husband was asking her. Her heart was beating quickly and her sensitive nostrils were still pinched from the harsh acrid animal-smell of the shadowy stranger in the upstairs hall. Stammering she said:

"I don't—didn't—expect to see anyone . . . I think it must have been a mistake. He'd come to the wrong address with some sort of"—Mariana's almond eyes widened with a sort of reckless innocence like the eyes of a child who has just discovered the possibility of inventing "truth"—"package like UPS. But not UPS—some other service."

"Yes? What other 'service'?"

"I—I don't know . . ."

"But he didn't 'deliver' anything, did he? Where is the package?"

"Package?"

Abruptly then as often he did, Pearce lost interest in interrogating

Mariana, as a predator loses interest in pursuing prey because the prey is revealed to be scrawny, elderly, or diseased, or because the predator isn't really hungry. With a mirthful knowing laugh—(but what was it that Pearce *knew*, Mariana wondered, that so unnerved her?—this was one of Pearce Shutt's mannerisms)—he brushed past her to the glass-front cupboard where liquor was kept. It was 7:28 P.M.: Pearce's first meeting at corporate headquarters in East Orange, New Jersey, had been at 7:45 A.M.; he would pour himself a glass of his favorite bourbon, seize a handful of Brazil nuts, and settle into his black leather La-Z-Boy chair in the TV room to watch news on three channels simultaneously until Mariana summoned him to dinner at which time Pearce would rub his hands zestfully together and mutter, with an air of just barely concealed impatience, yet boyishly, cheerily: "Well! Good! *I'm* starving."

Upstairs in the large house the rooms were empty—emptier than usual it seemed—no intruder. Of course, there could not have been an intruder. Mariana knew.

Yet the faint acrid sweat-smell of—someone, something—a male body at the height of arousal—remained in the corridor outside the bedroom . . . Pearce took not the slightest notice of it and so Mariana was left to conclude that she was imagining it, too.

A weekday evening like any other, Mariana thought.

So lonely!

*

And then, in the early evening of the following day, when Mariana was returning home from grocery shopping, she saw something moving in the dense shrubbery beside the driveway—a deer? a large dog? In the headlights of her car there was a flash of glaring eyes and swiftly then the creature turned, and was gone.

"Oh! God . . ."

Mariana would have liked to think it had been a deer—just a

white-tailed deer—there were many deer in Crescent Lake Woods . . .
Mariana didn't want to think that a creature of that size might be a
neighbor's dog, or a stray dog, wandering on their property.

Possibly, the creature could be a coyote. There were coyotes in this
part of northern New Jersey. Less likely, a wolf.

Only the rear of the Shutts' three-acre property was fenced. The
front was open to the road, though the house itself was some distance
from the road, at the end of a long circular driveway and near-invisible
from the mailbox.

And the house was dark!—darkened. Another time, Mariana had
driven away without having left even a single light on, as she'd driven
away without turning on the elaborate and expensive "security" system
that Pearce had had installed. If Pearce knew, he'd have reprimanded
her. *If the house is broken into, if valuable things are stolen, and the security
hadn't been turned on, the insurance company will refuse to pay us. Do you
realize what this could cost us . . .*

Mariana continued along the driveway. The headlights of her car illuminated the most harmless and familiar sights—the desiccated rem-
nants of flowerbeds, skeletal rosebushes, several leafless birch trees and
a swath of evergreens—whatever the creature was, it had vanished—
but no—there it was!—in the shrubbery at the garage—another time
came a flash of glassy-glaring eyes, predator-eyes, as the creature vanished into the shadows behind the garage.

Mariana wondered if it was frightened by the car, or—wanting to
hide from her, to prepare for an attack.

A dog-like creature, of the size of a German shepherd—its fur
seemed to be sand-colored, dark-mottled as if soiled—its ears pricked
up though oddly rounded, unlike a dog's ears. Mariana had the impression that the creature was oddly *hunched-over*—a primate of some
sort—like a baboon . . .

Panicked she thought *How will I get out of the car!*

She didn't want to turn the car around and flee—take refuge in a neighbor's house—like a silly, hysterical woman. Still less did she want to drive back into town where she had women friends, or call Pearce on her cell phone and arrange to meet him somewhere—these possibilities seemed excessive, unwarranted.

Pearce would have said *Call the police! 911! If anyone tries to break in or threatens you.*

"No one is threatening me. I am all right."

Adrenaline flooded her veins. All of her senses were aroused, alert to the point of pain. She knew herself observed from the dense tangled shrubbery at the side of the garage though she couldn't see the creature's eyes.

Tawny-golden eyes, they'd been. Not-human eyes.

For eleven of the nineteen years of their marriage Mariana and Pearce Shutt had lived in this large attractive pale-gray stone-and-stucco house—described by the architect as *French Provincial/contemporary*—set back from Crescent Lake Drive in a cul-de-sac, with frontage on Crescent Lake. It was the sort of house that corporation lawyers like Pearce Shutt lived in, as the truly large custom-designed "estates" in this affluent area of rural/suburban New Jersey were owned by corporation executives. They had no children—there hadn't been a time Pearce judged to be the absolutely right time in his career for the distraction of children—and so the house seemed to Mariana disproportionately large like a house in a malevolent fairy tale, subtly taunting, mocking its inhabitants.

At the sides and the rear of the house were many shrubs and tall trees and weather-ravaged flowerbeds—at the edge of the property, a deciduous woods bordering the lake—the creature could be lurking in any number of places, invisible. His—its—coat was spotted, soiled-looking—perfect camouflage. The property was fenced off at the rear to keep out marauding deer but frequently it happened that deer were sighted grazing on the lawn, having found a way through the fence, so the rear of the house certainly wasn't protected from intruders.

Dusk had come quickly on this grim November day—by late afternoon the earth had darkened, only the sky remained relatively light—riddled with clouds like grimacing mouths. Mariana would ordinarily have parked her car in the circle drive at the front of the house, where a door led directly into the kitchen; now, she thought she should park inside the garage, and shut the garage doors, before she left the protection of the car and entered the house. *It* would not follow her into the garage—would it?

The garage was large enough for three vehicles. Pearce had instructed Mariana numerous times to keep all the doors shut, even if she was just going out for an hour or so—it wasn't good to send a signal to any perspective burglar or home invader that no one was home in a house in Crescent Lake Woods where the minimum price for homes was in the area of two million dollars. Of course, Mariana often forgot, especially during the day; and so now one of the garage doors was up—(on Mariana's side of the garage)—and the other down—(on Pearce's side of the garage)—and she could have no idea whether the creature was already in the garage, having trotted ahead of her.

For the garage was so large, and its corners so shadowed; there was a phalanx of trash cans and recycling barrels; there were stacks of cardboard boxes, gardening tools, miscellaneous pieces of furniture; the wily creature could hide behind any of these, and Mariana wouldn't know until it was too late—until she left the protection of her car.

And the light inside the garage, emitted from bare bulbs—if you looked directly at this light, it was blinding; otherwise the bulbs cast a grudging sort of illumination, as if through gauze.

Slowly Mariana drove her car into the garage. Unlike Pearce's steel-colored Land Rover, Mariana's vehicle was slender, compact. She was prepared to back up swiftly if she saw something moving inside the garage. More than once she'd scraped the right-hand side of her car driving the car inside the garage—as Pearce insisted she do—and she dreaded this happening now, in this tense situation. She could see nothing in the garage—nothing that signaled danger—but in the rearview mirror there was only a shadowy haze like a TV screen gone dead—just outside the garage there appeared to be nothing at all.

Mariana was biting her lower lip. She'd begun to perspire inside her clothes.

She was calculating: the door that led into the back hall of the house was only a few yards away, directly in front of her car. She hadn't locked the door, she supposed—Pearce would have chided her, if he'd known—but often she forgot—or didn't think it was so very important; now, she could make a dash for the door and get it open and get inside within a few seconds; the groceries she would leave in the car trunk. Once she believed the car was inside the garage she punched the remote control to lower the garage door and at once there came a rattling thudding noise louder and more jarring than she expected, like hammers striking the roof of her car.

Narrowly the descending door missed the rear bumper and trunk of Mariana's car. Thank God! She'd done this correctly.

Mariana turned off the car motor. The sudden silence was unnerving.

Either she was alone in the garage now, in her car; or, the creature had slipped into the garage and was inside the garage with her.

Either she was safe. Or she was in danger.

How long should she wait? A predator could wait for a very long time for such is the predator's nature.

"I will. I will do it. I will be all right."

Mariana took hold of the car door handle. She was calm, determined. *He is in here with me. He is observing me. He has come for me.* She knew she must show no sign of fear, nor even of being aware of the presence in the garage; if there was a presence in the garage. She would behave as if she believed herself safe, alone—giving the predator no reason to rush at her—then opening her car door swiftly and scrambling out of the car and running to the back door where her slippery fingers fumbled at the doorknob but managed to open it—for, fortunately, the door was *unlocked*, as she'd left it.

Inside the house, Mariana shut the door quickly. She threw the bolt, and was safe. Relief flooded her veins, she felt close to fainting.

She would leave the groceries for later. When Pearce returned home she would return to the garage without his noticing, for certainly Pearce took little notice of what Mariana did while preparing dinner. She would tell him nothing of what had happened to her.

Safe inside the house! Inside the house! Thinking *So long as the door is locked, he can't follow.*

"WHY SO MANY LIGHTS, Mariana?"

"Because—I'm welcoming my husband home."

In a gesture of extravagance that was wholly unlike her, Mariana had switched on outside lights: lights at the front door, and at the kitchen door; floodlights on the roof of the garage; lights in the courtyard and lights illuminating the fountain in the pond and lights along the driveway to the road. Even the deck lights were ablaze, and floodlights at the rear of the house, not visible from the driveway.

With a giddy laugh Mariana came to her frowning husband, to kiss his cheek that was cold from outdoors. Pearce was too startled to kiss Mariana in return, or to embrace her; nor did Mariana embrace him, in the rough-textured dark woolen overcoat he hadn't yet unbuttoned and flung off.

And that night preparing for bed Mariana stared from the bedroom window down at the lawn that was sheathed in darkness now, and indecipherable. Her breath steamed the cool windowpane as she leaned near. Was there—something below? She stared until her eyes blurred with moisture but saw nothing, no one.

"Mariana? Where the hell are you? Come to bed."

"Yes! I'm coming."

" . . . at least, turn out the light."

Mariana turned out the light.

It was like Mariana to linger in the bathroom, before joining Pearce in bed. Often, by the time she came to bed, Pearce had fallen into a heavy sleep.

Though the bed was an enormous king-sized bed yet Pearce took up most of it, a dark hulk amid the bedclothes. Like a beached sea lion he snuffled, snorted, whinnied in his sleep; often he flung his legs about; by the morning he would have pulled out most of the bed-clothes, dragging them to his side of the bed; his face loomed like a large moon, riddled and rippled. In his sleep he frowned, grimaced, and often muttered—words Mariana couldn't decipher except to recognize as *legalese*.

Her poor husband! Litigator by day, litigator by night. Yet Pearce Shutt was so very successful, you had to concede that the effort of his professional life was worth it. *In law, winning is all. Coming in second is not an option.*

So Pearce often observed. This was not boastfulness but fact.

At the bedside Mariana heard a sound somewhere in the house—a creaking floorboard? a stealthy indrawn breath? Cautiously she went into the corridor—the carpet beneath her bare feet was thick, consoling—she made not the slightest sound, she was certain—there was a guest room at the end of the corridor—in the doorway she stood and saw in the shadowy interior—was it *him*?—or *it*?—an upright creature, on hind legs—no, it was a man—a man with an angular head, a snouted face—covered in something like fur, and the fur was sand-colored and speckled—spotted—the ears were oddly rounded though yet pricked-up, alert—his very fur shivered—an electric sort of life thrummed through his limbs that were lean but hard-muscled as his body was lean, angular, tense. Though Mariana stood less than ten feet away from him the creature—the man—didn't seem to be aware of her—unless he was pretending not to be aware of her; in a semi-crouch he stood beside a bookcase, and in his right hand he held a book, which he now quietly closed and replaced on the shelf.

The nape of his neck was dense and springy with fur—sandy-silvery-speckled fur—Mariana felt a sudden powerful urge to reach out and stroke that fur—and he seemed to be sniffing rapidly—sniffing *her*—though not turning to confront her, strangely—as a predator would have done by now. Mariana caught just a glimpse of his face, glittery mica-eyes veiled from her as if in—shyness?—slyness?—subterfuge?

He has come for me—has he?

Then, abruptly the figure was gone.

Mariana switched on the light but saw no one, nothing—the guest room was undisturbed, or seemed so; not only had the windows not been opened, but the curtains hadn't been disturbed; a small woven rug laid upon the carpet appeared to be untouched, though there were indentations—footprints, pawprints?—in the woven fabric. In the bookcase a single book jutted out—a paperback copy of Darwin's *Origin of Species*.

This had been one of Mariana's cherished books, from her undergraduate years at the University of Pennsylvania. She'd been a biology major—she'd intended to continue her studies in graduate school and get a Ph.D.—for the phenomenon of organic life fascinated her, with its myriad manifestations and seemingly inexhaustible permutations. She'd hoped to pursue a course of study in environmental biology though she'd been somewhat daunted by the fierce and fractious competition from pre-med students in required courses like organic chemistry and by the newer, computational sciences like molecular biology that had seemed to reduce the mystery of *animal life* to its most elemental and seemingly lifeless components . . . And there was the disappointment of her first year in graduate school, also at Penn, that had ended abruptly.

The paperback *Origin of Species* was still warm, as if the furry man had been breathing on it. There was a smell—a distinct, acrid, animal smell—like the smell of the other evening—in the guest room.

In a lowered voice Mariana spoke urgently, pleadingly—"Who are you? What do you want? Why—now?"

At the far end of the corridor, her husband slept in their bed, oblivious. And in this room, there was no one to hear.

*

"You will 'feel' the drill—and some 'tingling,' Mrs. Shutt—but at a distance. It will be like hearing voices in another room—when you can't distinguish individual words."

Dr. Digges's warm brown eyes, above the surgical mask that covered his mouth and nose, exuded an air of genial paternal authority.

Mariana was at the dentist's, for a complicated and costly dental-surgical procedure involving crowns on several upper front teeth. Dr. Digges had suggested both nitrous oxide—"laughing gas"—and novacaine; the first, to prepare her for the needle injecting novacaine into her gum, as the novacaine prepared her for enduring a procedure that would require as long as ninety minutes.

Dentistry for Cowards! was Dr. Digges's specialty. Mariana was grateful for as much anesthetic as she could get. Her pain threshold was not high. She was not a stoic. Even with nitrous oxide she was likely to be tense, anxious. Nor did she laugh. Not once, in the past, in Dr. Digges's chair, under the influence of nitrous oxide, had she even come close to laughing.

Dr. Digges's assistant Felipa, a buxom child-sized young woman with a brightly made-up face, said sweetly, "Mrs. Shutt, I will be tipping you back just a bit."

The dentist's chair was tipped back at a sharper angle than Mariana recalled. Her feet were raised, her head was lowered. Blood rushed to her brain. When Felipa placed the mask on Mariana's lower face, to administer the nitrous oxide, Mariana instinctively stiffened as if frightened to breathe deeply and give herself over to the curious, oddly distancing and depersonalizing narcotic.

She found herself staring at a glossy travel photograph on the ceiling directly over her head. The rugged coastline of the Greek island Santorini.

Dr. Digges's office was filled with brightly colored photographs of the dentist's numerous trips. Nowhere to look that wasn't glossy-gorgeous like a tourist's brochure: the Eiffel Tower, a Venetian canal, Roman ruins, the Acropolis, the Tower of London. The cliffs of Santorini against a ceramic-blue sky were jagged like teeth—like incisors—primitive—cruel-seeming—yet beautiful, romantic—Mariana stared, and her senses seemed to float—a wonderful airiness suffused her veins.

She smiled. Amid the cliffs of Santorini were wolf-like creatures, lean, lithe, just barely visible—but visible—their eyes glittering like mica and their tongues lolling as they trotted singly, in pairs, and in a small furry-speckled pack; some were adults, and some were cubs with the upright rounded ears and round eyes of children's stuffed toys.

Mariana must have smiled. She must have laughed aloud.

Felipa said, "Mrs. Shutt, this is good! Good to relax. Would you like your magazine? Dr. Digges is with another patient and will be a few minutes."

National Geographic had slipped from Mariana's fingers to the floor. Felipa picked it up and handed it to Mariana who'd been reading an article about a strange ritual—young Chinese women "betrothed" to dead men—for what bizarre reason, Mariana couldn't comprehend.

Why would one want to marry a dead man? Was it to be spared marrying a living man? Could one inherit property if a husband was already dead at the time of the wedding? Did the young Chinese brides want to be married to dead men or was this custom the wish of their families? And what of the "groom's" family? Mariana was trying to make sense of columns of print but her thoughts flew in all directions, her mouth kept smiling, she thought it was just so— funny . . . She began laughing as if she were being tickled though the gas—the nitrous oxide—hadn't yet begun—had it?—even as Felipa took the magazine from her fingers as it was about to fall to the floor again—"Mrs. Shutt? Are you sleepy?" Mariana stumbled on steps she hadn't seen—her eyes were shut—she was dazed, dizzy—falling, and clutching at something—someone. She'd fallen to her knees—her hands, and her knees—scrambling amid rocks . . . The face looming above her was one she knew well though she hadn't seen it in a very long time—a boyish face, somber and lean-cheeked, with a freckled skin and prominent ears.

" 'Robb Gelder.' "

"Who? Mrs. Shutt?"

Robb Gelder! It was he who'd appeared in Mariana's house, and somehow, too, he was the creature who'd frightened her when she'd returned home—*Robb Gelder*—whom Mariana hadn't seen in more than twenty years . . .

Mariana was astonished. Mariana gripped the arms of the dentist's chair to keep from falling out. In a faint wondering voice she said:

"A man I knew, Felipa. A young man. I mean—at the time. He was young at the time. But—I was younger."

So long ago! Mariana would have thought she'd forgotten Robb Gelder as surely Robb Gelder had forgotten her.

She'd known Gelder as a graduate student in the Ph.D. program in biology at Penn—he'd been an assistant in the lab to which Mariana had been assigned, under the direction of a senior professor renowned in his field of biological research and soon to win a Nobel Prize. Mariana had been intimidated by the renowned professor who'd scarcely acknowledged her presence except to stare at her from time to time as if he had no idea who she was.

In the lab, Mariana had reported to Robb Gelder. It was Gelder who oversaw the experimental work of the younger graduate students and Gelder upon whom Mariana had come to depend more than she would have liked.

She asked Felipa what did it mean—"If you see someone who isn't there?"

"Like a ghost, Mrs. Shutt?"

A ghost? Could Robb Gelder be a *ghost?* Mariana didn't want to think so.

"Oh no—he didn't seem like a ghost. He didn't behave like a ghost. I'm sure he wasn't a ghost. He was much more solid. He left footprints, he had a—smell . . ." Mariana had begun to shiver, recalling.

"Mrs. Shutt, could be he died. And his ghost was summoning you."

Felipa spoke somberly, as one who'd had some experience with ghosts.

"Oh, but—I don't think . . . Robb Gelder is too young to die."

"Mrs. Shutt, nobody is too young to die."

Rebuked, Mariana could think of no reply. The airy lightness that had permeated her brain—had been making her laugh—turned cold suddenly. *Nobody is too young to die!*

This was true of course. This was absolutely irrefutably true.

As if she'd spoken too harshly Felipa relented, "Could be he's having some bad time, Mrs. Shutt, in his life, and he's thinking of you—like sending a prayer."

Felipa spoke in a gravely poetic way that was very touching.

"I hope Robb isn't—hurt. He would still be young . . . fairly young."

In fact Robb Gelder had been a slightly older graduate student, as Mariana recalled. In his late twenties perhaps, when Mariana had known him. Now he would be in his late forties—at least Pearce's age. Mariana felt a pang in her chest at the prospect of seeing him again.

Felipa asked, "This is a man, Mrs. Shutt? Yes? Someone—close to you?"

Mariana felt her face burn. An airy sort of laughter gripped her, like a swarm of small moths.

Though Mariana was forty-three, she did not feel as if she were forty-three. She did not even feel as if she were twenty-three. (She'd been twenty-one when she'd known Robb Gelder, in her brief and not very happy single year in graduate school.) Absurd, to be thinking of Robb Gelder! Feeling such emotion for a man she hadn't seen in twenty-two years, and knew nothing about. It wasn't that they'd lost contact with each other—they'd never really been *in contact* with each other.

Mariana had been the youngest and most inexperienced individual in the biology lab, and one of only two women. She'd felt like a swimmer caught in a riptide—often she couldn't understand what was being presented in the most matter-of-fact way, and her own presentations were nightmare occasions for her, fraught with anxiety and dread. She'd had the desperate thought that her professors, who were all men, had sized her up within the first week or two, were not impressed and were not about to change their minds.

Though he'd been enormously busy with his own research, Robb Gelder had taken time to meet with Mariana. She'd had difficulty with her experiments—he'd tried to guide her through them. He'd been supportive, patient, kind. At times, his patience had seemed strained—but he'd never spoken sarcastically to her. Unlike the other male graduate students, he'd never made a sexist remark, of which Mariana was aware. He hadn't been a particularly attractive individual, superficially—often he was unshaven, and his skin was lumpy and blemished; his hair was lank, sand-colored, and likely to be dirty; his clothes were rumpled, and likely to be dirty; when harassed and anxious, he smelled of his body. Addressing the lab he spoke in a stiff, self-conscious manner that undermined the originality and intelligence of what he had to say; a sharp question from the senior professor who headed the lab threw him into confusion, though he knew the answer perfectly well; at his most nervous he breathed through his mouth, and spoke haltingly as if to forestall a stammer. But his eyes were greenish-hazel, and seemed to Mariana beautiful.

She hadn't fallen in love with Robb Gelder, she was certain!—there were other men she found much more attractive, who were attracted to her. One of these was Pearce Shutt.

Abruptly in the spring of her first year Mariana's graduate studies were terminated. She could not have been surprised when her advisor summoned her to speak with him, to inform her that the graduate committee wasn't recommending that she continue in the program; yet she'd been crushed, terribly hurt. For all that she'd known she was having trouble, and couldn't seem to compete with other graduate students, she'd somehow hoped that—she'd wanted to hope that—some allowance might be made for her, because she'd tried so very hard; some sort of suspended judgment . . . But in an instant in her advisor's office, as the older man stared coldly at her as if waiting for her to leave, she'd felt that all she had worked to establish—the days, weeks, months of assiduously studying, her experimental work and her effort of presenting herself publicly—being *positive, feminine, sweet*—had been swept aside like the petals of a Japanese tulip tree in a violent rainstorm.

She'd left her advisor's office stunned as if the man had slapped her face. She would come to think that he'd spoken to her in this way because she was a woman—an attractive young woman with long thick pale-blond hair to her shoulders, who didn't dress like the other female graduate students in tattered jeans and pullovers; men didn't want to take her seriously. Nor did women scientists want to take her seriously. There was, in the most seemingly neutral of circumstances, a distinct sex-consciousness, a prevailing sexual rivalry. For all of biology—all of *life*—was about sex: sexual attraction, sexual intercourse, reproduction of the species. That was all that life *was*.

In the corridor of the biology building she'd encountered Robb Gelder and before Gelder could speak—even as he smiled at her, and prepared to say hello—Mariana told him bluntly that she'd been dropped from the program. She wouldn't be working with him that summer—(as she'd planned)—and she wouldn't be returning in the fall. In Gelder's face she saw—she would fix upon this, afterward—not quite so much surprise as she might have expected to see. She thought *Of course! He's one of them.*

He'd been consulted about her. He'd been frank about her. He hadn't shielded her from the others. In a sudden fury Mariana cut him off as he was expressing sympathy for her, suggesting that maybe she could try another school, or maybe, if she wanted to teach biology, she could enroll in the school of education and get a teaching degree, she'd interrupted saying that really she didn't care, she'd come to dislike the program at Penn, she'd come to almost dislike science, the life of a scientist, if the scientists at Penn were representative. Robb Gelder stared at her in surprise as she said, with a bitter twist of her mouth, "Well— I'm going to be engaged anyway. I'll be getting married and moving away from here. This is really for the best."

Rudely she'd turned away from Gelder before he could say anything further. She wasn't hurt so much as she was angry, furious. She hadn't wanted to see Robb Gelder again. He'd been her only friend yet she felt that she hated him, for he'd betrayed her—he hadn't helped

her, and so he'd betrayed her. It was a male-female thing, a sex-thing.
She was the weaker of the two, it had been incumbent upon him to
help *her*—and he had not. She never wanted to see Robb Gelder again,
nor had she wanted to think about him. She would seek out men like
Pearce Shutt who took for granted their superior strength, and would
protect her.

It wasn't equality Mariana wanted—except nominally. In truth it
was dependency, and an acknowledgment of dependency. A woman is
loved precisely because the man is strong enough to love her. A man
who was a woman's equal would be a weak sort of man—because he
was her equal.

Robb Gelder hadn't tried to contact Mariana after their final en-
counter. All that had been between them had vanished as if it had
never been. She'd become engaged to Pearce Shutt, and she'd married Pearce Shutt, and hadn't given a thought to Robb Gelder except
when she'd seen references to his work in the newspaper—in the *New
York Times* science section she'd read about the Gelder experiments
involving animal behavior and animal "languages" and she'd felt a pang
of something like envy, and regret; but only in passing. Once, Pearce
said, "What on earth are you reading, Mariana?"—curious that Mariana was reading anything in the paper with such concentration; and
Mariana told him she was reading about "animal communication"—a
series of experiments conducted by a biologist she'd known in graduate
school.

Pearce asked to see the paper, laid it down beside his TV chair and
never again touched it so far as Mariana knew.

" 'Robb Gelder.' He can't not be alive."

Merely out of curiosity Mariana looked up *Robb Gelder* on the Internet. She had no intention of contacting him. It was a surprise—a
pleasant surprise—to discover that Robb Gelder had had so produc-
tive a career: after getting his Ph.D. from Penn he'd had a post-doc

appointment at UC–Berkeley; he'd taught at UC–San Diego, the University of Chicago, and Cambridge University (England); he'd had countless fellowships, awards, and grants from the National Science Foundation, and elsewhere; he'd spent years in Africa, studying the behavior of "social carnivores"; at the present time he was a senior associate at the Bangor Institute for Advanced Study in Maine where he headed the Bangor Field Station for the Study of Ecology and Animal Behavior. He'd become a specialist in spotted hyenas.

Spotted hyenas! These were native to Africa. Yet, when Mariana researched *spotted hyenas* on the Internet, she saw that they closely resembled the creature she'd seen in the shadows outside her house.

She thought *Robb has been thinking of me. That's it!*

She sent an e-mail to Robb Gelder at the Bangor Institute asking if he recalled her, saying she was traveling to Bangor soon to visit a relative, and would like very much to visit his famous hyena farm.

Almost immediately she received an e-mail reply—

> Dear Mariana—
>
>   Please come to Bangor whenever you can. I will take you on a tour of my spotted hyenas. I think you will find them beautiful animals that have been ignorantly disparaged and "demonized" by humankind. Of course I remember you! In fact—it's very strange—I was thinking of you just the other day—not sure why.
>   Sincerely,
>   Robb Gelder

Gelder set up dates for Mariana to choose, and she chose. She was intrigued by her own brashness, which wasn't like her; and when she told Pearce that she was going away for a day or two, not asking his permission but simply telling him, she was surprised at her own equanimity in the face of his astonished disapproval.

"You're going away? To Maine? Without telling me? To see a cousin?—who is this cousin? Have I met her?"

Yes, Mariana said. He'd met her cousin Valerie a long time ago—at their wedding.

"Don't you remember, Pearce? You said you'd liked her—you thought she was 'sensible.'"

Pearce frowned. Pearce was not one to readily admit that he'd forgotten anyone, or anything; he could not bring himself to admit that he didn't remember Mariana's cousin Valerie.

"I didn't know that you have relatives in Maine."

"I don't have 'relatives' in Maine—just Valerie. She's divorced, and she teaches high school biology, and she's just recovering from breast cancer surgery, and I think I should go see her. For just a day or two."

The syllables *breast cancer surgery* were subtly repellent to Pearce, she could see. He asked why would Mariana want to visit her, if she scarcely knew her—"Does she want you to come?"

"Of course she wants me. She invited me."

"But why?"

Mariana was beginning to feel anxious, agitated—as if her husband were in fact mocking her relationship with a cherished girl cousin. *Of course* men were doubtful of such intimate bonds since they had so few themselves . . .

"Because Valerie is lonely. She needs me. She says—'I'm thinking of you, Mariana. Please come see me.'"

To this, Pearce could make no reply. *Breast cancer surgery* had unmanned him.

Mariana kissed her husband's cheek that was hot with indignant blood. She would be back, she promised, by Thursday—or Friday at the latest. And she would call.

"You'll 'call'! Isn't that thoughtful of my wife."

With bitter amusement Pearce spoke as if knowing—suspecting—

that *my wife* would betray him. But in what way, he could have no idea.

Of course I remember you! In fact—it's very strange—I was thinking of you just the other day.

Alone—it was the longest trip by car she'd ever undertaken alone—Mariana drove to Bangor, Maine. She stayed overnight in a motel somewhere in Massachusetts, her dreams were confused, tumultuous, rife with exertion. In dazzling bright November sunshine she made her way to the Bangor Institute for Advanced Study which was two miles north and east of Bangor and there she was directed another mile along a hilly rural road to Professor Gelder's field station—low-lying buildings, chain-link enclosures, several pickups and vans and unmistakably in the air a pungent odor of animal urine.

A small woman with a wizened face came trotting to her, with a smile—"Mariana? Dr. Gelder is waiting for you. Come with me."

Mariana was thrilled. She believed this was the emotion she felt—excitement, anticipation—and not rather anxiety. She glanced about at the buildings in the cold autumn sunshine, the fenced-off enclosures, young assistants in jeans, hooded jackets, boots. The perky little woman with the wizened face was one of these young assistants who'd grown old in the service of Dr. Gelder's animal labs.

How strong, the animal-odor! Mariana's nostrils pinched. Was she the only one who noticed it?—of course, the others were accustomed to the smell. So this was the "field station"—an outdoor variant of a scientist's laboratory. Something like this might have been her life—her professional life—if she'd continued as a research biologist.

There came a low whooping cry—a greeting: "Mariana?" A man in a bulky jacket approached her at a trot—a man with a battered face, wind-whipped silvery-sand-colored hair—shyly smiling, his hand extended—"It's me—Robb."

Mariana stared at this middle-aged man—of course, this was Robb Gelder—her friend of twenty-two years ago . . . Boldly he'd taken her hand to shake it—she felt something strange about the hand—she saw that two fingers were missing.

"Oh, this? Sorry! A little accident I had a few years ago, in Africa."

Robb Gelder laughed as if the memory were something private, embarrassing and yet cherished.

"One of your spotted hyenas didn't tear off your fingers, did he?"

" 'She,' actually. Yes."

Mariana was trying to smile. The mood between them was exhilarating, jovial. She was conscious of her heart beating rapidly and a sensation very like a swoon coming over her, as if the earth had tilted beneath her feet.

Robb took Mariana's arm, as if in disbelief—was she real? He stared bluntly at her, and leaned close. Mariana could smell his breath—a meaty, earthy smell—a faint under-smell of decay like something over-ripe. Here was a middle-aged man with a creased face, a lopsided smile framing uneven stained teeth, in a woodsman's jacket festooned with zippers and pouches, mud-splattered trousers and boots. If Mariana had seen him on the street—would she have recognized him? Would she have wished to recognize him? How happy he was to see her, yet nervous, visibly tremulous, like one who can't believe his good luck. "I would know you anywhere, Mariana! You've changed very little."

Mariana laughed, drawing back from Robb Gelder just slightly; she wasn't accustomed to being so *stared-at*, so *concentrated upon*, and from someone so physically close to her, his breath in her face.

Physical closeness with her husband was very different. There were—still—intimacies of a kind between them, but Pearce was not very much aware of Mariana; wherever his mind was, it wasn't likely to be on *her*.

"I've changed entirely. I'm a married woman . . ."

"But—have you had children?"

"No. And you?"

Robb smiled, and Robb shrugged. He had three children, he said, now fully grown, adult—"Not in my life right now."

"And—your wife?"

" 'Wife'? No. Not for—a while."

A look of longing and loneliness came into the man's face. His stained teeth glistened. Mariana felt a swirl of vertigo—*This is why he has summoned me. He wants me, he's bereft.*

There was a curious childlike frankness about this man—this stranger—as if he weren't entirely accustomed to human contact, for he continued to stand just slightly too close to Mariana, and continued to stare at her. She had the uneasy idea that surreptitiously, Robb Gelder was *sniffing* her . . . His nose was of no extraordinary size but the prominent, dark nostrils contracted and expanded.

With a snap of his fingers Robb summoned the little wizened-face woman and sent her scuttling off to prepare coffee in his office. He would take his visitor on a tour of the field station and return to his office in about twenty minutes.

"So wonderful that you're here, Mariana! You've come . . . *here*."

Walking with Mariana, fingers gripping her upper arm as if he feared losing her, Robb asked her about her life since he'd seen her last at Penn—had she become a biology teacher?—had she continued her interest in science?—and what of her marriage, had she married a scientist? Mariana laughed at the thought of Pearce as a scientist—he hadn't the temperament, he certainly hadn't the patience—briefly she told Robb about Pearce in the only way Pearce could be summarized— "He's a litigator. He's chief counsel for Extol Pharmaceuticals. He's very successful." Mariana heard her own words with something like chagrin. *Successful!* How vulgar that sounded—if *success* mattered. "He's a very intelligent person—I mean, it's a certain sort of intelligence. He's a nice person . . ." Mariana paused. In fact, was Pearce a nice person?

"Did you—do you—regret not having children?"

A peculiar question to ask within minutes of their meeting! But Mariana understood the biologist's preoccupation with reproduction, genetics. Another woman would have been offended—Mariana answered frankly: "I might have regretted having children, with Pearce Shutt."

Robb nodded gravely. His fingers had not relinquished their grip on Mariana's upper arm.

They were approaching a series of enclosures, on a concrete walkway. Robb was telling her that the foremost spotted-hyena field station was at Berkeley: the Bangor field station was smaller, but in other respects the equivalent. Certainly, he and his assistants were as dedicated. Their ideas were as original. Mariana was having trouble concentrating as Robb spoke, feeling blood rush into her face—what had she confessed, to Robb Gelder? To a man she scarcely knew? *Might have regretted having children, with Pearce Shutt.*

The words had seemed to leap from her, impulsively. Not only had Mariana never spoken such words before in her life, she had never had such a thought until now.

"Here—here's Naxos and Troy."

The spotted hyenas froze in place, staring from about fifteen feet away. Their blunt snouted noses shifted and shivered and their mica-eyes glittered. The smell of animal urine was very strong here, almost overwhelming.

"Naxos? Come here."

The smaller of the two hyenas came forward, slowly. The larger, at the rear of the enclosure, remained unmoving, closely observing.

"Here's a visitor, Naxos—'Mariana.'"

The hyena inclined its head. Its rounded ears pricked. The rapid oscillations of the damp, dark nose were evident.

Robb had brought Mariana to the first of the chain-link enclosures, which contained just two spotted hyenas. The enclosure resembled a zoo cage open at the rear so that the hyenas had access to a larger, outdoor space.

Robb was cooing at the creature, poking his fingers through the wire mesh invitingly. Though Mariana made no move to approach the cage, Robb motioned for her to stay back—*he* would approach the cage; he'd stepped over a white stripe painted on the concrete, about eighteen inches from the chain-link fence which Mariana supposed to be a warning not to come any closer to the cage.

"Naxos is just a year old. I helped raise him—we're 'bonded.' Eh, Naxos? Good boy . . ."

Mariana held her breath as the dog-like creature approached Robb Gelder's extended fingers—three fingers and a stubby thumb were all that remained on Robb's right hand. Though the sharp stained teeth were bared, and the tongue lolled, and the eyes glowed and glittered like glass come coldly to life, the hyena lowered its head as if in deference to the man and allowed Robb to stroke it. The low, rounded rump quivered with mute animal pleasure.

"They're from the African savannah, originally. I mean—the clan. We established the spotted-hyena field station here in 1989 and it has continued ever since. Spotted hyenas reproduce reasonably well in captivity."

"It's a—he's—a beautiful creature . . ."

Mariana spoke with enthusiastic insincerity. Though the coarse silvery-tawny-spotted fur was in fact attractive and the intensity of the animal-stare suggested an almost human attentiveness. Mariana supposed you might fall under the hyena-spell even as the rank hyena-smell ceased to make your nostrils pinch. She held her breath hoping the animal wouldn't suddenly tear off her friend's hand.

"Thank you! Yes, some of us think so. No animal has quite the undeserved reputation as the hyena—the 'laughing hyena.' Jackals, vultures, any sort of scavenger—you'd think that people would be intelligent enough to realize that, in the ecological scheme of things, all creatures are 'equal'—all have 'equal' status. Without scavengers, without maggots—where would we *be*?"

Mariana tried to think. Where would we *be*?

In the voice of boyish earnestness Mariana recalled from their days at Penn, Robb told Mariana that he had fourteen spotted-hyena adults at the field station—seven females and seven males. There was an alpha female, and there was an alpha male. These were related hyenas, in a strict pack relationship. The clans were matriarchal—comprised of subgroups of mothers, daughters, and offspring; in the wild, adult males appeared as "immigrants" from other clans. What was exceptional in spotted hyenas was that the females were larger than the males, more aggressive and more dominant in social situations; the alpha female had dominance over the alpha male, and her offspring had dominance over the offspring of other females in the clan. All of the females mated and had offspring but the alpha-female offspring were dominant over the offspring of the other females.

"The most extraordinary feature of spotted hyenas is that the female external genitalia are 'masculinized'—the clitoris has evolved to a considerable 'pseudopenis'—and there is no external vagina. The female spotted hyena urinates, copulates, and gives birth through the clitoris."

Distracted by the dangerous animal on just the other side of the fence, tilting and bumping its head against Robb's maimed hand, now making a low soft grunting sound, Mariana wasn't sure she'd heard correctly. Clitoris? *Pseudopenis?*

Robb continued: "The female clitoris expands almost exactly like the male penis, and to the same approximate length. It isn't quite understood why. You would think that androgens are responsible—converted to testosterone at various stages in the hyena's development—but we haven't found evidence for this. When the female gives birth it's through the narrow, tunnel-like organ—the very tip of the clitoris—it can be a difficult birth sometimes." Robb spoke gravely as if he'd witnessed such difficult births upon more than one occasion.

Mariana shuddered. How awful! She remembered how, in the interstices of her schoolgirl fascination with biology, she'd been overwhelmed by the purposelessness of such facts of animal life.

She knew—Darwin's great theory of evolution was one of natural selection and the acquisition of random features of survival—no, not the acquisition, for that was the Lamarckian heresy—was it?—only just random, chance, purposelessness . . . A biologist like Robb Gelder would laugh at her if she uttered such words as *acquire, purpose*.

Possibly she'd been defeated by this principle, as by her advisor's chilly condescension. A woman more than a man is likely to believe in purpose in life, she must believe that she herself has some purpose—otherwise, how to endure?

"But it must be dangerous, working with these animals. Even if you've 'bonded' with them . . ."

"Well, yes. Mistakes are made. But we love our spotted hyenas here at the field station—it's exciting and exhilarating work. One day we will discover why, alone among the hyena species, the spotted hyena female is the one with the 'pseudopenis'—unless our colleagues at Berkeley discover why, first."

They walked on. Mariana noticed now that Robb was walking with a very slight limp, favoring his left leg. She didn't want to ask what might have happened to him.

"My limp? You've noticed?" Robb chuckled, stroking his left upper thigh. "This was an accident, really—a quintessential accident. Not carelessness. When the first of the hyenas arrived at the field station here . . ."

In an offhand voice he told an alarming tale meant to amuse as well as to impress. Mariana winced, hearing.

"Well—this is a mammalian species in which cubs have been observed to attack each other *at birth*."

Robb shook his head, smiling. Imparting such brutal information seemed to evoke in the biologist an air of admiration, even pride.

Mariana noted that her old friend's face was both freckled and pitted. His skin was coarser than she recalled, very likely from having been exposed to the African sun, and wind; the pores of his nose were riddled with minute bits of dirt like buckshot. And there was the meaty-smelling breath, an odor of earth, dried blood . . . And the greeny-hazel eyes now less distinct, behind wire-rimmed bifocal glasses. She found herself staring at him with a curious sort of tenderness.

He has summoned me here. This is why I am here. But why?

Robb was saying that he'd become interested in spotted-hyena research as a consequence of post-doc work he'd done at Berkeley in animal social behavior and reproduction—"Definitely, the spotted hyena is the most exciting animal to work with! Two of my close friends were drawn into monkey research and my wife—ex-wife—worked with marmosets—but those of us who work with spotted hyenas feel a special mission, I think. The spotted hyena has such a lurid, unmerited reputation—we want to redeem the species. For instance, in the eye of the credulous public, hyenas are perceived as 'cowardly'—'vicious'—inferior to lions, their predator-rivals—and this is wholly unmerited." Robb spoke vehemently, stroking his upper left thigh.

In the next enclosure several hyenas were trotting about excitedly, as if Naxos and Troy had subliminally alerted them to expect a visiting stranger. These were Mei-Mei, Cubbie, Baxter, Kimber, and Condoleezza. Robb summoned the little wizened-faced assistant to feed them—"It's almost lunchtime. We won't disturb their schedule by much." Of the several hyenas, the largest was clearly dominant over the others; this was Condoleezza the alpha female, Rob explained, who ate first while the others kept at a little distance pacing anxiously about and emitting low cries and whimpers. Mariana had to resist an impulse to hide her eyes—the hyena-feed was so brutal, so bizarrely sensuous, it had almost an erotic component; it was not at all pleasant to observe. Under what terrible circumstances, Mariana wondered, might *she* devour food in such a way?

She could not imagine. There were no such circumstances. She would rather starve, she thought. There are some acts a *human being* will not perform.

The little woman in denim jeans, bulky denim jacket and with a wool cap pulled low on her forehead, seemed to take a special pride in the hyenas, and in the rapacity of hyena appetite, glancing up at Mariana with a touchingly intimate smile. Robb said, "Mariana, this is Dana—she's been here at the station from the very first. We all go back a long time, Dana, don't we?"

Dana laughed a low, thrilled chuckle. Yes, they did!

Though Mariana had been a serious student of biology she had never worked with "social carnivores" and the feeding-spectacle unnerved her, for the meat Dana had pushed into the enclosure could have been a part of a human carcass, a torso and legs; though it was in fact, as Robb explained, a deer carcass—"There's a supplier in Oakland that delivers." The devouring was voracious, nonstop, efficient and terrible to see. Splattered blood, bits of bone, gristle!—the deep guttural warning-growl in the hyena's throat like a malevolent purr. Mariana would have liked to have made some sort of intelligent observation—*Are human beings the only animals for whom food has taste?*—but the hyena-meal was too distracting, and the intensity with which Robb Gelder watched, from just outside the chain-link fence, was disturbing. When greedy Condoleezza at last allowed the others to approach the remains of the carcass, each fell upon it panting and ravenous, devouring every bit of the meat—every bit of bone, gristle, blood—only a damp greasy spot remained on the concrete floor which the smallest of the hyenas licked with wistful eagerness.

Mariana said, faintly, "Why—there's nothing left at all. They've eaten it all."

Robb Gelder and Dana laughed, as if proudly.

"They can eat even if they're not—totally—'hungry.' Eating is life to them."

"Eat, sleep, copulate, reproduce—defend their kill against lions—that is life to them."

"Well, they also *nurse*. The females."

"And of course they fight. Even the cubs fight."

"And cubs *play*. It's fascinating to watch them."

There was nothing playful about the hyenas now, having finished the last of their meal and still clearly hungry; licking their bloodied muzzles and staring with glassy intensity at the two-legged creatures on the other side of the chain-link fence. The stumpy hind legs were taut with muscle, the lowered tails motionless as if poised with animal cunning.

To disguise her nervousness Mariana said, with schoolgirl brightness, "Do you think that *Homo sapiens* is the only species for whom food has actual *taste*? I mean—more than just . . . devouring."

"Well, Mariana—most of the world's population eats to live. The idea of 'taste'—of cultivating 'taste' in food—is a luxury of the 'first world,' overall." Robb spoke in a kindly professorial manner, yet Mariana knew herself rebuked. "In nature, life is mostly finding food—eating. If the effort ceases, life ceases."

Dana nodded, with a grim smile. So small was this middle-aged woman, so gnomish and slight in her denim clothes, she might have been a malnourished child in some desolate Third World setting. Yet her gnome-face was creased with smiles, you would have to conclude that her life was a happy life, in the service of Professor Gelder.

Squatting just a few inches outside the enclosure, murmuring to the nearest hyenas as if they were adorable puppies, Robb said: "Come say hello to Mariana, guys! Baxter, Cubbie—come!"

Without thinking—meaning simply to be friendly, agreeable, despite her revulsion—Mariana came forward stepping over the white stripe painted on the concrete, which was grimy in front of the cage; at once Robb pushed at her legs, pushing her back—"Mariana! No"—just as the tawny eyes of the nearest hyena leapt onto her, and the blood-stained teeth flashed in a maniacal grin. There was a rush inside the cage, excited barks, yips. Mariana felt foolish, as well as faintly sick.

"I'm sorry! I forgot."

"You were in no danger, Mariana! But it's a good idea to keep back of the white line."

Surreptitiously Mariana glanced at her wristwatch. How exhausting the hyena-tour was! She felt as if she'd been staring at hyenas, as hyenas had been staring at her, for a very long time, though it was less than a half hour since she'd arrived at the field station.

But Robb was eager to show her the rest of the spotted-hyena enclosures which were open-air, on the other side of the cages; there were two of these, each as large as a half-acre, with chain-link fences to a height of about twenty feet. Uneasily Mariana wondered if a hyena might manage to crawl—claw his way—over this fence; she made certain that she was nowhere near it, keeping Robb Gelder between herself and the hyenas as he led her along the walk. In a low, caressing voice Robb called to the hyenas—"Ranger! Blondie! Heath! Cybele! Come say hello to Mariana"—but the hyenas froze in place, staring. Almost, you might think the curious-shaped animals with their distinctive spotted coats were domestic dogs of some sort, wolf-related; except for their short hind legs and their hard alert stare of utter resolution and concentration, a sort of *concentration of hunger*, of the sort Mariana had never seen in any domestic dog.

Suddenly, as if a signal had passed among them, the clustered animals broke, began to trot about agitatedly, emitting low yipping cries. It was clear that they were communicating with one another, and not with their smiling master.

Shivering Mariana thought *If they could get free, they would devour us. Even Robb. All of us. Nothing would remain.*

What would Pearce think, if such a hideous thing happened to his wife? How could Pearce Shutt explain to his associates at Extol Pharmaceuticals that something unexpected and extraordinary had happened to his wife—*Mariana was killed, devoured by hyenas. She was devoured totally and not a trace remained.*

Mariana wondered: could an insurance investigator demand that the stomach contents of a hyena be examined? But no insurance investigator would have the knowledge to act so quickly, before the contents had passed through the hyena's stomach. And there could be no autopsy since no trace of the body remained.

Such morbid speculations! Mariana could not understand where they derived from.

Seeing her tense face, and that she was smiling strangely, Robb gently laid a hand on her arm. "Don't worry, Mariana—they can't get free. And if they did, I would protect you."

In Robb Gelder's office, which was a large, cluttered space with imitation maple wood walls festooned with photographs and drawings of spotted hyenas, Robb showed Mariana a film he'd made with a federal grant on spotted-hyena "social behavior"—female and male hyenas deferring to a swaggering alpha female; six-month cubs meekly deferring to the just slightly larger cubs of the alpha female; lean-shanked brother-hyenas grooming one another; a mother-hyena briskly grooming a daughter; a male hyena mating with a female— awkwardly, since the male's hind legs were short and the female, larger than the male, appeared exasperated with him, lifting her lip in a jeering sort of snarl as he fumbled to mount her; a pregnant hyena giving

birth, over a period of many minutes—so bizarrely, expelling with difficulty what looked like clumps of wet-matted fur through the tendril-
like organ that was the pseudopenis-clitoris, quite the most ghastly
thing Mariana had ever seen close-up, as the birth was the most ex-
cruciating birth she'd ever seen, leaving her sickened, faint. Even the
mother-hyena appeared exhausted, confused. *To what purpose such a
folly of nature? And why am I here, with this man I scarcely know, staring
at it?* Only footage of tiny blind-looking hyena cubs nursing at their
mothers' teats was pleasant to see though Mariana prepared herself
against a sudden eruption of violence among even these tiny creatures
resembling a child's stuffed toys.

Next, Robb showed Mariana photographs taken in the African savannah, of himself as a younger man, alone and with others, and with
spotted-hyena cubs; in several photographs there was a frowning young
woman, and Mariana wondered if this was the ex–Mrs. Gelder, but
could not quite bring herself to ask. On Robb's desk and shelves were
framed photographs of children, obviously his children for all resembled him about the eyes and nose; but no photographs of the mother.
This suggested to Mariana that Robb and his wife had not parted
amicably and was this a good thing, from her perspective—or not-so-
good? (A man's feeling for the next woman in his life was likely to mimic
his feeling for the most recent woman in his life, she had been given
to know.) Most of the wall space in the office was covered with hyena
photos and drawings, some of them cleverly executed like cartoons,
with captions beneath—two spotted hyenas with laptops, one saying to the other THIS IS THE GREAT THING ABOUT THE INTERNET,
NO ONE KNOWS YOU'RE A SPOTTED HYENA. Everywhere Mariana
looked were more hyenas, a genealogical chart of hyenas of biblical
proportions—names, dates, numerals. Perky little Dana had made
coffee, and had brought sandwiches which Mariana and Robb ate together, seated at a table overlooking the rear of one of the open-air

hyena enclosures; Mariana had not eaten breakfast that morning, in excited anticipation of visiting Robb Gelder, and should now have been very hungry, but found that she had little appetite—her first mouthful of a ham and cheese sandwich made her vaguely nauseated as if with the memory of something best forgotten.

Dana had brought spring water in transparent blue plastic bottles—this, Mariana drank thirstily. How parched her throat was, and her lips! As if she'd been in some wild, dry place for days.

Like the hyenas in the enclosures, that had seemed to communicate with one another subliminally, Robb Gelder's assistants must have known of Mariana's presence for they dropped by his office as if casually; casually too, Robb introduced her—"This is Mariana. We were in graduate school together at Penn."

Mariana was touched that Robb should think of her in this way, or that he should speak of her in this way, for it would have been more accurate to say that Mariana had been a student of his; it was kind of him to suggest that Mariana might still be a scientist of some kind and not rather the wife of a pharmaceutical lawyer in rural-suburban New Jersey.

With each introduction Robb Gelder seemed to speak more tenderly of Mariana, and more familiarly; he'd finished both his sandwiches and hers, and was gazing at her with warmly moist eyes. Again Mariana saw tiny nicks, scars, and indentations in her friend's skin—there was a sizable scar, comma-shaped, near his hairline, and his sandy-silvery-wavy hair was in need of washing. Yet his boyish expression and a sort of youthful glow to his skin made him appear attractive, even handsome. Oh—was she *falling in love* with this man whom she hadn't seen in more than twenty years . . . She'd begun to feel acutely self-conscious, anxious. Where Robb Gelder and his crew of assistants were very casually dressed in stained denims and khakis and muddied boots, Mariana was wearing sharply creased black woolen slacks and a tiny, tight-fitting embroidered beige cashmere jacket over a turtleneck sweater; her ankle-length coat was pale lavender suede and her boots were Italian black-leather. In Manhattan, both she and Pearce shopped at Berdorf Goodman—but only when the beautiful designer clothing was on sale. Seeing gnomish Dana with her pixie-face creased from smiles, so very eager to please her master, Mariana felt something like panic. This was not the place for her!

It was thrilling to Mariana, to know that Robb Gelder was attracted to her; that he remembered her so clearly, after more than two decades; yet it was a different matter, to have stirred the sexuality of an adult male, and this Mariana didn't want, not right now. Nor did she think that she would want it, later. Her marriage with her husband had long become sexless, as it was emotionless; a cordial sort of relationship, forged in mutual responsibility; this was an ideal sort of marriage for a woman like herself, as it appeared to be an ideal sort of marriage for her husband; and if Pearce was unfaithful to her, on one or another of his business trips, what was the harm to *her*?—how he spent his evenings away from home did not truly engage her any more than the choice of meals he had on those occasions, or if he had a late-night cognac from the minibar in his hotel room. But if she stayed longer here, Robb Gelder might misunderstand.

Mariana was on her feet, reaching for her coat—without waiting for Robb to help her with the coat. She thanked him for the tour, she shook his maimed hand and released it quickly. "This is a remarkable place, Robb—I'm very grateful to have been taken on a tour."

"But—Mariana—you're leaving so soon? Didn't you say you were staying overnight in Bangor? At least, for dinner?" Robb appeared stunned with disappointment.

In a bright quick voice Mariana said, "My cousin Valerie—in a suburb of Bangor—that's why I came—I'll be staying with her. Maybe I didn't explain in my e-mail, the poor woman is just my age and she has had breast cancer surgery."

Breast cancer surgery did not so clearly repel Robb Gelder, as it had Pearce Shutt. But in the face of these words, Robb could think of no adequate reply.

Reluctantly Robb walked Mariana to her car. His limp was more pronounced now, almost the man seemed to move with a sideways scuttle, as if one of his legs were shorter than the other; he must have been deeply hurt and confused, he could only repeat that he'd thought she would be staying longer and that they might be having dinner that night in Bangor. At Mariana's car there was a tense moment when Robb seemed about to take hold of her shoulders, and kiss her; but Mariana shrank away, with what might have been a look of apology, and regret; and so Robb thought better of touching her, only just staring at her morosely as she backed her car around and drove away. In the rearview mirror she saw the man's diminishing figure, his hand lifted in farewell, a fond, faint, wistful smile on his face fading as she pressed on the gas pedal.

Driving back to New Jersey, Mariana lapsed into a kind of trance. Her heart beat slowly, calmly. Whatever danger there had been—she'd eluded the danger. The cold-glassy predator-eyes fixed upon her, the panting tongues dripping saliva, the bloodstained teeth—Robb Gelder's maimed hand closing about her upper arm, and his kindly, warm gaze fixed on her face: she'd eluded it, she'd escaped.

Another time she stayed in a motel in Massachusetts, and slept a dreamless sleep. In the morning she remembered she'd forgotten to call Pearce—for the second time.

"Now, it's too late. I'll be seeing him tonight."

*

. . . unbearable exquisite sensation in her jaws, her throat and torso and running down her body into her bowels, into her groin and legs, hard-muscled

thighs and calves and what joy in running, what joy in running at a fast panting trot beside her companion, a romp by moonlight, there is no emotion more exquisite than this joy of the body in its running, the sensation in the jaws which are hard-muscled as the legs, hard-muscled the scalp at the very top of the skull that allows the jaws to snap open, the sharp teeth to sink into the soft sweet panicked flesh of the prey, side by side pursuing the prey, side by side romping in the snow-stubbled field behind the darkened house through skeins of tilting trees, the edge of a thinned-out suburban woods of deciduous and evergreen trees and underfoot sharp serrated broken things, the scent of something hot-blooded and panicked is a torment to them unless they can seize it, sink their sharp teeth in it and tear, tear and chew and grind and swallow, the smell of panic is the smell of blood, her companion is laughing, barking-laughing in a way to torment her, ripples of unbearable exquisite sensations are coursing through her supple body, she is close behind her companion, she is impatient and yearning and in an instant they are on the terrified creature, seizing the squealing thrashing furry creature in their jaws, tugging/tearing, the rabbit's shriek pierces the moonlit silence, they have torn the living rabbit into pieces and within seconds they have devoured the still-pulsing flesh, their powerful incisors have torn, their powerful back teeth have made of the flesh a liquidy sinewy substance to be swallowed in great panting ravenous gulps, the spine of the rabbit has been shredded, and devoured, and the small knobby skull shattered like clay, the spongy rabbit-brains sucked and swallowed and each hair of the rabbit's soft dark hide, each drop of the rabbit's meek blood, of the creature piteous and desperate to live but a few seconds previously not a trace remains—not a trace in the snow-stubbled field behind the darkened house that is one of a constellation of darkened houses in which human inhabitants sleep in ignorance of the terror of torn-apart flesh as of the joy of the predators' bodies and now truly they are ravenous—the predators tawny-eyed panting and slathering saliva trotting by moonlight, softly laughing together, long low whoops of animal laughter deep in the throat and in play the male nips at

the female's heels, in play the female feigns tearing at the male's throat, her
sharp incisors draw blood from one of his ears and now truly the female is
ravenous, both female and male primed to hunt for once the bloodlust has
been quickened it will not readily abate and now—where?

"MARIANA. This is good news, I would have thought."

Pearce was staring at her. His dark-blooded fleshy face loomed above her disapprovingly. *He knows* she thought, panicked. Then *But what can he know?*

"Were you even listening?"

"Yes! Yes, I was listening of course. The corporate 'retreat'—"

"In St. Bart's this year."

"St. Bart's! That's wonderful."

"Last week in January."

"*That's* wonderful."

Quickly Mariana went to get a calendar. Fortunately, the calendar included the first month of the new year. Each of the January days was blank. And beyond the month of January there was nothing—the calendar had come to an end.

"St. Bart's is even nicer than Bermuda. I'll look forward to this."

"Yes, I think so. I think you should look forward to it."

Why did Pearce speak so—*condemningly?* Since Mariana had driven to Bangor, Maine, to visit her very sick cousin, Pearce had behaved with an air of hurt reproach like one owed an apology.

Mariana tried to recall St. Bart's. She'd gone to so many Caribbean resorts with Pearce, she could not distinguish one from another, for in all instances they'd mostly stayed within a hotel compound; except for brief guided-tour trips into "native culture," her experiences of the Caribbean islands, Mexico, and coastal Venezuela had blurred together like wetted Kleenex.

"There will be a cruise, too. Ty Hemmings's yacht."

Ty Hemmings was CEO of Extol Pharmaceuticals. Mariana had been on Hemmings's dazzling-white Catalina yacht several times. She bit her lower lip, trying to smile. A wave of utter nausea swept over her. Brightly she said, "Maybe we can fly down with—is it Kevin and Sarah?—you know, that nice couple from Far Hills—he's a lawyer, too—we spent time with them last year, in Jackson Hole. We could share a—"

"Tyrell is no longer with Extol, I'm afraid."

"No longer with Extol!"

"In fact, Kevin has been gone at least eight months."

"But—where did he go? Was he—transferred?"

"I'm sure I have no idea, Mariana. You look as shocked as if these people were our close friends."

"They were—nice people . . ."

In fact, Mariana couldn't recall their last name. She dreaded Pearce asking her but clearly the subject no longer interested him.

It was several days after Mariana returned from Bangor. These days, and these nights, she'd been unusually restless, distracted. Her sleep was erratic and disturbed and she would have said dreamless except dream-shreds returned to haunt her during the day at weak moments, making her heart jump, and her mouth water with a terrible intensity of thirst, or hunger; there was a hard, harsh pulse in her groin, a yet more terrible intensity she could not identify except to know that she had never experienced it before in this household. She found herself lapsing into an open-eyed trance while driving her car, or preparing meals, or preparing for bed; her mouth was frequently dry, and her eyes welled with moisture; she felt as if she were under a spell, hypnotized—by something subaqueous—not visible surfaces but the deeper being itself. With a pang of yearning she thought *Is there something beneath, waiting? Does this something know me?*

Pearce hadn't asked her much about her Bangor visit. But then, it wasn't like Pearce to inquire into Mariana's life apart from her life with him.

Pushing her hair back from her forehead in a way to signal headache, unease, exhaustion she'd told him that her cousin Valerie was terribly sick, she'd lost thirty pounds and it was heartbreaking to see her and to see her children—the oldest was eleven, the youngest six— looking so anxious; and Pearce murmured something husbandly and placating that at the same time signaled *Thanks! That's enough* and when Mariana glanced up she saw that he'd moved away, and in the adjoining room TV voices flared up, companionable and familiar.

That night in bed Pearce slept heavily, turned away from Mariana; whether she couldn't sleep for his snoring or whether she could not have slept in any case, Mariana didn't know, but after a discreet interval she slipped from the bed and went along the corridor to the guest room—the room in which a copy of Darwin's *Origin of Species* was still slightly protruding from the bookshelf—and in that bed she lay deliciously alone, drifting to sleep as if sinking slowly beneath the surface of dark water and suddenly there came an arm—a man's hard-muscled arm—along her side—in her silk nightgown she was sleek, slender— for a long moment fixed in place as if mesmerized, or paralyzed—then, she felt a surge of strength in all her limbs—she felt the kick of joy— sheer rapturous joy—in her chest, and in her throat; though trying to tell the man in a hoarse whisper *No! You shouldn't be here, he has a gun—a rifle; no please, I can't*—even as she and the man were grappling together, in the bed; it was a bed with a quaint brass headstead; Mariana was pleading with him, begging him *No!—please*; Mariana was pushing at him, clawing at him; yet at the same time she and the man were no longer in the bed but were descending the darkened stairs and the irises of their eyes were dilated so powerfully, they could see in the dark; only the faintest moonlight was required, for them to see in the dark. At the rear of the house they were on all fours, in the snow-stubbled grass, and in an adjoining field; there was a brackish smell from the lake, beyond the icy banks where a dark current ran swiftly, shattering rays of moonlight; her heart beat in such happiness, she laughed aloud; her companion was laughing aloud; her shoulders and chest were thick with muscle and her back and haunches and at the nape of her neck hairs bristled in anticipation; her companion was nipping at her playfully, and to draw blood; for it was playful, to draw blood; it was very exciting, to draw blood; she was made to realize how bold, how brash this male creature was, to approach her; to approach a female; for her sharp incisors could tear out his throat, if she wished; at a fever pitch of excitement they were trotting side by side tongues lolling and slathering saliva and the smell of panicked prey embold-ened them, something small, furry and shrieking was lifted in their jaws, tossed into the air and seized in mid-air and devoured in mid-air, flesh blood bones gristle; on the redwood deck above the snow-stubbled grass there had come a two-legged figure to observe them, an individual whose face was hidden in shadow, a thick-bodied man, short of breath, panting; for this man was unaccustomed to physical exer-tion, and excitement; a cowardly hunter, who would hunt his prey from a little distance, thrilled at the prospect of killing at a little distance; Mariana was astonished seeing him on the redwood deck above her and her companion, in the excitement of the moment she'd forgotten the man's name, and even that he had a name; that he was an individual man, and her husband; or, he had been her husband when she'd lived in that house with him. She knew to think almost calmly *He will kill us! That is the coward's power.*

The hunter lifted something to his shoulder, and aimed: a rifle, or a shotgun. There came a sharp retort, and a smell of something singed, and at once Mariana and her companion leapt instinctively apart so that the hunter above them couldn't sight them together in the scope of his weapon; for neither had been hit, and each knew exactly what stratagem to undertake, again by instinct and without needing to communicate; bodies carried low against the ground and heads lowered they trotted in opposite directions in the snowy grass beneath the deck; again there came another deafening shot, a hard-cracking shot that had to be a rifle and not a shotgun; for this was the weapon Mariana's husband had used, deer hunting years ago; cursing them now, cursing them as filthy beasts the hunter hurried to the farther end of the deck, leaning against the railing; for he was very short of breath, and in poor physical condition; lifting his weapon and aiming—but uncertain, where he meant to aim—as Mariana pads soundless behind him without his knowing to leap onto his back, in that instant bringing the hunter down, and causing his weapon to fall harmless onto the redwood deck, of no more consequence than a toy gun; Mariana's mate has leapt up onto the deck to join her as their prey thrashes on the deck screaming and in mid-scream silenced for in that instant the hunter's throat is torn out; they are tearing at the heavy, limp, flaccid body, the belly is ripped open, entrails torn out; the softer, exposed parts are devoured first, then smaller bones, and then larger bones, backbone, thigh-bone, femur—skull—soft spongy brains sucked out and swallowed until at last nothing remains of the prey except a damp greasy dark-tinged stain in the redwood deck; nothing remains except mangled, bloodied and unrecognizable clothing, and the dropped rifle; for already the pair have departed, already they are flying over the snowy crust through the forest where the night lies all before them, where to roam.

IV

SAN QUENTIN

How you kill a person, he is asking.
How a person *die*, he is asking.
What it mean—*kill, die*—he is asking.
Enrolled in Intro Biology to seek *why*.

HIS NAME IS UNPRONOUNCEABLE—*Quogn*. He is five feet one inch tall. He can't weigh more than one hundred pounds. He is not a scrappy featherweight with swift lethal child-fists like rock, he is a slight bald boy with a curved back. His face is a patina of scars and blemishes and his minnow-eyes are shy behind his black plastic glasses that fit his narrow head wrongly. Smiling eager in Intro Biology to show how serious he is saying, How is a person *die*, how that happen. Is like an animal maybe but *why*.

He thinks of this all the time he says. Like wake or sleep or in-between. Some-kind voice saying to him *How you did this thing, how this happen, you!*

And she your old sister she be good to you.

——

SAN QUENTIN: where you never meant to do what you don't remember you were accused of doing so long ago it almost doesn't matter
where you were when it was claimed you'd done what you were accused
of doing which of course—you swear—you hadn't done, or not in exactly that way, and not at that time.

THEY WEAR long-sleeved white T-shirts beneath short-sleeved blue
shirts with P R I S O N E R in white letters on the back. They wear
blue sweatpants and at the waist in white letters C D C R and on the
left pant-leg in vertical white letters

P

R

I

S

O

N

E

R

and all of their clothing loose-fitting as pajamas.

THERE IS SOMETHING in his mouth that causes his words to
emerge contorted and bright with spittle. There is something in his
throat that stammers like a small frog in spasm. The minnow-eyes glimmer and dart. He is a diligent student, he will read slowly and in silence
pushing his stubby forefinger along lines of print. He will hunch his
shoulders close to photocopied pages from *Life: The Science of Biology*
which is a massive textbook too dangerous to bring into the facility.

There comes a squint into the ruined boy's-face. There comes a look of intense fear but determination. With a plastic spoon he "dissects" a sheep brain in the biology lab. Under the instructor's guidance, he and eight other inmate-students. The "dissection" is clumsy. The sheep brain resembles chewy leather. His lab partner has a dark face like erosion and dreadlock hair to his shoulders. He is explaining he is not sure he had ever seen a *live* sheep—maybe pictures, when he be boy in school in San Jose. He is saying why does a *live thing* stop being *live*— what makes a *live thing* be *dead*. One minute and then the other—and be *dead*.

He wonders if the *live-thing* be like fire that it be blown out and gone or if the *live-thing* be like Holiness that it not be killed but taken up to Heaven.

He has question is easier for a thing to *live* than to *die*—like weed? Like cockroach?

There are ten inmate-students registered in Intro Biology but always each week one will fail to come to class. Yet never *Quogn*—he is most eager student.

Never can you really understand what Quogn is saying. Yet you nod, smile and nod for you are weak in such ways.

You have learned, Quogn has enrolled in Intro Biology before. Several times it may have been. For he is not so young as he appears, for he appears scarcely more than sixteen. So small, and his back curved so you feel sorry for him but also exasperation and impatience for he speaks slowly and with difficulty and with a look of wonderment— How is possible, a thing *die*? What is it mean, *take a thing life from it—how?*

He is a "lifer"—sixty years to life.

Each class is three hours. Three hours!

In San Quentin, time passes slow as backed-up drains.

In San Quentin, murderers dressed like a softball team.

San Quen-tin, voluptuous sound!

San Quen-tin, a hard caress.

Each class he is grimmer, broke-back like an upright snake and staring with minnow-eyes at the instructor. Shy and clumsy unless he is resentful and furious with the plastic spoon, that cracks between his stubby fingers with a startling little *crack*! that draws the other inmate-students' eyes to him.

Is a split plastic spoon now a weapon. You will wonder.

Your heart cringes. Such wonderment, you keep out of your eyes.

Wants badly to know, it is all the God-damn fuckin wish he has to know, how you can kill a person *living*, how does a person *die*. For does the person who die say to herself it is *all right now* to die, she is sick tired fed-up and *to die*, or is it the other way—it is the one who kill who is the cause. *Tryin to figure this out, there is some answer to this to be revealed.*

Through the semester he stare at the lecturer, and at the blackboard where the lecturer scribble words with colored chalk. At lab time the others in P R I S O N E R clothing avoid little Quogn like you avoid a little mangy sick dog might suddenly yip and bury ugly yellow teeth in your ankle. Wants so bad to figure these facts but the weeks pass, the dry cold winter season is past and it is spring and the sun blinding just outside the Quonset-hut classroom where the prisoners go singly to use the outdoor urinals glimpsed from behind the white horizontal bar P R I S O N E R across the back of the blue shirt for nowhere is P R I S O N E R to be avoided, you have made of yourself a ridiculous sight, no one dares laugh.

And now it is ending. And now, it is last week. He has not passed Intro Biology—(again)—for he has not done most of the work and what work he has handed in, is incomprehensible like a child's scribbling in pencil on sheets of torn and curiously soiled paper. Yet he is not angry with instructor, or does not give that impression. He is sad, he is anguished-seeming not angry, his blemished face contorted as if in the pain of actual thought saying he think about it all the time but don't know more than ever—what it *is*.

Stil I am not given up. I have sixty-year yet, to figure out.

WHY THERE be spiders there—these place I am put. They said, you have hurt & you are bad person to be punish & I tell them, I am not that one, but I am thinking it is the same one, the knife-for-cutting fish in his hand and the handle slippery like fish-guts.

How it began Mam say she love both us like the same. Mam say of my old sister she is not a lit girl any longer & Mam say, she my lit girl.

She also my lit girl til I am deadandgone.

She be my old sister from before daddy be with us.

They said, It is best thing for she, & for you. You are sugar-blood-dibetees. You are fat. For she fat lady, in the place where I was waiting by the chairs, where you can sit & drink from—in your hands, & the water spil out but you can lick with the tongue like a cat-lick. I heard boy say, That lady so fat—man she is fat. So they laugh. & one say,

Oh—*her*. & they look at me where I am waiting. I am face like head, too big face.

Like a faucet turned on—hot. & no one to turn it back. The sharp thing that was in my hand, that came to hurt her, that Mam could not take from my fingers, she too fat to take breath. I was shamed, my old sister so fat they laugh at us, and Mam like to say, they both my lit babies.

Daddy is not there now. They say Daddy is *here*—in this place I am put to be punish. But in the yard where I see him it is *not Daddy* but some other & a mistake to stare, it will be hurt to you, if you stare.

Finly when it was over, they came for me where Mam told me hide under the kitchen where they be spiders in your hair & eyelashes & if you open mouth to breathe, in mouth—nasty!—the light was bright & their voices loud & they say *What did you do! What did you do!* & it was never explained to me either, all those years ago.

Intro Biology I am taking, this is why. I am not given up hoping please you will help me.

ANNIVERSARY

Never be alone in the facility—even in the 'safety zone.' Always be in the company of at least one other person."
Never be alone. This was wise advice.

"THE INMATES use urinals in the yard—try not to look in that direction."

She looked, of course—she and her companion both, in a nervous and involuntary reflex—but there was no one at the long trough-like urinal against the side of a building, nor was there anyone at the toilet—a lone, terribly exposed lidless toilet like an installation in an art exhibit—a few yards from the urinal.

Vivianne's companion and co-instructor in the volunteer-teaching program asked why was the outdoor toilet so public?—he hoped it wasn't to embarrass and humiliate the inmates.

Their guide, a civilian who was a co-director of the State Prison Education Program, said, not sharply, but with an air of subtle reprimand: "Of course not. If you saw what 'toilets' were provided for inmates in the yard a few decades ago, you'd know what an improvement this is."

RESPECT IS the key. You must respect the inmates in order that the inmates respect you.

THEY'D DRIVEN to Hudson Fork, New York: the Hudson Fork Maximum Security Correctional Facility for Men. It had been a drive of nearly two hours but during that time they had not spoken, much—to Vivianne's disappointment her young companion/co-instructor had talked on his cell phone for much of the trip, to a series of friends. And then, yes, as if he'd only just realized, he'd shut up his phone to discuss with Vivianne the "expository writing" course they were to teach together for the next ten weeks—Vivianne as Cal Healy's assistant, since she'd applied late to the program, and had had no previous experience teaching in a prison.

Vivianne said she'd photocopied an essay by James Baldwin, she thought they might pass out to the students, to read for the second class meeting. Cal said, "Great! I have lots of things for them too." But he didn't tell Vivianne what these things were, for his cell phone rang at that moment.

IT WAS early Sunday afternoon. The chill October sun was high overhead and in the near distance behind the weatherworn prison wall topped with cruel-glinting razor-wire was a mountain like a painted backdrop on a stage.

The mountain, in the southern Catskills, was partly covered with fir trees and a scattering of deciduous trees with bright splotches of foliage like a Fauve painting. It seemed to loom close beyond the prison wall like a taunt but had to be miles away.

What would Vivianne have been doing on this bright-chilly October Sunday, in her old, lost life? It did no good to wonder.

Hudson Fork was one of the older prisons in the New York State prison system, originally built in 1891. Of course it had been partly rebuilt, remodeled. But the old buildings remained, like fossilized rock.

Until 1967, Hudson Fork had executed men. Now the old death row quarters had been refashioned into a part of the prison yard that housed the Education Unit office and classrooms.

"The inmates joke about 'ghosts,'" their guide told them. "They're referring to the old death row prisoners and they aren't serious—anyway, most of them."

There were forty-three hundred prisoners in this facility designed to hold approximately two thousand men. Yet, there could not have been more than forty inmates scattered about the vast open space inside the prison—the "yard."

In their blue prison-issue the inmates resembled actors in a desultory and uncoordinated action in which no single individual was prominent—some were making their way, with a kind of studied slowness, around a weedy track, which brought them in proximity with the civilian-volunteers on the other side of the wire-mesh fence. Vivianne was surprised to see an older man, in his sixties at least, wispy-bearded as a figure out of mythology, walking with a cane.

An unexpected number of the men were middle-aged and a majority appeared to be Caucasian unless you looked more closely—to the far left of the yard, in a scrubby-grassy area abutting a protective stucco wall where there was a primitive basketball court and a hoop with frayed netting, young African-American men shot baskets and milled about restlessly.

Elsewhere, in their sequestered corners of the yard, were Hispanic men, "mixed-blood" men, a very few Asian-Americans.

Why are you here, why'd you sign up?—Vivianne was asked by her companion/co-instructor Cal Healy, and she told him because she wanted to help prisoners adjust to life outside prison—"I want to be *of help*."

In fact, not all of their inmate-students would be paroled any time soon, or possibly ever: this was information the civilian-volunteers didn't generally know.

Vivianne's response was awkwardly pious, but true: she did not add that in this late phase of her life, to be *of help* was all that remained.

In turn, she'd asked Cal Healy why he'd volunteered and he'd said, "For a selfish reason, I suppose—I can list this course on my résumé, when I'm looking for a job." He paused, and laughed, as if he'd said too much. "And I want—like, to *contribute*. I want to be a part of— y'know—making things better for 'disenfranchised' Americans."

Cal Healy was a tall slight-bodied young man in his late twenties who wore a baseball cap pulled low on his forehead, a nylon parka, cor-duroys. He'd described himself to Vivianne as a "social-eco-activist" enrolled in the Ph.D. program in social psychology at SUNY Pur-chase. Vivianne wondered if he resented her as a co-instructor or if he was grateful for her presence, as he'd said: "We can't teach in the prison alone, y'know. The class I assisted for, last spring, there were three of us—plus the primary instructor."

Vivianne liked it that she, with her lengthy teaching career, and her administrative career, was now "assisting" a young Ph.D. candi-date with virtually no experience in teaching. There was something consoling about this like the sensation she felt—sometimes—waking abruptly from sleep without remembering where she was, what time in her life it had become.

The Education Unit was inside the prison facility, a sequence of wood frame buildings with a look of the temporary, like Quonset huts.

In the Education Unit were an office and several classrooms and to access this space, you had to pass through three checkpoints manned by prison guards; the Unit was segregated from the prison itself and from the yard by a twelve-foot wire-mesh fence topped with razor-wire. Several inmates, including the old man with the cane, passed close by on the other side of this fence, staring at Vivianne and her companions, covertly; it was eerie, how neither the inmates nor the civilian visitors acknowledged one another, despite their physical proximity of only a few feet.

Vivianne only just glanced at the inmates in their blue prison-issue clothes, and looked quickly away.

Her social instinct was to smile, nervously. She knew it was an instinct to be resisted.

This was a season in her life when often helplessly she glanced at strangers—felt a premonitory kick in her heart—and looked quickly away.

Of course you won't see him. How could you hope to see him.

In her profession she'd met so many people, she'd shaken the hands of thousands of people, locked eyes with so many—sincerely, for the most part—for Vivianne Greary was indisputably a *sincere person*—yet in Hudson Fork Correctional Facility she seemed to have forgotten, or mislaid, her composure.

She could not determine why: she knew there was no danger to her, physically. Not behind the wire-mesh security fence, and not in the presence of guards.

The inmates in the yard were observed, too, continuously by armed guards in watch towers. No gesture of theirs could go unnoticed, unrecorded.

A woman, sighted by inmates in the yard, would naturally be of interest—any female, any age.

Though there were a number of female volunteers in the program. And, to Vivianne's surprise, there were a number of female guards in the all-male facility, who wore uniforms identical to the male guards' uniforms and were, at a short distance, indistinguishable from the men.

Did Vivianne imagine it?—the female guards at the checkpoints, scrutinizing civilian volunteers, seemed even more disapproving than the men.

Greary, Vivianne C. had had to show her driver's license and photo I.D. several times and she'd had to print and sign her name several times so that the name might be matched with a roster of "cleared" names provided by the State Prison Education Program. The tender inside of her right wrist was briskly stamped with an invisible code, to be checked when she left the facility.

Civilians were warned not to "wash off" the invisible ink.

If they did, they might be detained for hours. Possibly, the prison would be locked-down.

The prison guards wore military-looking uniforms the color of brackish water. It was indeed difficult to distinguish between female and male in these singularly ugly clothes.

"Ma'am. Lift your arms please."

A stout unsmiling black woman had drawn a wand over Vivianne— across her shoulders, her chest and back, along the length of her legs, and behind her legs—sounding impatient with her.

"Ma'am—turn around."

The guard had seemed annoyed by Vivianne as one who, judging by her age, her demeanor, her tasteful but clearly expensive black-woolen clothing, was out of place in Hudson Fork.

The presence of civilians in the maximum-security prison was offensive to many of the guards, for civilians were a potential source of danger. At the three-hour orientation class Vivianne had attended two weeks before, she'd learned that the prison had a no-hostage policy.

Some of the volunteers had laughed, hearing this. Their laughter was edgy, anxious. What did *no-hostage policy* mean, exactly?

Vivianne hadn't had to ask. She knew: if prisoners take hostages, there would be no negotiating for their release.

"MA'AM? Sign here."

Greary, Vivianne C. Co-Instructor English 101.

What relief to her, that no one knew her here! Her identity was no more and no less than that of the other civilian instructors: a person who'd volunteered to teach in a maximum-security prison for men, to be *of help*.

This was a new life. A remnant of a life.

Or maybe not a life but a shrewd stratagem for getting through the day, the week, the weeks, a month.

"Now, through here. All of you show your I.D.s to the guard—hold them up so she can see them."

A small contingent had gathered in the holding-cage—both civilians and guards on their way into the inner facility. Without needing to be told, the civilians let the guards—silent, unsmiling, indifferent to the courtesy—go ahead of them.

Vivianne, who'd hiked as a girl, and continued to walk distances as often as she could, was made just slightly breathless by the walking—uphill, and down—inside the prison walls. Even Cal Healy was becoming winded.

The distance from the front gate to the Education Unit at the far end of the yard must have been a quarter mile, most of it outdoors.

Above the Catskill Mountains, the sky was massed with clouds that seemed to have blown up from nowhere: cumulus clouds bearing shadowy pouches of rain, like just-visible tumors.

As the sun faded, the air turned colder. Already when Vivianne and Cal had hurried from his car, parked in the distant visitors' lot by the river, they'd shivered in the gusty air blowing off the choppy slate-covered Hudson River.

Oh why am I here. Why, this terrible place!

She'd laughed, she'd been so chilled, and so discomfited.

She'd laughed, her life of which she'd once been so proud had become ridiculous as a weathered old wind sock whipping in the wind.

STILL: she held herself in perpetual readiness—(how exhausting this was, her slender body taut as a bow!)—that if somehow she failed to see him—(through the wire-mesh fence, for instance, with its look of latticed neurons)—he might see *her*.

HERE WAS A SURPRISE. Vivianne supposed it was a disappointment.

Sunday classes at the prison were scheduled at the same time as once-weekly visiting hours. This was unfortunate!

Was this deliberate, was it a hostile act, to force the prisoners to choose between taking a course and seeing visitors?—indignant Cal Healy had to ask. And Mick McKeon said, in a lowered voice, so that no guards or prison authorities might overhear, "Well—try to see it this way. Visiting hours are likely to be Saturday or Sunday—weekends. Classes are usually weekdays. Why they've scheduled these Sunday classes at the same time as visiting hours I'm not sure, no one in the program knows, and we can't really ask. We are here—we are *in here*—only because the prison authority has allowed us in. We have no rights and privileges and our prison program can be canceled at any time."

"But it's hostile, then? Essentially."

Since they'd arrived at the prison Cal Healy had become increasingly excitable. Initially he led Vivianne to believe that he had taught a course at Hudson Fork, but in fact he'd only assisted another instructor for just two class meetings. At the checkpoints he'd been edgy and defensive; he'd been stunned when a guard told him he hadn't been "cleared"—his name hadn't been on the roster—until it turned out, after closer inspection, that *Cal Healy* was on the roster, at the smudged bottom of a printed page.

(Had the guard meant to harass him? Or had it been a simple mistake?)

At the final checkpoint Cal had been informed by a guard inspecting his clothing that he couldn't remove his jacket inside the facility since he was wearing, beneath, a gray-green shirt that might be confused, at a distance, with blue—no civilians were allowed into the facility wearing blue.

Cal had begun to protest—his T-shirt wasn't in any way *blue*—but the guard only just repeated, his shirt might be mistaken for blue by a sentry in one of the towers.

Cal had promised, he would only remove the jacket when he was in the classroom, not outdoors. But the guard insisted, he could not remove the jacket anywhere inside the facility, since he was wearing a T-shirt that might be confused with blue.

Furious, Cal zipped up his jacket. His lean young face had been suffused with indignation. Vivianne had felt for him the kind of concern—sympathy tempered by exasperation—a mother might feel for a headstrong son.

Now as Cal complained to Mick McKeon of the prison authorities and of the state legislature that had recently rescinded a bill providing state funds for prison education and rehabilitation, Vivianne only half-listened, in silence. She'd become a quiet woman, a brooding woman, one who *half-listens*. She recalled how in her old, lost life she'd been a lively and provocative conversationalist—she'd been a popular teacher and administrator—but none of that mattered now, and certainly not in this place where no one knew her name. She'd taken to heart what incoming volunteers had been told at the orientation meeting: *Don't expect answers to your questions from prison authorities. Don't trust your judgment and never rely upon "common sense" inside the prison.*

This, too, was good advice. Vivianne had lost all faith in her own judgment and she could not believe that "common sense" had any relevance to the world she'd come to know.

In the Education Office they'd signed another roster—printed their names and signed and indicated the date and time—and again showed their photo I.D.s. And another time led back along the now rain-wetted wooden ramp, again passing close by the open urinal less than twelve feet away on the other side of the wire-mesh fence. Vivianne wasn't a squeamish or even a fastidious woman—she didn't think so—but she couldn't imagine finding herself in such close proximity to men using the urinal just outside the Education Unit.

This curious awkwardness had not been mentioned at the orientation meeting though the instructor—a woman of about thirty-five, with a plain fierce face—had stressed the importance of "respecting" the prisoners' privacy: not to ask personal questions, and not to share personal information.

It was crucial, the volunteer instructors were warned, to avoid "familiarity"—"over-familiarity"—with their inmate-students.

Never touch a prisoner, even lightly on the wrist.

Never position yourself close to a prisoner.

Never come up behind a prisoner unannounced.

Never engage in flirtatious banter with a prisoner.

Never give a prisoner your telephone number and address.

Never give a prisoner any gift however small. And never any money.

Never accept a gift from a prisoner however small.

Never deliver any message even a verbal message from one prisoner to another, this is a felony.

Mick McKeon was saying: "The area we're in, which is the only part of the prison you will ever be in—is a 'safety zone.' It's completely surrounded by this fence—twelve feet high, with razor-wire at the top. Only inmates cleared for classes are allowed in here through the checkpoint. And we are only allowed in here, through the checkpoint. At the end of your class which should be ended promptly at 4:30 P.M.—no earlier, and no later—I'll try to get back to escort you through the checkpoint. If I'm held up, I'll send my assistant Dana. We can't ask officers to escort us. Remember what you were told at orientation: never leave the men in the classroom alone, not even to look for me or Dana. And never walk alone anywhere—always be with another instructor or with an escort."

Cal objected: "The men cleared for our classes aren't 'violent offenders'—that's ridiculous. I thought it was policy, no prisoner who's had behavior issues is cleared for the program."

"These are prison regulations, Cal. Forget 'common sense.'"

McKeon singled out a key from a ring of many keys to open the classroom door. Inside, the air was chill and damp. A smell of something dark, melancholy like the stirring of rotted leaves—Vivianne felt a touch of vertigo.

Thinking *I am strong enough for this. I have never been a weak woman—you will see.*

SHE'D TAUGHT for much of her adult life. She'd been a dean, and even a college president—of a highly regarded liberal arts college in the lower Hudson Valley. Still she was on the faculty of the college though she'd retired as president after twelve years and now she was taking a much-postponed sabbatical in what she didn't want to think, from a purely statistical perspective, might be called the "twilight" of her career.

No one knew her name here: this was relief!

This was freedom, and relief.

Vaguely the prison education organizers knew who *Vivianne Greary* was, or had been. They'd welcomed her request to be a volunteer instructor with an excited flurry of e-mails.

Since the state legislature had cut aid to prison programs, the program had to depend upon private donors. Vivianne would pay for the photocopying that her part of the course required and Vivianne would have happily donated books to the class—except there was the prison regulation, no gifts to prisoners.

"Not even books?"

"Not even books."

They—the new instructors—had been bemused to learn that hardcover books could not even be brought into the facility, along with more plausible contraband—money, keys, cell phones, computers, tape recorders, cameras, wallets and purses, shoulder bags, any and all weapons and sharp objects.

Hardcover books, which with their "sharp" edges might be used as weapons.

And chewing gum—which might be fashioned, in some ingenious Smokey Stover–way, to thwart locks.

The classroom to which Mick McKeon had brought them was larger than Vivianne would have expected, and not nearly so dreary—two walls were lined with windows. Still, Cal Healy complained that the tables weren't positioned for teaching—the room must have been hastily, carelessly cleaned, and tables and chairs shoved about.

Long ago as a graduate student Vivianne had taught night school at a branch of the state university in Yonkers, New York. Her Ph.D. studies were in political science and philosophy but she'd been grateful to teach remedial English and expository writing whenever she could, as her young husband had also been grateful for these arduous, low-paying jobs. In fact, there had seemed to both Vivianne and her husband a curious sort of romance, gritty, melancholy, exhausting, in such expenditures of spirit.

Of course, they'd been young. Newly married, and young.

Often Vivianne had had to drag and shove desks around, before her students arrived; she didn't so much mind doing this now, as a way of working off nervous tension.

There were seven tables in the classroom, each accommodating six students. At the front of the room there was a smaller table, for instructors. A portable blackboard—that is a "white-board." And on the floor, a podium.

On the wall beside the door, a clock with prominent numerals and hands. The time was 1:24 P.M.

"Your students will start arriving in a few minutes. Don't forget to have each one sign the class roster at the start of class and at the end—they can just initial their signature, at the end."

One of McKeon's assistants came into the classroom carrying an awkwardly large cardboard box of supplies: yellow tablets for the students, white note cards, pencils, a copy of the class roster for the instructor and a copy for the students to sign. There was photocopied material to be passed out at the first class meeting—(material that had had to be cleared by the prison authorities, two weeks before)—and there was a small blue plastic cube, set by the assistant in a prominent position on the instructor's table.

McKeon pointed at the little blue cube: "This is crucial, Cal—Vivianne. Be sure you don't let this out of your sight and that you return it in the box, to the office, at the end of the class."

"Why? What is it?"

"A pencil sharpener."

"A pencil sharpener!"

The little blue cube contained a sharp piece of metal, like a razor that could be used as a weapon, McKeon explained.

"Your classroom supply-box will be inventoried. Make sure this pencil sharpener is in it."

Cal laughed, as if he'd never heard anything so ridiculous.

"Our students aren't going to cut one another's throats! These are serious students, enrolled in the degree program. I remember from last spring—they're decent guys. The last thing they're going to do is fuck up getting out of here."

"They might not cut anyone's throat themselves," McKeon said, "but they might sell the sharpener to someone else. That's why we have to take precautions."

Still, Cal seemed skeptical. Vivianne thought the precaution made perfect sense.

"I'll keep my eye on it, Mr. McKeon! Thank you for the warning."

AT LAST, at 1:40 P.M., the first students began to arrive.

Explaining there'd been a slow-down at the checkpoint—some problem with the guards' break.

One by one, the inmate-students entered the classroom. A figure passing by the window on the ramp—in the doorway, a stranger—as Vivianne felt again that quick absurd thrill of anticipation, or hope.

And the immediate rebuke *He isn't here. Can't be here. What are you thinking!*

Her heart beat painfully. A fine scrim of sweat broke out beneath her arms. Her black woolen clothing—a short, trim jacket, fitted trousers—was too warm suddenly.

Her black cashmere-wool coat she'd neatly draped over the back of a nearby chair.

She'd brought no handbag with her, no wallet. You could enter the prison with only a photo I.D., pens and papers, car keys, a handful of tissues stuffed in a pocket. Other possessions had to be left behind in a locked car trunk.

As the inmates entered the classroom they came first to the instructors' table where Cal and Vivianne were standing, to introduce themselves, and shake hands.

This was a surprise! In all of Vivianne's experience no students had behaved in this formal way. Not even graduate students arriving for a seminar.

There was *Hardy*, and there was *Athol*. There were *Junot, Claydon, Evander, Floyd*. There was an older man, an African-American with a creased dark face whom others called *"Preach"*—there was a limping older white man with a cane, in his sixties at least, with a soiled-looking skin, dented hairless head and an incongruously cheery expression who greeted Cal Healy with a firm handshake and Vivianne with a courtly smile and a mock-bow: "Ma'am, howdy!" His name was *Conor O'Hagan* which rolled off his tongue like an Irish stage name.

There was *Darl*. There was *Matthias*. There was *Yusef*.

It was something of a shock—a pleasurable shock—to feel her thin hand gripped warmly in the hand of a stranger.

Do not hug inmates or engage in other intimate forms of physical contact. A brief handshake is permitted.

There was a lone, slight-bodied Asian boy with a shaved head and a squinting smile, or grimace; unobtrusively he slipped into the room, taking his place at the far left against a wall, not coming first to the instructors' table to introduce himself. (Vivianne deduced from the class roster that his name had to be *Quogh Nu* which was—Vietnamese?) The most flamboyant students were a tall spidery-limbed Dominican with shoulder-length dreadlocks—this was *Ramirez*—and a heavyset Hispanic with a battered handsome face, mournful eyes and an affable manner—*Diego*.

Vivianne saw that the men didn't segregate themselves in the class-room according to race but it was clear that they were sitting as far from one another as they could.

Cal Healy suggested that the men "come a little closer"—"to make it easier to communicate"—and the men laughed as if he'd said some-thing funny.

Diego, who was sitting in the first row, explained that, in his cell, if he leaned his back against the wall and stretched out his legs—"like this, see, man?"—he could press the soles of his feet against the wall.

Meaning, their cells were so small, and these were double cells—naturally the men wanted as much space around them as they could get, when they were out of their cells.

Cal caught on, belatedly. A blush rose into his face. The men laughed, not unkindly.

"Oh yeah—right. I get it. Sit where you want to, sure. The impor-tant thing is . . ."

The class began, somewhat awkwardly. Cal seemed to be confused—looking through papers in a manila folder, searching for the class roster which had been removed from the cardboard box and set on the table. Vivianne located it for Cal, but when he took it from her he'd become distracted by something he was telling the students, and set it down absentmindedly without asking the men to sign it.

Vivianne saw a figure passing by the front windows of the class-room, outside. She felt an immediate visceral response—a small kick of the heart.

Telling herself *You must stop. This is absurd. He will not . . . this is not . . .*

She understood: it was the logic of dreams. In a dream you have no comprehension of time, or plausibility; anything, all things, can hap-pen in a dream. And you have no volition, you can't save yourself from the folly of hopeless wishes.

Without a warning knock the door was pushed inward. A burly guard in a khaki-colored uniform stood in the doorway. At first he said nothing, but seemed, by the quick-darting action of his eyes, to be counting the inmates.

This wasn't one of the friendly guards, clearly. The man scarcely glanced at Cal who was smiling awkwardly at him and he ignored Vivianne entirely. He asked for the sign-in roster which he wanted to check and when Cal was forced to stammer apologetically that he hadn't "gotten around yet" to having the roster signed, the guard told Cal to pass the roster around the room and he'd wait.

In silence the roster was passed around the room and the men signed their names.

You could feel the tension, the hostility in the air. Where a moment before there'd been an air of affability, anticipation.

It was inevitable, inmates hated guards. Guards hated—or distrusted—inmates. In this unnatural setting, individuals yet behaved naturally.

Volunteer instructors were inclined to take the side of their students, against the guards. But Vivianne understood how the guards— this guard, surely—resented prisoners receiving special treatment from civilians.

The program offered college-level courses, like English 101.

Vivianne had seen, in front of the prison gate, in a patch of tended ground in which there was a flagpole with a weatherworn American flag at half-mast, a monument to the guards who'd "given their lives in the line of duty"—about twenty names, since 1928.

She'd asked, why is the flag at half-mast? Had someone died?

But no one in Vivianne's little group knew. Not even Mick McKeon knew. And no one wanted to ask the grim-faced guard awaiting them at the first checkpoint.

It took several minutes for the guard to check the inmates in the classroom against the class roster and a printed list in his hand and when at last he returned the roster to Cal it was with an expression of scarcely disguised contempt; he told Cal to "be sure not to forget" to have the inmates sign out at the end of class.

"If there's a fuckup, there could be a lockdown. No one would get out of here for hours."

Still the guard addressed Cal, ignoring Vivianne. She saw the hot quick blood in her young co-instructor's face and she said with a bright smile, "We will, officer! Thank you."

WHEN SHE'D been a girl Vivianne had only to enter an unfamiliar place to feel that something special might happen, someone special might appear—and her life would be changed. She'd stepped into new settings with an air of romantic expectation—and some anxiety—and one day it happened, she met someone, someone special, and her life was changed.

And so, now that he had departed from her life, she'd become susceptible again to the old yearning, though decades had passed and she was so much older: yet, so strangely, the same person still, the same eager naïve hopeful girl.

So badly wanting to be *of help*.

Her husband had often spoken of volunteering for such work—when he retired, when he had more time.

Having *more time*—this is a curious concept!

Now, there was *time*. Vast, choppy, slate-colored and with no perceptible beginning, or end—the direction of its current, like the Hudson River in certain weathers, indeterminate.

———

REPEATEDLY THEY'D been warned: you will not be allowed to wear blue into the prison.

For blue was the prisoners' color, exclusively.

Guards wore khaki-colored uniforms. Prisoners, blue.

In fact, blue over white. And their prison-issue sneakers were white.

Prison attire as a form of correction, punishment. A way of taking from the prisoner his identity, and making him ridiculous.

P R I S O N E R in stark white letters on the backs of the inmates' (blue) shirts.

On the right legs of their (blue) pants stark white vertical letters

P
R
I
S
O
N
E
R.

At the waist of the (blue) pants, stark white initials N Y S D C R— NEW YORK STATE DEPARTMENT OF CORRECTION AND REHABILITATION.

Civilians could not be allowed to wear blue or any combination of colors like stripes that might be confused with blue by sentries in the watch towers for, if there was a "disturbance" in the yard—a sudden melee—(how often did this happen, the uneasy volunteers wondered)—sentries would command inmates to throw themselves on the ground and individuals who failed to obey, and remained standing, would be in danger of being shot down.

A civilian wearing blue would be in danger of being shot.

At the orientation meeting one of the volunteers identified herself as a "nurse by training" who was already co-teaching in the maximum-security prison at Auburn, but wanted to expand her time "inside" by volunteering here, too. With a small glow of pride the woman told the group that she'd been volunteering for prison work for thirty years.

She had a bulldog face, plain, squinting, somber. Her dark hair was short and wiry. She wore jeans and a denim jacket and hiking boots.

Not long afterward, the instructor brought up again the subject of "familiarity"—"over-familiarity"—with inmates. She warned of becoming "emotionally dependent" upon prison work: "If you discover that the emotional center of your life is in the prison, and your visits are the highlight of your week, you might want to reconsider your volunteer work, and cut back a bit."

These remarks seemed to make no impression on the woman who'd identified herself as a nurse. Vivianne felt a stir of embarrassment for her.

She thought *That would never happen to me.*

Her husband had expressed the intention to volunteer in prison education, when he retired. But why prison, Vivianne didn't know. And which prison. She must have asked him. She would not have asked him more than once.

He'd had a way—so subtle, for he was a subtle man—of discouraging Vivianne's curiosity when it seemed to him misplaced or intrusive, without saying anything specific, often without saying anything at all, only just frowning, glancing away—signifying *Excuse me but this is private. I'd prefer not to discuss this though I love you and respect you and my reluctance to answer is not a rebuke.*

She'd sometimes taken it as a rebuke, of course. But she had never doubted that he'd loved her.

———

SHE WAS introduced by her young co-instructor as "Vivianne Greary—a renowned university professor and scholar" and himself as an "aspiring social-eco-activist." In the course they would be reading "exemplary expository" essays and writing essays themselves. There was no textbook—photocopied material would be passed out at each class meeting, to be read for the next week's meeting. Both Cal and Vivianne spoke—she saw the men's eyes glide onto her, with a kind of affable interest; not sexual, not aggressive. She was sure of this.

The mood of the inmates was *eager*. At least, those men who were seated near the front of the room, who lifted their hands to speak, who'd had experience in previous courses.

Not all had been in the program before, but almost all. The young Asian-looking man at the back of the room, gazing with a sober impassive face at the instructors, seemed out of place, even disoriented. And one of the older white men, also at the back of the room, but nowhere near the young Asian, was frowning and sucking at his lips in a way that would have been distracting if he'd been sitting nearer.

What was this inmate's name?—Vivianne had a vague recollection of a strange, cumbersome name—*Ardwick*.

She would check the name roster, unobtrusively.

The man might have been in his early sixties. He had a blunt shaved head, a face that looked as if it had partly melted away. And much of his face was obscured by dark-tinted glasses. His short-sleeved blue shirt was loose-fitting as if it were the shirt of a much larger man and the sleeves of his white T-shirt straggled over his hands. Something in the way he stared at the instructors—at *her*—made Vivianne uneasy though you would not have guessed by Vivianne's classroom manner which was smiling and pleasant, upbeat.

Yet, she kept looking at the man at the back of the room—*Ardwick?*—*Oldwick?* His first name, too, was unusual—*Elias? Ezra?*

She thought *He has shrunk. This is not the self he remembers and so he is baffled, he may be angry.*

Yet, the class was going well. The men took notes on yellow prison-issue tablets. Cal wrote on the blackboard. The men were diligent as students of another era. Already one of the younger black men had lifted his hand for permission to come forward to use the pencil sharpener.

"'Scuse me, ma'am?"—then, "Thank you, ma'am!"—as if Vivianne had dominance over the little blue plastic object.

Vivianne was reminded of her old, lost life as a university instructor—before she'd earned a Ph.D., before she'd acquired a reputation, and tenure.

Night-school classes were like boat-crossings on rough rivers—you just hung on, you rowed your heart out, you *made it across.* And what pleasure in that kind of teaching, that had little to do with the refinements of university teaching of advanced classes, scholarly research. The prison situation was not very different from night school, Vivianne thought. You did not expect brilliant students, you would be pleasantly surprised always by a few students who worked hard, did good work, became your friends . . .

She'd photocopied a section from James Baldwin's "Notes of a Native Son" to pass to the students. The assignment was to read it carefully and respond in five hundred to one thousand words which they would read aloud at the next class meeting—"But only if you feel comfortable with reading aloud." Vivianne had seen looks of dismay in several faces.

She suggested to Cal that maybe the men might volunteer to read the Baldwin essay aloud, just to make sure they understood it, and then they could ask questions if they had any; Cal seemed to agree, this was a great idea, then recalled suddenly that he'd forgotten to ask the students to introduce themselves, to say why they were taking the course and what they hoped to get out of it, which was suggested as first-class procedure, and so—maybe they'd better do that, first.

"Then, we can read from the essay. OK?"

Cal Healy was an inexperienced instructor, that was the problem. And the prison-situation seemed to have made him anxious. Vivianne would have liked to touch Cal's wrist, to calm him: to ask him to speak less rapidly, and maybe less; to allow the students to talk more. She would have liked to seize his hand to reassure him, as an older teacher, as an older woman—but of course she couldn't embarrass the young man in front of their students.

One by one, the men gave their names. Why they were taking the course, what they hoped to get out of it.

With a broad smile Conor O'Hagan said he was taking the course because he was going to be paroled in four months—"And I'd have to pay for it, outside."

Ramirez said he was taking the course because he never learned nothing much in high school—"They just pass you along, man."

Diego said he was taking the course because he wanted to "improve" his mind—"If you can *write*, man—you can *think*."

Others echoed Diego, and others said that they were taking the course because it was a requirement in the degree program. The Asian boy Quogh Hu at the back of the room spoke reluctantly at first and then in a rapid, heavily accented English which Vivianne couldn't understand; very likely, Cal couldn't understand either. But both said, "Good! Good."

The last to speak was the frowning man in the dark-tinted glasses who'd been staring at Vivianne as if lost in a dream. He hadn't been paying attention, it seemed, for another inmate had to prompt him to reply in a stumbling voice: "Why I'm h-here . . . here . . . why I am *here*, is because . . . This is where . . ."

His words trailed off, eerily. There was an awkward silence in the room.

There came "Preach" to the rescue asking the instructors why'd they come here?

"Man, you got to tell us, too! It's your turn."

Cal answered first, reiterating his initial introduction and adding that he was a "social-eco-activist" who'd lived most of his life in the vicinity of the Hudson Valley and who hoped one day to "travel extensively in the Far East."

Vivianne saw the men looking at her, expectantly. Until now she'd felt obscured by Cal Healy; she'd felt protected by him, despite his inexperience and awkwardness. She heard herself say, smiling, or with an attempt at a smile, "Today is my fiftieth wedding anniversary. My husband has been dead for two years—so anywhere I am, on this day, is like any other."

The room was utterly silent. Vivianne's co-instructor stared at her. What had she said? The words had glided from her, like liquid. The men regarded her with grave and astonished expressions. Even the frowning man at the back of the room. Quickly Vivianne said, "Please don't misunderstand. There is nowhere else I would rather be, that I can be, right now. And so—I am here, in my first volunteer class at Hudson. With you."

Her face beat with blood. What had she said!

She'd meant to be casual and entertaining. She'd meant to be the opposite of self-pitying, self-revealing. She'd meant just to explain *why*—but it had come out wrong.

For the first time, she saw herself as more than ridiculous—she saw herself as arrogant, indifferent to her husband's memory. She was making her way in the world as if he had not died—as if he had not lived.

The horror of her selfishness washed over her, like dirty water.

She'd been counseled *You must move on. You must live your own life.* It was a lie, she'd wanted to believe. A selfish lie. And she knew this. And the men staring at her knew this.

———

THE REMAINDER of the class passed quickly.

Quickly and jarringly like a boat in a choppy river, that is not quite entirely out of control.

Vivianne was distracted by a roaring in her ears. Though Vivianne addressed the class, explaining the assignment to them; giving them some background to James Baldwin—"By consensus, one of the very best American essay-writers of the twentieth century."

She hoped that the African-American men in the class would admire Baldwin, and wouldn't find his elegantly structured prose difficult. She hoped they wouldn't think that she and Cal Healy were being patronizing, to pass out this essay, on a passionately black subject, to the class.

She hoped that the others wouldn't resent the assignment, with its racial subject.

There was a brief discussion, involving just a few inmates. The men who'd been speaking at first continued and others, at the margins of the seating, looked on in silence; not unfriendly, Vivianne thought, only just not inclined to speak.

Or maybe the mood of the class had shifted. Maybe, when Vivianne misspoke. Her face was still warm with blood and pulses rang hot in her ears.

What did you say! Oh what did you say! To strangers.

Somehow, the subject of ghosts came up.

Vivianne had no idea why. It had been originally planned by the instructors that their students would write fifteen-minute impromptus in each class, to habituate them in writing spontaneously and easily; volunteers would read their impromptus aloud. But somehow it happened, they'd begun to run out of time. Cal Healy had talked too long about topics for term papers later in the course and Vivianne hadn't been watching the time, and would not have wanted to interrupt him, if she had.

How quickly the subject of ghosts emerged! Soon it was clear that the men believed in ghosts; even a drawling pigtailed man who looked like a drug dealer in a Hollywood film believed. Vehemently he said, "If you passed by the north-gate unit"—(this was what Vivianne thought he'd said, but she wasn't altogether sure)—"you'd believe, too."

This must have been the old death row, Vivianne thought.

"You mean actual *ghosts*? Like—of the dead?"

Cal spoke with an air of mild incredulity as if he weren't certain whether the inmates were joking.

"Man, yes! They be *actual ghosts*. Like—*dead folks*."

The men were nodding vigorously. Clearly this was no joke.

"There is ghosts! Ain't no sligh'est doubt, there *is ghosts*."

"Preach" spoke definitively. There was nothing deferential about the man now, he knew what he knew and no white civilians could dissuade *him*.

Heedless, Cal tried to argue. In the way that one might argue in a university setting, speaking of "superstition"—the need for "evidence"—"proof." The men listened to him resentfully.

Vivianne wanted to touch Cal's wrist lightly—*Enough! You've made your point.*

Cal was forgetting one of the cardinal rules of volunteer prison-work: you didn't speak ironically or sarcastically to the inmates, even when their ideas were untenable; you were to respect their ideas, and to speak carefully to them.

Outside the prison, you could speak dismissively of ghosts; in the prison, evidently, you had better take ghosts seriously. Vivianne understood.

"Ma'am? What d'you say?"

One of the young black men—*Junot? Evander?*—was addressing

Vivianne. In his voice there was both deference—for an older, white-woman teacher—and a subtle air of intimidation.

Vivianne said, with a strange little smile, "On the subject of 'ghosts'—through the millennia—thousands of years—all the evidence is not yet in . . ."

Her voice trailed off weakly but this was a shrewd answer.

Vivianne was wishing that Cal would curtail the discussion, which was lively but aimless, threatening to veer out of control. Hadn't they intended to do something with the class? To have the men begin to read the Baldwin essay, aloud? Even as Vivianne remembered this, she was forgetting it; Cal seemed to have forgotten entirely.

At the back of the room, the scowling man in dark glasses. Or maybe he wasn't scowling, maybe Vivianne was misreading him.

And cheery Conor O'Hagan with his dented-looking bald head, his bleary eyes in which a sort of malicious merriment shone. He waved his surprisingly sinewy arm to be called upon, as in a classroom, but spoke loudly interrupting others; Vivianne saw a lurid flamey-red tattoo on his right forearm.

These are criminals, you must not forget. These men have hurt others. You must not ever forget.

Of the fourteen men in the class eleven were "lifers"—their sentences were indeterminate, depending upon their behavior in the prison. Vivianne gathered from what she'd been told that the average prisoner at Hudson Fork was classified as a "violent felon" though it wasn't likely that inmates in the education program were among these.

The older black man, for instance—"Preach." And Diego with his courtly way of speaking. And—was it Floyd?—a boyish-looking black man with a scarred face and a friendly smile . . . Vivianne felt a surge of something like affection for these strangers, as she'd often felt for her night-school adults decades ago when she'd been a new, young teacher, younger than most of her students.

The warning was: you do not ask inmates about their personal lives, and particularly you do not ask inmates about the crimes for which they were convicted, and you do not ask inmates about their prison sentences.

Vivianne thought *But why would I ask? The fact of our lives is—we are here.*

THEN, IT ENDED.

With rude abruptness, ended.

At 4:18 P.M. there was a sharp rap at the door.

The same burly guard stood in the doorway.

"This class has to end now. Men return to your cell-blocks."

A cruel sort of pleasure in this announcement. As if to say *This bullshit is over. Get the fuck back where you belong.*

"But—why? Class is almost over."

Cal spoke more pleadingly than defiantly. Vivianne was relieved, her co-instructor was intimidated by the guard.

No reason was given. The guard repeated his command and the men stood and prepared to leave. There was no murmuring, and there was no opposition. In the guard's presence—(and you could see another guard out on the ramp)—the men were stiff, wary.

Talking of ghosts had stirred the air. Their talk had animated both inmates and instructors. But in an instant, that was ended.

"Well! We'll say good-bye, then—until next week."

"Yes, good-bye—until next week."

"If you have any questions about the assignment . . ."

Vivianne spoke in her quick warm friendly voice, that rarely failed to put others at ease. But the men were captives who'd been given orders they could not disobey, most of them scarcely glanced at her now, or at Cal standing disconsolate and abashed at the front of the room.

Only Diego lingered for a quick question addressed to Vivianne—a strange question—"Ma'am? Did you know James Baldwin like—in person?"

"Why, n-no . . ."

"You wasn't his, like, teacher? I guess?"

Rudely the guard snapped his fingers at Diego, as you'd snap fingers at a dog, to hurry him along. Vivianne saw the look of hurt and chagrin in the man's eyes. She said, smiling, as if to soften his disappointment:

"No. I wasn't James Baldwin's teacher."

This would make an amusing anecdote to tell her friends, who'd tried to dissuade her from prison teaching.

The men left. The guards followed close in their wake. Cal was cursing after them—"God damn *fuckers*. You see the looks in their smug fucking faces!"

Vivianne was grateful that one of the guards had been a black man—her co-instructor couldn't rant about racism, at least.

Cal and Vivianne were putting things back in the cardboard box when they both realized, seeing the class roster, that they'd forgotten to have the men sign out.

The men had signed in—there were fourteen printed names and beside each a signature. But in the sign-out column there were only blanks.

Cal said: "God damn! God damn *cocksucker*."

Vivianne, too, was dismayed. She could not comprehend how they'd forgotten the roster—a second time—except that the class had ended so abruptly. And why hadn't the guard asked them about the roster? As he'd asked them, at the start of class?

Then, Vivianne saw that the little blue plastic pencil sharpener seemed to be missing.

Panicked, Vivianne looked for it on the floor beneath the instructors' desk.

Trying to remember who'd used it last—which of the inmates had signaled for permission to come to the table and taken up the little blue plastic cube to sharpen his pencil, like a dutiful child. *And when Ms. Greary wasn't looking, he'd slipped it in his pocket. Was that what had happened?*

"Do you think he was serious? There might be a lockdown? Because the men didn't sign out? Oh, Christ."

Cal was slamming supplies into the cardboard box. His face was contorted as if he were about to cry. Vivianne tried to console him—really, she didn't think the prison could be *locked-down* for such a trifle—the guards had seen the prisoners leave the classroom, surely they'd checked their names against their own list. It had to be that the guard meant to harass the instructors—Vivianne was sure. At the same time she remembered that *common sense* did not apply in prison.

More seriously, the little pencil sharpener seemed to be missing.

Certainly there had to be a razor-sharp piece of metal inside it, however small.

Vivianne hesitated to tell Cal about this second blunder. She would take responsibility for it herself—she'd promised to watch over the little plastic cube and somehow she had failed. How stupid! Unlike Cal who was cursing the guards, Vivianne could only curse herself.

Cal didn't seem to be noticing how Vivianne was searching for something in the classroom, stooping to look beneath the tables, and the inmates' chairs. He had no sense of her desperation, even as she was determined to disguise it.

"*He* could have said something, the son of a bitch! Fucking prick! He was hoping the roster hadn't been signed, that was why he broke up the class when he did. *God damn.*"

Vivianne knelt, groping beneath a table. Nothing here but tiny clumps of dirt from the inmates' sneakers. Her face was pounding now

with blood, she had never felt so despairing. Her life had become yet
more ridiculous, in the very effort to be *of help*.

Then, without a word to Vivianne, as if he'd forgotten her entirely,
Cal slammed out of the classroom carrying the roster. He was oblivious of the fact that he wasn't supposed to step outside the classroom
alone, and he wasn't supposed to leave his co-instructor alone.

Vivianne called: "Cal? W-Wait . . ."

She might have run after him. But—the pencil sharpener!

She felt a chill panic, alone in the room.

This room that, a few minutes before, had seemed so lively—so
filled with *life*.

But the men had been ordered to their cell-blocks: she couldn't possibly be in danger.

(Presumably, all the men in the prison? Or—just the men in a particular cell-block?)

Vivianne stood uncertainly. She would have followed Cal except—
there was her coat on a chair behind the instructors' table. She went
to get her coat and kicked something and sent it skittering along the
floor—the pencil sharpener?—but no, only a pencil.

She could have wept aloud. Though possibly, this was funny.

An amusing anecdote to tell her friends. Her husband . . .

Vivianne took up her coat which was made of soft black wool. Not
knowing how to dress for the prison she'd worn black: a short black
woolen jacket with little gold buttons, tapered black woolen trousers,
black leather boots. And the black overcoat with deep pockets into
which she'd thrust her leather gloves: one glove in each pocket.

Here was a small triumph: when Vivianne checked the coat pockets, there was a glove in each. She hadn't lost her gloves, at least.

She'd given up looking for the blue plastic pencil sharpener. She
left the classroom and stepped outside—the air was colder, the sky a
scoured-looking gray. Next door was another classroom where a sci-

ence course was being taught; she wondered if Cal had gone in that direction or if he'd headed back to the Education Office, along the wooden ramp.

She was angry with her co-instructor for leaving her—but of course he'd panicked also, he hadn't been thinking clearly. She could hardly blame him, he'd felt under more pressure than Vivianne had felt. Yet neither Cal nor Vivianne seemed to have been thinking clearly for the past two hours. Entering Hudson Fork Correctional Facility for Men had seemed to effect a kind of shift in Vivianne's brain as if a tiny knob had turned, and she'd lost her power of concentration.

She was staring at a row of men, three or four men, blue-clad, with stark white letters P R I S O N E R across their backs, on the other side of the wire-mesh fence. They were facing a wall—what were they doing at the wall?—and no guards in sight.

The men didn't see Vivianne, yet. She felt a curious sense of elation, of intense relief, as if she'd already died, and had become invisible. She had crossed over to this desolate place, as to a region in Hades, not one of the spectacular fiery regions where savage punishments were exacted but one of the more ordinary regions where a smell of backed-up drains, the exhaustion of sleepless nights and headache-wracked days prevailed. This region of ghosts, of the damned who'd become ghosts, and it was no different from her ordinary, posthumous life.

One of the inmates on the other side of the fence turned, adjusting his pants. Of course, he'd been at the urinal—Vivianne had totally forgotten the urinal, and the warning about not looking at men using it.

The inmate saw her. He was coarse-faced, with spiky red hair and a smudged white skin. He shouted at her, something ribald, jeering.

All of the men turned. All saw her.

They were furious, jeering. They were thrilled to see her—whoever she was: one of the civilian volunteers, looking lost.

Lost, and terrified.

Vivianne stammered an apology, backing away. Badly she wanted to hide her face, so ashamed.

The men were shouting after her. Blindly she turned away.

She had no idea where she was going. She knew that she should not return to the classroom—she'd be trapped inside. But she wasn't supposed to walk alone to the Education Office and she wasn't sure where it was.

She found herself in a cul-de-sac, at the end of the ramp. She must have stumbled in the wrong direction. But maybe there was a way out, here? She saw a door—but it was a classroom door, and the room inside was darkened.

She would have to flee in the other direction, to get to the Education Office—but if she did, she would have to pass by the men at the urinal, whose loud excited voices were terrible to hear.

"Ma'am! Howdy."

She turned. She felt a touch on her shoulder. Another touch, a lover's caress. A face loomed beside hers, pitying, with a look of sorrow, but revulsion too, disgust, for the woman had insulted his manhood with her condescension; with her ridiculous female vanity, that had taken root in grief; between his fingers the little razor was gripped tight, drawn against Vivianne's throat, beneath her chin, a quick slash, the blink of an eye, the intake of a breath, mercy—for here was the angel of mercy, clad in blue.

They would discover Vivianne Greary missing, amid the confusion of an unexpected lockdown. They would discover Vivianne Greary fallen and lifeless on the wooden ramp behind the entrance to the Education Office, at the very end of the ramp, bled out.

———

"NEXT TIME. Next time will be different."

Cal Healy was driving, erratically. He was chagrined, excited, talking rapidly and obsessively of the "fucking-stupid" mistakes they'd made. He did not spare Vivianne, as he did not spare himself. To the left, the Hudson River looked like molten lead. There was no beauty to the wide choppy river, that reflected a sunless sky. Vivianne had given up listening to her companion's ranting words. They'd both been reprimanded by the Education Office coordinator; they'd had to copy the men's names from the sheet of paper the men had signed, onto the formal roster-sheet; it had taken them what seemed like a very long time. Vivianne's head pounded with pain. Her eyes stung with tears like acid, or blood. She was exhausted, wounded, like one who has been stricken, her throat slashed. She was finished, she'd bled out. She heard herself say:

"Next time. Yes."